THE BIG GAMBLE

ALSO AVAILABLE IN BEELER LARGE PRINT BY
MICHAEL MCGARRITY

Hermit's Peak
Mexican Hat
Serpent Gate
The Judas Judge

THE BIG GAMBLE

A Kevin Kerney Novel

MICHAEL MCGARRITY

BEELER LARGE PRINT
Hampton Falls, New Hampshire, 2002

Library of Congress Cataloging-in-Publication Data

McGarrity, Michael.
  The big gamble / Michael McGarrity
     p.   cm.
  ISBN 1-57490-437-X (alk. paper)

Cip data was not available at the time of publication.

Published in Large Print by arrangement with
Dutton, a member of
Penguin Putnam, Inc.

BEELER LARGE PRINT
is published by
Thomas T. Beeler, *Publisher*
Post Office Box 659
Hampton Falls, New Hampshire 03844

Typeset in 16 point Times New Roman type.
Sewn and bound on acid-free paper by
Sheridan Books in Chelsea, Michigan

For Steve Rush, a gifted psychologist and my first clinical supervisor, who taught me not to take things in life personally, and Di Bingham of Brisbane, Australia.

ACKNOWLEDGMENTS

Sheriff Tom Sullivan of Lincoln County, New Mexico, helped me gain insight into the operation of his department. My thanks go to him for giving me valuable information and several good ideas for the book.

Mrs. Genora V. Moore and Gene and Barbara Thornton graciously allowed me repeated access to the family ranch outside of Santa Fe. My thanks go to them for giving me a chance to find the perfect piece of land where Kerney could build his home.

CHAPTER 1

THE CEMENT BLOCK WALLS OF THE ABANDONED building kept the fire fairly well contained until the roof ignited. Then wind whipped burning embers into the dry grass along the shoulder of the highway. In the predawn light, Deputy Sheriff Clayton Istee watched the volunteer firefighters chase down and drown rivulets of orange flames that snaked quickly through the grass. A year of drought had made any fire dangerous, and the incessant spring winds that rolled across Carrizozo and the surrounding rangeland could easily transform a cinder into a catastrophe engulfing the whole valley.

Flames licked through the boarded-up side doorway and the long opening at the front of the structure, which had once served as a counter for baskets of apples and jugs of fresh pressed cider. Under a steady stream of water from a pumper truck, the remnants of the roof crashed in, showering brilliant pinpoint sparks into the sky, momentarily illuminating a large, somewhat-faded plywood sign nailed to the building that read:

ELECT PAUL HEWITT
LINCOLN COUNTY SHERIFF

Hewitt was Clayton Istee's new boss. Three months ago, after five years with the Mescalero Tribal Police, Clayton had accepted the sheriff's long-standing job offer. His decision hadn't made his mother or his wife particularly happy, but Clayton was glad to get away from the petty politics and cronyism of the tribal administrators.

1

Ray Bonnell, the volunteer fire chief, stepped up to Clayton's side. One of Paul Hewitt's best friends, Bonnell could be found just about every weekday morning having an early cup of coffee with the sheriff at the Dugout Bar & Grill. In his sixties, with the thick upper body of a man who'd spent a lifetime doing hard physical work, Bonnell was a third-generation native of the valley. He ranched, owned a local propane gas delivery company, and ran the fire department in his spare time.

"Smell that?" Bonnell asked.

Clayton nodded.

"Know what it is?" Bonnell asked.

"Burned flesh," Clayton answered.

"Yep. You got yourself a crispy critter inside. Let's just hope it isn't somebody we knew, or worse yet, somebody we knew and liked. Best to tell Sheriff Hewitt."

"He's already rolling," Clayton replied. "ETA ten minutes."

Bonnell smiled. "Paul said you were a good one. Guess I don't need to tell you how to do your job."

"I'll take all the help I can get, Chief," Clayton said.

"Then help yourself to the spare pair of Wellington boots in the back of my truck," Bonnell said with a laugh as he moved away. "You're gonna need them. After we soak down the inside of that fruit stand it's gonna be a soggy, god-awful mess."

All the burned grass along the roadside had been covered with dirt and doused. Firefighters walked in circles around the charred patches of earth checking for hot spots, hosing down anything that looked like it could combust or flare up again. At the burned-out building two men on ladders directed high-pressure jets of water into the guts of the structure.

Soon murky black water started oozing out the door frame. Clayton went to Bonnell's truck, got the rubber boots, and put them on, figuring whatever crime scene evidence there was inside the building had to be pretty well trashed. Nothing could be done about it. Putting the fire completely out was the first priority, especially since the warmth of the early morning sun topping the mountains had stirred up strong gusts coursing out of the canyons.

The men on the ladders shut down their hoses. At the front of the burned-out door Bonnell motioned for Clayton to join him. He plodded toward Bonnell in the squeaky rubber boots.

"This place hasn't been used for years," Bonnell said, shining his light inside. Most of a plank floor at the back of the structure had been burned away, revealing a partial basement.

Bonnell froze the beam of his flashlight on what appeared to be a pile of burned rags under a window. "There's your crispy critter," he said.

Clayton nodded. He could see a seared, blackened forearm and hand protruding from the rag pile. "What's with the basement?" he asked.

"It was probably a cold-storage cellar for produce," Bonnell replied as he swept his light back and forth. "We're looking for fire behavior here, Deputy. So far I don't see anything abnormal. The flames burned up and out, just like they were supposed to."

"Are you calling it accidental?"

"Not yet, but I don't see a burn pattern that suggests an accelerant was used."

Clayton gazed at the deep pool of black water that was quickly draining into the cellar. "What a mess."

Bonnell snorted and slapped Clayton on the shoulder. "Come on, Deputy, let's get in there, get muddy, and find out what we've got."

"First, I'd better call for the medical examiner," Clayton said.

Bonnell pointed at a firefighter coiling hose at the back of the pumper truck. "We've got one right here," he said. "Shorty Dawson will be more than willing to declare the victim dead."

Clayton thought about the mess inside. Mud, debris, and charred pieces of the roof filled the enclosure, a lot of it covering the body. Conditions would make extracting the victim and searching for evidence time-consuming and tedious. Allowing too many people inside would only make it worse.

"Have Dawson make a visual inspection from the doorway," Clayton said. "I want to limit entry to just you and me until the crime scene techs arrive."

"I'm sure Shorty will oblige," Ray Bonnell said. The sound of a siren made him glance down the highway in the direction of Carrizozo. "Here comes your boss. Shall we wait for him before we get started?"

"Might as well," Clayton replied. "When we get inside, I want you to do exactly what I say."

"Now that the fire is out, it's your show," Bonnell replied.

Paul Hewitt watched his young deputy work. Major felonies were not commonplace in Lincoln County, New Mexico, and while it was quite likely that the John Doe inside the fruit stand had died by accident, Clayton Istee was treating the investigation as a homicide, which was exactly the right thing to do.

Hewitt had aggressively recruited Clayton because of

4

his college education, five years of patrol experience, and extensive training in major felony investigations. He'd kept a close eye on Clayton since his arrival and was pleased by the young man's work ethic, his professional conduct, and his seasoned patrol skills. Now, for the first time, Hewitt had a chance to observe Clayton conducting a crime scene investigation, and he liked what he saw.

After photographing and videotaping the scene, Clayton had approached the search for evidence as if it were an archeological dig. With Ray Bonnell's help he'd uncovered a partially burned backpack, a few charred remnants of a cheap sleeping bag, two empty pint whiskey bottles, some partially burned pieces of mud-encrusted firewood, singed scraps of a wool blanket, and a disposable cigarette lighter.

The firefighters and their equipment were long gone, the sun was high in the sky, and the day had heated up when the two men took a break.

Ray Bonnell leaned heavily against the front of Paul Hewitt's slick top unit, smearing dirt on the paint. "Looks like our John Doe burned himself up," he said to Paul. "I'd say the point of origin for the blaze was the sleeping bag under the victim, probably started by a spark or a cigarette. My guess is that he built a fire to keep warm, slugged down two pints of whiskey, passed out, and never woke up. He may have died from smoke inhalation. We'll know for sure after the autopsy."

Paul nodded in agreement and looked at Deputy Istee, who was splashing water on his grimy face. He'd removed his uniform shirt and shucked his weapon and equipment belt. His jeans and tee shirt were stained dark brown and he was covered in mud. "Any ID on the victim?" Hewitt asked.

"Negative, so far," Clayton replied. "I still have to search the body and the backpack."

"He was probably a drifter," Hewitt said. "Wrap it up here as soon as you can."

Ray Bonnell shook his head. "Can't do that, Paul."

"Why not?" Hewitt asked, scanning Bonnell's face.

"We've got another body, Sheriff," Clayton said, "and what looks like a completely different crime scene."

"Show me," Hewitt replied.

Clayton took the sheriff to the doorway, clicked on the battery-operated flashlight, and beamed the light into the back part of the dark cellar.

Hewitt saw an exposed skull with a fractured forehead, covered with patches of what appeared to be leathery skin. Pressurized water from the fire hoses had revealed some of the torso and Hewitt could see what looked like swaths of fabric.

"It's a female skeleton," Clayton said. "The fracture to the skull was most likely from a blunt-force instrument. A clutch purse was buried with the body. According to the driver's license inside the purse, the victim's name was Anna Marie Montoya. She had a Santa Fe address."

"You're sure this is a separate incident?" Hewitt asked.

"There's no way she was killed in the fire," Bonnell said from behind Hewitt's shoulder.

"Any guesses on how long the body has been here?" Hewitt asked.

Clayton shrugged. "Her driver's license expired ten years ago."

"Let's hold off on doing any more until the state police crime techs get here," Hewitt said.

6

"Are you going to give the investigation to the state police?" Clayton asked.

Hewitt had recruited Clayton to complete the staffing of his major felony investigation unit, made up of three specially trained field officers. His twelve-man department was too small and underfunded to manage felony cases any other way. But with the addition of Clayton, Hewitt now had a unit that could do a hell of a lot more than take a report, collect evidence, interview witnesses, or get an occasional voluntary confession from some feebleminded perp.

At least, he hoped they could. Up to now, the unit was untested. It was time to see what they could do.

"It's your case, Deputy," Hewitt said. "Call in the team."

Clayton stripped off his plastic gloves. "I'll get them rolling."

Ray Bonnell watched Clayton walk to his unit to make the call. "I think you hired yourself a good one, Paul," he said.

"I do believe you're right," Hewitt said.

"How come I'm all dirty and you're all spick-and-span clean?" Ray asked, brushing dirt off his pants and eying Hewitt's freshly pressed shirt.

Paul Hewitt smiled. "You do look a mess, Ray. How about you wipe the dirt off your face, wash your hands, and I buy you some biscuits and gravy?"

"I could use some breakfast," Bonnell replied.

Sergeant Oscar Quinones and Deputy Von Dillingham arrived in a hurry. Clayton briefed them, paying particular attention to how the men reacted to the news that he'd been assigned by the sheriff as lead investigator. He didn't need an attitude flashed at him

7

for being placed in charge.

Quinones didn't even flinch. A retired border patrol supervisor who'd been with the department for five years, he'd worked on many task forces, investigations, and multiagency operations run by lower-ranking officers.

"Where do you want us to start?" Quinones said when Clayton finished.

"We'll work it as two separate crime scenes," Clayton said, looking at Dillingham for a reaction, "starting with the male victim. Search the body and the backpack, and bag and tag all evidence. Then we'll do a field search around the perimeter."

Dillingham pulled a toothpick from his mouth and smiled. "What about the female victim?"

"We treat it as a buried body and do an excavation," Clayton said. "But not until victim number one is removed and all evidence recovered."

"Sounds like a plan," Dillingham said.

The crime scene techs appeared as they were finishing up the perimeter search. Motorists passing by slowed down to check out the emergency vehicles parked just off the highway, creating a potentially hazardous situation. At Clayton's request, another deputy was sent out to keep traffic moving and the curious locals at bay.

The officers and the techs worked deep into the night. Piece by piece, they brought out an accumulation of trash, broken pieces of old wooden fruit baskets, bits of rope, a rotting ball of twine, and several cracked glass gallon jugs. In the cellar, they used tweezers, paint brushes, magnifying glasses, trowels, and other small tools to dig around the female victim for evidence. The most surprising discovery came when the female

8

skeleton was finally unearthed. Patches of leathery skin showed that the dry cellar had caused a certain degree of mummification. Bits and pieces of apparel still covered parts of the trunk and lower extremities. Earrings lay next to the skull, and a turquoise and silver ring loosely encircled a finger bone.

By the time the search concluded and the bodies were removed, midnight had come and gone. Another hour passed doing some preliminary paperwork. Clayton released Quinones and Dillingham and drove home feeling fairly certain, based on a missing-person report in the computerized National Crime Information Center's files, that the dead woman was Anna Marie Montoya, who had disappeared from Santa Fe without a trace eleven years ago.

A match of the victim's teeth with dental records would make the identification conclusive. The state police tech supervisor promised to track down the dental records first thing in the morning and call him with the results.

The Istee family lived on a dirt road just outside the tribal village of Mescalero. Nestled in tall pines at the end of the lane, the house had two bedrooms and only one bath, which was woefully inadequate for a family of four. Soon his son and daughter would need their own rooms, so next up on Clayton's home improvement list was a master bedroom and bath off the living room, away from the children, which he would build himself. He'd spent hours drawing up the plans and figuring out a budget with his wife, Grace. Financially, he could swing it. But with the new job, finding the time to do it was the problem.

In the kitchen Clayton stripped off his dirt-caked

clothes, cleaned up as best he could at the sink, and slipped quietly into bed without disturbing Grace. He slept hard until his son, Wendell, jumped on the bed to wake him up.

"Mommy says you made a big mess in the kitchen," Wendell said when Clayton opened his eyes.

Wendell, age three and fast approaching four, had recently turned into something of a motormouth, and Clayton was secretly hoping this new behavior wouldn't last too long. "Your mother said that?"

"Uh-huh. The floor and the sink are all yucky."

"Go clean it up for me," Clayton said.

"Mommy already did."

"Then go away and let me sleep," Clayton said.

"No."

"Why?"

" 'Cause it's breakfast," Wendell said.

"Okay, I'm up."

Clayton pulled on a pair of jeans and a tee shirt, and with Wendell leading the way, found his wife and his two-year-old daughter, Hannah, at the kitchen table.

"I got him up," Wendell said proudly as he slid into his chair.

The family took its meals at a table in a dining nook adjacent to the kitchen. After tearing out a partial wall that originally separated the two areas, Clayton had added a bay window to bring in light and create a feeling of openness. He took his chair at the head of the table, which gave him a view of the woods at the side of the house, and smiled at his wife and daughter.

In her high chair, Hannah, who considered herself an adult, spooned cereal into her mouth and looked at her brother with quiet, thoughtful eyes. Then she wrinkled her nose at him.

"She made a face at me," Wendell said.

"Yes, she did," Clayton said. "Eat your breakfast." He turned to Grace. "I caught a homicide case yesterday."

"You were so late coming home, I thought something important might have happened," Grace said.

"What's a homicide?" Wendell asked.

"A very bad thing," Clayton said, rubbing Wendell's head. "Almost as bad as interrupting people when they're talking."

Wendell dropped his eyes and stuck a spoonful of cereal in his mouth.

Keeping Wendell quiet with occasional long, cool looks, Clayton summarized his activities at the fruit stand for Grace.

She listened without interruption. "It sounds very complex," she said when Clayton finished.

Clayton nodded. "It was."

"Well, you said you wanted a job with a challenge."

"Are you being sarcastic?" Clayton asked. He studied his pretty wife's face, searching her calm dark eyes for any sign of discontent.

"What's sarcastic?" Wendell asked.

"We'll look it up together in the dictionary later, Wendell," Grace said gently. "No, I'm not. You have to stop thinking that I'm unhappy because you changed jobs."

"You've been complaining that I'm hardly home."

"Not complaining, just noting." Grace looked at her children and smiled. "We all miss you."

"You should smile more," Clayton said.

"It is not my nature," Grace said, as her smile widened.

"You're so modest," Clayton said, teasing.

Grace lifted her chin. "Of course, I'm a respectable, married woman," she replied, teasing him back. Her expression turned serious. "You've been among the dead. Wear something black today to protect against the ghost sickness."

Clayton nodded. "I may have to go up to Santa Fe."

"I'd like to go with you," Wendell said.

Hannah banged her little fist on the high chair's hinged table. "I get down now," she said.

Grace released her and put her on the floor. She made a beeline for Clayton. He picked her up, put her on his lap, and gave her a kiss.

"When will you know?" Grace asked.

"I'll call you later today."

In the 1960's a beautiful two-story red brick courthouse on the main street in Carrizozo had been demolished and replaced by a nondescript building constructed on the same site. Clayton had only seen pictures of the imposing old courthouse, but those photographs looked a hell of a lot more inviting than the sterile functionalism of the present building.

Tucked away in part of the courthouse, the sheriff's department suffered from a serious lack of space. Clayton used a small desk pushed up against a wall in the hallway that led to the supply closet to do his paperwork and organize all his supporting documentation.

First he worked on the John Doe case. Based on the remnants of information found in the backpack, the victim was likely one Joseph John Humphrey, a homeless Vietnam veteran originally from Harrisburg, Pennsylvania.

Among Humphrey's few belongings was the business

12

card of a Veterans Administration alcoholism counselor in Albuquerque. He spoke to the counselor, faxed a copy of Humphrey's driver's license photo to the man, and got a quick identity confirmation. He also learned that Humphrey had been diagnosed with inoperable liver cancer and had no more than three months to live.

After disconnecting, he phoned Shorty Dawson, the ME, for a preliminary cause-of-death report.

"I can't tell you anything definite," Dawson replied. "The victim's flesh and clothing were melted together. The body is gonna have to be peeled like an onion. Then they can open him up and take a look inside."

"Where's the body now?" Clayton asked.

"In Albuquerque," Dawson replied. "We should get the final autopsy results by tomorrow. But, tentatively it sure looked to me like the guy sucked down carbon monoxide."

"How could you tell that?" Clayton asked. "The flesh was too burned to show any discoloration. Even if the skin had looked cherry red, lividity isn't conclusive for carbon monoxide poisoning."

There was a short silence before Dawson replied. "Look, Deputy, I said my opinion was just tentative. My job is to find the victim legally dead and offer an informed opinion as to cause and time of death. We'll both just have to wait for the autopsy to find out what really killed him."

"Thanks, Mr. Dawson," Clayton said.

He hung up wondering if Humphrey had committed suicide to avoid letting the cancer kill him. That didn't make any sense. Humphrey could have chosen many easier, less horrific ways to die than by smoke and fire. Maybe it was an accidental death. He decided to stop speculating about it until the autopsy report came in.

He filled out his paperwork, including a notation that if no family members could be found—the Harrisburg police were still looking—Humphrey's VA counselor would arrange to have the body cremated and interred in the National Cemetery at Fort Bayard, outside Silver City.

Humphrey's status as a Nam vet made Clayton think about his natural father, Kevin Kerney. He knew very little about Kerney's service experience other than that he'd served as an infantry lieutenant in Vietnam during the latter stage of the war. Until six months ago, Clayton hadn't even known that much. Then he'd busted Kerney for trespassing on Apache land, which ultimately led to his mother's disclosure of the long-kept secret of his father's identity.

Clayton had learned that his mother had once been Kerney's college sweetheart. She deliberately became pregnant without Kerney's knowledge just before he'd graduated and gone off to serve in Vietnam. For almost twenty-eight years, neither father nor son knew of each other's existence.

Clayton was still struggling with it all. He had no idea how Kerney was coping. What he did know was that Kerney had recently been installed as the Santa Fe police chief. He gave a passing thought to calling him to ask for information and assistance in the Anna Marie Montoya case.

He reached for the phone and pulled his hand back. Late last year, Kerney had stood on Clayton's front porch and given him two ten-thousand-dollar certificates of deposit for Wendell's and Hannah's education, with no strings attached. At the time, Clayton had been both stunned by the gift and suspicious of it. Thinking back over the event, which he'd repeatedly

14

played through his mind, Clayton knew he'd handled it badly. Instead of being gracious, he'd challenged Kerney's gift-giving motives and failed to thank him for his generosity. Finally he'd never followed through on a promise to invite Kerney and his wife to dinner, in spite of Grace's nagging him to do so.

Because of his bungling, Clayton felt the opportunity to develop some sort of relationship with Kerney had come and gone. He didn't know what he could do, if anything, to set things right.

Although he lacked final confirmation that the earthly remains of Anna Marie Montoya had been discovered, Clayton had enough evidence to move ahead. The clutch purse with the ID, the jewelry and bits of clothing found at the scene that matched information contained in the NCIC missing person report, and the size and sex of the body made it almost positive. It was time to get rolling. He called the Santa Fe Police Department, identified himself, and got put through to a detective sergeant named Cruz Tafoya.

Tafoya heard Clayton out before asking questions. "Were you able to confirm the victim was killed at the crime scene?"

"No," Clayton replied, "and I don't think we'll be able to. Any trace evidence was washed away. Personally, I think she was killed elsewhere and then buried in the cellar. It's only five feet deep by eight feet square."

"So the killer had to know about the cellar," Tafoya noted. "Is the fruit stand still in use?"

"It's been abandoned for years," Clayton replied. "We're looking into who owns the property."

"Good idea," Tafoya said. "You're gonna want a copy of our case file."

"Roger that."

"I'll put one together. Should I mail it or will you come and get it?"

"I'll let you know," Clayton replied, thinking he needed to clear travel plans with the sheriff. "But I'm probably coming to Santa Fe sometime soon."

"I'll have a detective update the file," Tafoya said. "At least the family will have some peace of mind about what happened to the victim."

"Yeah, there's that," Clayton said. "Once I get a positive ID, will your department notify the family?"

"Ten-four."

"I'll need to talk to the detective who handled the case."

"If he's still around," Tafoya said.

"Can you find out?" Clayton asked.

"Give me a minute."

In the receiver Clayton heard movement, footsteps, silence and then paper shuffling followed by Tafoya's breathing.

"Well, what do you know about that?" Tafoya said into the telephone.

"What?" Clayton asked.

"The original primary investigator on that case was our new police chief."

Clayton grunted in surprise. "Could you have Chief Kerney call me?" He rattled off his phone number.

"You got it," Tafoya replied.

Clayton hung up and walked to the sheriff's office. Paul Hewitt looked up from some paperwork on his desk and wondered why Clayton, who'd been relieved of patrol duties to work the homicide, had decided to wear a black cowboy shirt on a day that was going to be much too warm for such a garment.

"Would you like an update on the cases, Sheriff?" Clayton asked.

Hewitt gestured at a chair. "Have a seat and fire away."

Clayton left Sheriff Hewitt's office with authorization to conduct his investigation in Santa Fe, as needed. He was given a travel, meals, and lodging allowance and told to stay within budget or make up the difference out of his own pocket. He found Sergeant Quinones and Von Dillingham in the small staff lounge, inventorying evidence and doing paperwork.

"The county clerk's records show that the fruit stand is owned by Hiram Tully. He's got a Glencoe address," Quinones said, handing Clayton the information.

"I'll go talk to him," Clayton said.

"Are any autopsy reports in yet?" Dillingham asked.

"Not yet. Shorty Dawson thinks Humphrey died from carbon monoxide poisoning, but he's not sure."

"Shorty loves to play pathologist," Quinones said, logging an evidence bag on an inventory sheet. "We're almost done here. What's next?"

"Field interviews," Clayton said. "Find out if anyone who lives near the fruit stand saw or heard anything before the fire broke out. I'll be back to assist as soon as I can."

"Roger that," Quinones said, turning his attention to the bagged and tagged evidence.

Clayton left the office and drove the state road that took him past the burned-out fruit stand, through the ranching town of Capitan, and on to the historic hamlet of Lincoln, where rows of lovely old territorial buildings along a narrow pastoral valley drew tourists in search of the Billy the Kid legend.

17

Where the road ended at the Highway 70 junction, Clayton swung west toward Glencoe and found his way to the Tully place. A small valley settlement on the Ruidoso River surrounded by national forest, Glencoe consisted of farms and orchards, a post office, and a few businesses along the highway that funneled traffic east and west over the Sacramento Mountains.

The Tully ranch house was a beautifully maintained, low-slung, whitewashed adobe hacienda with a deep veranda. Several hundred yards behind the house the river wandered against the base of the mountains. On either side of the ranch house, apple orchards in early bloom fanned out and rolled down to the riverbank, putting a sweet scent into the air.

Early-to-leaf mature poplar trees overhung the residence, branches shimmering in the midmorning sun under a gentle breeze. Large ornamental evergreens bracketed carefully tended flower beds that bordered a semicircular driveway.

Clayton parked his unit, walked the gravel path to the veranda, and knocked on the front door. The woman who answered appeared to be in her late twenties, close to his own age. Attractive in a wholesome way, she had short-cut blond hair, hazel eyes, and perfectly straight white teeth.

Grace had already warned Clayton that Hannah would need braces. How she knew that with Hannah still years away from losing her baby teeth was a mystery to him. He identified himself to the woman and asked to speak to Hiram Tully.

"My grandfather recently had a stroke," the woman said. "He's in the hospital in Roswell."

"And you are?" Clayton asked.

"Page Seton," she said. "Why do you need to speak to

my grandfather?"

"He's listed as the owner of an abandoned fruit stand on Highway three-eighty. It burned down last night."

"Really?" Seton said. "Was anyone hurt?"

"Two bodies were found inside."

Seton's eyes darkened. "That's terrible. Were they killed in the fire?"

"We're still investigating the cause of death," Clayton answered.

"That place has been boarded up for years. I drive by it all the time."

"Do you or any members of your family ever stop to inspect the property?"

Seton's expression tightened. "There's been no reason to. Whoever those poor people were, they trespassed. That property is posted with a keep-out sign. Are you suggesting negligence?"

"That's not the focus of the investigation."

Seton's look darkened. "I'd better contact our lawyer anyway."

"Maybe you should," Clayton said. "Who has access to the property?"

"Just the family, and the realtor who has it listed for sale. We've been trying to sell it, but nobody is interested in an acre of highway frontage outside of town without water or electricity."

"Have you rented it out in the past twelve years?"

"Not to my knowledge. But my father would know for certain." Seton pulled her chin back and gave Clayton a chilly look. "Why twelve years? The stand has been there longer than that."

"I'm just gathering information, Ms. Seton. Who's the listing agent?"

Seton gave Clayton the name of a Carrizozo realtor.

"How long has it been up for sale?" Clayton asked.

"Ten years or more," Seton replied.

"Are you aware the fruit stand had a cellar?" Clayton asked.

Page Seton nodded. "The cellar served as cold storage for our apples and fresh cider."

"When was the last time it was used to sell fruit?" Clayton asked.

Seton paused. "Twenty years. Grandfather shut it down the year I turned seven."

"Has anyone—family, employees—been there since then?"

"It's impossible for me to answer that question," Seton replied. "We have seasonal workers. Some of them return every year, others will pick one crop for us and never come back, and there are always a few we have to let go. As far as family goes, you'll have to ask, and it's a pretty big clan, Deputy."

"The names and phone numbers of family members involved in the business will do for now," Clayton said.

"What exactly are you investigating, Deputy?"

"Unattended deaths, at this point, Ms. Seton. Has the fruit stand been used for any other purposes?"

"Such as?"

"Parties, beer busts, a make-out place?"

Page Seton looked upward as if to seek divine relief from stupid questions. "Not by me, Deputy, and certainly not by any member of the family that I know of."

"I'll need those family names and phone numbers," Clayton said.

While Seton assembled the information, Clayton asked a few more questions. He left knowing that the Tully ranch and farm had been a family business for over a hundred and twenty years, that Page Seton was the financial officer of the company, and that the ranch operation was headquartered on the east side of the Capitan Mountains, where her parents, Morris and Lily Tully Seton, were staying while the spring works, a semiannual cattle roundup and calf-branding event, took place.

Clayton also learned that Hiram Tully's stroke had not hampered his ability to communicate. He decided to interview Tully first and then swing by the ranch on the back road to Capitan. In his unit, a four-by-four Ford Explorer, Clayton keyed the microphone and checked dispatch for messages. No calls had come in from either the Santa Fe PD or Chief Kerney, but the state police crime scene supervisor reported that a match had been made with the skeleton found in the cellar and Anna Marie Montoya's dental records.

Clayton's interviews with Hiram Tully and Morris and Lily Seton served only to confirm what Page Seton had told him. He came away thinking that he'd accomplished nothing more than eliminating some highly unlikely suspects. The chances of solving an eleven-year-old homicide were slim at best. If no creditable leads materialized, background investigations on everyone in the Tully family would need to be done.

He looked over the list of family members Page Seton had provided. Excluding the four people already interviewed, another eight would need to be contacted. He'd ask Quinones and Dillingham to start the ball rolling if they came up empty on the field interviews near the crime scene.

Even without any tangible progress, Clayton remained pumped about his assignment. He was particularly eager to go to Santa Fe and do some real digging into Anna Marie Montoya's past. Besides, it would be a kick to clear a case that had stymied Kerney. He smiled at the prospect of it.

The day was more than halfway gone. With all that was left to do, Clayton figured he had another full day or two of work before he could leave for Santa Fe. He called the tribal day-care center where Grace worked as a teacher and told her that he wasn't going out of town right away.

"When will you go?" Grace asked.

"I'm not sure yet," Clayton said. "Maybe the day after tomorrow.

"Sometime soon, I think all of us should go to Santa Fe."

"I can't take you and the kids with me."

"I know that," Grace said. "I'm thinking of a weekend family outing."

"If we left early in the morning, we could make it a day trip," Clayton said, thinking about how pricy Santa Fe could be.

"That wouldn't be enough time," Grace replied.

Since neither Clayton nor Grace worked in high-paying professions, Clayton constantly worried about family finances. "I thought we were saving money to build the addition," he said.

"A weekend trip to Santa Fe won't bankrupt us, Clayton."

"Yeah, you're right."

"Will you be home for dinner?"

"I don't see why not."

"I'll see you then," Grace said before hanging up.

He checked in with dispatch. Kerney still hadn't called back. He gave his ETA to Carrizozo and told the dispatcher he'd be at John Foley's real estate office

22

when he got into town.

The office was in an old building where Central Avenue curved and became E Avenue. One of the town's first permanent structures, it had started out as a tin shop in the early part of the twentieth century. Foley's late-model Cadillac was parked at the side of the building.

Inside, Foley pressed a cup of coffee into Clayton's hands and sat with him, making small talk. A big man in his late seventies, Foley had slightly hunched shoulders and carried some extra pounds around his midsection that spilled over his tightly cinched belt and showy turquoise and silver buckle.

With some difficulty, Clayton guided Foley to the topic of the fruit stand. After talking about the fire, he got a short history of Foley's failed attempts to sell it. He asked if Foley had records on any prospective buyers that went back eleven or twelve years.

Foley shook his head. "I only keep information about potential clients who are solid prospects. I don't recall ever showing that property to a serious client. It's too far out of town to have any commercial value and there's no water, phone, or electricity to the property line."

"When was the last time you were out there?" Clayton asked.

"Let me think," Foley replied. "Two, three years ago. I showed it to a fella who was interested in starting a flea market and living on the property. But he didn't want to invest any money in extending the utilities and digging a well."

"Did you ever go into the fruit stand?"

"There was no need to," Foley said. "According to the Ruidoso newspaper, you found a murder victim in that fire."

"I didn't realize that information had been released."

Foley handed Clayton the newspaper. Sheriff Hewitt had not only briefed the press about the homicide, but had gone on at some length about assigning his highly qualified Apache deputy, Clayton Istee, as lead investigator.

Clayton folded the newspaper, gave it back to Foley, thanked him for the coffee and his time, and left the office. He understood the sheriff's decision to go public about the homicide, but he would have liked to have been forewarned. He also wondered when all the sheriff's self-congratulatory public and private back-patting about hiring an Indian cop was going to end. Soon, he hoped. It was getting tiresome.

He sat in his unit and wrote up some notes before checking in with dispatch. Kerney still hadn't returned his call, and Quinones and Dillingham were reporting that no useful information had been gathered so far in their field interviews. But on a more positive note, there weren't any anxious messages from the sheriff asking for a status update.

He reached Quinones by radio and got the names of people who still needed to be contacted. If he hurried a bit, he could finish his part of the canvass, go back to the office to finish his paperwork, hold a quick team meeting, and call it a day.

CHAPTER 2

BACK LATE FROM AN ALL-DAY MEETING IN Albuquerque, Kevin Kerney sat in his office and paged through the Anna Marie Montoya missing person file. Until yesterday Montoya had never been found and the investigation had remained officially open, although not actively worked for some time. There were periodic entries by various detectives summarizing meetings and phone conversations with family asking if any new information about Montoya's whereabouts had surfaced, along with unsuccessful query results from other law enforcement agencies regarding the identification of human remains found elsewhere.

Notations in the record showed that every year on the anniversary of Montoya's disappearance, her parents met with a detective sergeant to ask about progress in the case. One supervisor had scrawled in the margin of the supplemental contact report, "These sweet people foolishly refuse to give up hope."

Kerney shared the detective sergeant's sentiments. Based on what was known about Montoya, she was an unlikely candidate to go missing, so foul play was the only scenario. He scanned the woman's personal information. Born and raised in Santa Fe, Anna Marie, age twenty-nine, was about to earn a master's degree in social work when she disappeared. She lived in an apartment with a roommate, her best friend since high school. She was engaged to be married to a young, up-and-coming businessman, had a good job lined up after graduation, and worked as a part-time counselor at a youth shelter. She had strong ties with her family and a tight-knit circle of friends.

Montoya's roommate reported her missing on a day when the major crimes unit was busy busting a burglary ring, so Kerney, then serving as chief of detectives, handled the call. Montoya had failed to return overnight from an evening reception for graduating students held near the university campus in Las Vegas, fifty miles north of Santa Fe.

Kerney had run his inquiry according to the book and come up empty. Montoya's car, which was found at a shopping mall parking lot in Santa Fe the day after her disappearance, provided no clues or evidence of foul play. People at the reception remembered Montoya leaving the gathering alone. All in attendance had strong alibis for their whereabouts during the remainder of the night. Family, friends, and coworkers knew of no troubles which would have made Montoya want to go missing. Her fiancé, who'd spent the night Montoya vanished in the company of his roommate, reported no problems with their relationship. Faculty members at the school of social work disclosed that Montoya stood near the top of her class academically, had congenial relationships with instructors and fellow students, and had evidenced no signs of stress, unhappiness, or depression.

With nothing that pointed to a motive or a suspect, Kerney had dug for some dirt on Montoya, hoping to uncover a shady tidbit about her past or a shabby little secret. Nothing incriminating had surfaced. Anna Marie had been a solid, upstanding young woman who'd lived a respectable life.

He'd interviewed casual male acquaintances and all the men who lived in the apartment complex where Montoya resided in the hopes of finding someone who fit a stalker profile, but nothing emerged.

He studied the woman's photograph, taken just a few weeks before she vanished. She had round, dark eyes that looked directly at the camera and seemed to hide nothing, full lips that smiled easily, a quizzical way of holding her head, and long curly hair that fell over her shoulders. It was an intelligent face that held a quiet, sincere appeal.

The telephone rang and Kerney picked up.

"I thought you might be working late," Sara said.

Kerney smiled at the sound of his wife's voice. "How are you?"

"Tired of being a pregnant lieutenant colonel in the army," Sara replied. "Emphasis on the word pregnant."

"Protecting the country from known and unknown enemies while having a baby does seem a bit inconvenient," Kerney said.

Sara laughed. "The pregnant part is slowing me down and I don't like it. I have to sleep for two, eat for two, and basically think for two. It's distracting me from my career path."

"Does that mean you won't be the honor graduate at the Command and General Staff College ceremony?"

"I will be the biggest blimp of an officer to ever waddle up to the stage and receive that high honor," Sara said.

Kerney let out a whoop. "You got it!"

"You're first supposed to say that I will look beautiful at the ceremony, pregnant or not. Indeed I did, by two tenths of a percentage point. And if you're not here to see me graduate, I'm divorcing you for mental cruelty and emotional abandonment."

"You are beautiful," Kerney said. "I promise to be there. But it's still a whole month off."

27

"And you won't see me until then," Sara said.

"You can't break away for a weekend at all?" Kerney asked.

"I've way too much to do. Besides I'm not sure you want to see me minus my girlish figure."

"I'll stare at your chest," Kerney said.

"Even that has enlarged a bit."

Kerney laughed. "I've heard from Clayton in a roundabout way."

"Really? Tell me about it."

Kerney gave her the facts about the missing person case he'd handled eleven years ago, and Clayton's discovery of Anna Marie Montoya's remains.

"Sometimes fate smiles on you, Kerney," Sara said when Kerney finished.

"Meaning what?"

"Now you have a perfect opportunity to connect with Clayton. Use it."

"I tried that before, remember?"

"You've had three, maybe four conversations with Clayton in your lifetime, all in the space of a few very intense days. That hardly constitutes a major effort."

"The effort has to be mutual," Kerney said.

"You cannot tell me that Clayton isn't at least a little bit curious about who you are on a personal level."

"He hasn't shown any interest," Kerney said.

"Oh, stop it, Kerney," Sara said. "You sound like a little boy with hurt feelings. Just because Clayton didn't follow through on a dinner invitation he hastily suggested, after you left him speechless by establishing a college fund for his children, doesn't mean he's cold to knowing you."

"Maybe you're right."

"So?"

"So, I'll try to be a grown-up."

"Good. If I were with you, I'd be giving you sweet kisses right now."

"As a reward for trying to be a grown-up?" Kerney asked.

"No, as a prelude to wild, abandoned sex. I'll talk to you soon, cowboy."

Kerney hung up smiling and returned his attention to the Montoya case file. What had he missed in the original victim profile? Unless Anna Marie had been abducted and killed randomly by a complete stranger, events in her life should point to a motive for murder.

He'd found nothing when the case was fresh, and now surely people had scattered, memories had dimmed, and hard physical evidence—if any was to be found—had vanished.

Kerney sat back in his chair and inspected the two framed lithographs Sara had helped him select for his office. One, a winter scene with a solitary horse grazing in a pasture, was centered above a bookcase on the wall opposite his desk. The second image showed an old cottonwood in summer, branches dense with leaves. It hung next to the office door.

At the time, he'd teased Sara about picking out such serene, idyllic images to hang on a police chief's office walls.

"These are reminders," she'd replied.

"About?"

"Places we need to find when we're together."

"For what purpose?" Kerney had asked.

"Are you dense, Kerney? Look at that cottonwood tree. Look at that pasture. What would we most want to do in either setting?"

"Just checking."

Kerney put the remembrance aside and flipped through the Montoya case file one more time. It was Deputy Sheriff Clayton Istee's homicide investigation now. He'd heard through the cop-shop grapevine that Clayton had recently switched from the tribal police to the Lincoln County Sheriff's Department. He called the sheriff's dispatch number, left a message advising Clayton he'd be available to discuss the Montoya case first thing in the morning, locked up his office, and walked downstairs through the quiet, almost-empty building to his unmarked unit.

Clayton bypassed the office and started work interviewing ranchers and home owners he'd missed yesterday. By the fifth stop, the responses became predictable. The canvass had turned into a see-nothing, know-nothing Q-and-A exercise. Nobody knew diddly or had a shred of useful information. Once the formality of being questioned was out of the way, everybody tried to get some juicy gossip-talk going. He just smiled and shook his head in reply.

He contacted Sergeant Quinones and Deputy Dillingham by radio, who reported similar dead-end results. Dispatch called to advise that the local crime-stoppers organization had put up a thousand-dollar reward for any information leading to the arrest of Anna Marie's killer. The news gave Clayton a touch of renewed enthusiasm.

When asked if he'd ever noticed anyone suspicious hanging around the fruit stand, one old rancher took off his cowboy hat, scratched his head, gave a Clayton a sly smile, and allowed that sometime back he'd seen Paul Hewitt nailing an election sign on the building. With a straight face Clayton promised to question the sheriff. In response the rancher grinned and said he'd like to be there to see it.

At the end of a ranch road a pickup truck outfitted with a rack of emergency roof lights and sporting a volunteer-firefighter license plate pulled off the pavement and stopped just as Clayton closed the gate behind his patrol unit. Shorty Dawson, the medical examiner, got out and hurried toward him.

At no more than five feet four inches, it was clear how Dawson came by his nickname.

"I've been looking all over for you," Dawson said, squinting up at Clayton, who topped out at five ten.

All the firefighters had radios equipped with the department's police band frequency. "Did you try calling me?" Clayton asked.

Dawson shook his head and shifted a wad of chewing tobacco from one cheek to the other. "I didn't want to do that. Too many people listen to police scanners. You know that John Doe that got burned up in the fire?"

"His name was Joseph Humphrey," Clayton replied curtly, out of respect for the dead man's ghost.

"Whatever," Dawson said. "You were right, the fire didn't kill him. According to the pathologist in Albuquerque, he took a knife blade through the heart."

"Thanks for telling me," Clayton said casually as he wrapped the chain around the gatepost.

Dawson eyed Clayton, waiting for more of a reaction. After yesterday's phone conversation with the deputy he half expected a smug response. "It sort of complicates matters for you, I guess," he said, smiling apologetically.

Clayton shrugged. "Not really. I've been treating it like a homicide all along."

Dawson drove off, thinking Deputy Istee needed to

31

loosen up and be a little more friendly if he wanted to get along in Lincoln County.

Paul Hewitt, who had been a police commander down the road in nearby Alamogordo for twenty years before coming home to run for sheriff, sat behind his desk and listened as Clayton Istee talked.

In his late forties, Hewitt, who stood six one when he squared his shoulders and straightened up, was a big-boned man. He carried a scant ten pounds more than his playing weight as a high school lineman. Hewitt's best cop attribute was an ability to adopt a frank, honest interest in whatever he was hearing, no matter how boring or revolting the subject might be. It had paid dividends for Hewitt over the years in terms of managing people and catching bad guys.

Clayton reported that the canvass had been finished with no positive results, and that Quinones and Dillingham were visiting local businesses in Carrizozo and Capitan on the chance that Humphrey might have stopped to buy booze or a meal as he passed through the towns.

Hewitt nodded and smiled as Clayton pitched him with a plea to be allowed to work both homicide cases, all the time thinking that it made no sense all. He wondered why Deputy Istee wanted to juggle two major felony murder investigations, especially when one was a cold case that might prove impossible to solve, especially by long distance.

Clayton stopped talking. Hewitt leaned forward, put his elbows on the desk, and said, "I think the Humphrey homicide needs to be our priority."

"I understand, but I'd still like to keep working the Montoya case."

Hewitt smiled sympathetically. "Let's concentrate on the most recent crime. That's where we have the greater chance of success."

"I'd hate to see the Montoya investigation go on the back burner."

"I don't think the Santa Fe PD will let that happen."

"The body was found here. It isn't their jurisdiction."

Clayton sounded uptight. Hewitt muzzled a quizzical look. "As far as we know, the crime occurred in Santa Fe. That gives them jurisdiction. Have you got a problem with the PD that I need to know about?"

Clayton shook his head and stopped arguing. "No. I'll fax everything to them right away."

Hewitt nodded. "If you need me to grease some wheels in Santa Fe, let me know."

"That's not necessary, Sheriff. The officer who originally handled the case is now the police chief."

"Kerney was the primary? That should get the case some serious attention. Do you know the chief?"

Clayton hesitated. "Yeah, I met him a few times when he was down here working those campground murders."

"I've known Kerney for years," Hewitt said, relaxing against the back of his swivel chair. "Some may disagree, but I think he's a good man and a damn fine cop. How do you plan to proceed with the Humphrey investigation?"

Clayton laid it out. He'd make some calls to Veterans Administration employees who had dealings with Humphrey, get as much background information as he could, and then start tracking down others who knew the victim.

"You're going to have to spend some time in Albuquerque," Hewitt said.

"I'm going up there today. If the Santa Fe P.D. sends

some people down here while I'm gone, will you ask Sergeant Quinones to keep an eye on them?"

Hewitt kept his tone amiable and his smile bland. "What aren't you telling me, Deputy?"

"Nothing," Clayton replied, rising from his chair. "I just want to make sure I stay informed. Who knows? There's a chance the murders could be linked. I'll call Santa Fe now."

"Good deal."

From the hallway desk, with people brushing past him on their way to and from the supply closet and the access corridor that led to various other county offices in the courthouse, Clayton read through the Montoya autopsy report and called Kevin Kerney.

"What can I do for you, Deputy?" Kerney asked.

"My boss is kicking the Montoya homicide investigation back to your department," Clayton said.

"That makes sense," Kerney said flatly. "Update me."

Clayton summarized the autopsy findings. "I'll fax you a copy of the report," he said.

"Get it to me ASAP," Kerney replied.

"I'll do that," Clayton said.

"You don't sound too happy about giving up the case," Kerney said.

"Don't worry about me."

"I was only making an observation, Deputy."

"It sounded patronizing to me, *Chief*."

"Let's change the subject."

"What good would that do?" Clayton asked.

"It might give you understand that you have my goodwill."

"That's very generous. What do you want to talk about?"

"Forget about it," Kerney said after a pause, barely

keeping an edge out of his voice. "I'll handle the Montoya case personally. Keep me informed of any new developments."

"I've told you what I know," Clayton said, checking a surprised reaction.

"You may learn more," Kerney said. "Since we share jurisdiction, let's set aside any personal issues and agree to cooperate."

"Do you have personal issues with me, Chief?" Clayton asked.

"It's more like a question," Kerney answered. "Why, whenever we talk, do you seem intent on pushing my buttons?"

"I can't get into any of this now," Clayton said.

"Then get your head around this thought," Kerney said, unable to keep the bite out of his voice. "I understand that you consider me nothing more than a sperm donor. I accept that, and if we can't be friends, fine. But at the very least, let's deal civilly with each other as professionals. In fact, Deputy, I expect no less from you."

The point struck home and Clayton clamped his mouth shut. In this situation with any other ranking officer from another department, he never would have acted so impertinently. "Agreed," he finally said.

"Good enough," Kerney said before he hung up.

Kerney got in his unit and drove off to meet with George and Lorraine Montoya, Anna Marie's parents. In the last two months, he'd stopped participating directly in departmental operations, particularly those of the major crimes unit, and shifted his emphasis to purely administrative oversight. The change followed the murder in early February of Phyllis Terrell, an

35

ambassador's wife. Kerney's investigation had set off a chain of events that resulted in his being harried and watched by government spies, placed under electronic surveillance, fed disinformation, and forced to accept a trumped-up solution to the case, spoon-fed to him by the FBI—all to enable the government to keep secret a state-of-the-art intelligence-gathering software program.

His efforts to get to the truth of the matter had ended in an assassination attempt against him and Sara by a U.S. Army intelligence agent. The agent had bushwhacked them on a rural New Mexico highway during a winter snowstorm as they returned from a meeting with the murdered woman's father. Fortunately, they had survived, but not the assassin.

The experience had shaken Kerney's trust in his government and heightened his paranoia about the intelligence community. Privy to information about the government-decreed killings of citizens, Kerney could not assume that he, Sara, or their unborn child were safe from retaliation, or would ever be. The spycraft organizations involved in the cover-up could easily decide their knowledge was a dangerous, unacceptable liability.

To cope, he'd been steering a survival course by keeping a low profile and operating on the assumption that he was still under surveillance, and probably would be for some time to come. It was the right thing to do, but it left Kerney with a caged feeling. He hoped that taking on the Montoya homicide follow-up investigation would lift his spirits.

In truth, hunkering down and concentrating on management issues had paid good dividends. Deadwood had been cut, response times on calls had improved, the percentage of cleared cases had increased, and a new pay system for patrol officers was about to be established that would bring their salaries in line with plainclothes personnel. Still, Kerney couldn't bring himself to get jazzed about his successes.

George and Lorraine Montoya lived on a dead-end dirt lane within easy walking distance of the historic Santa Fe Plaza. On the fringe of a prestigious neighborhood, the lane consisted mostly of two rows of modest homes, all built just before or after World War II. The few houses that had changed hands from Hispanic to Anglo ownership were easy to spot. Enlarged, lavishly landscaped, and given the Santa Fe look, they dwarfed the simple farm-style cottages that were so out of vogue among the gentry and the new-rich immigrants.

Kerney had called ahead to arrange a meeting with the elderly couple, and they were waiting on a small porch when he pulled to a stop behind a beautifully maintained old pickup truck parked in a gravel driveway. Both looked apprehensive as he approached. Mrs. Montoya, a short, round woman, clutched a string of rosary beads. Her husband, equally round and just a few inches taller, seemed to flinch as Kerney drew near.

On the telephone, he'd given no reason for his visit other than to say he had fresh information to share. A deep sadness showed on their faces as he reintroduced himself and shook George Montoya's hand. His palm was moist and his grip vise-hard.

"Our Anna Marie is dead, isn't she?" George Montoya asked.

"Yes."

He let go of Kerney's hand and gestured at the screen door. "Please tell us what you know," he said, his voice cracking.

Inside, Kerney sat in the front room with the couple. Nothing in the room had changed in the years since his last visit except for a new television and an oak stand to hold it. On the walls hung Mrs. Montoya's stretched canvas embroideries of New Mexico songbirds—at least a dozen—all nicely framed. Kerney recognized a flycatcher, a warbler, and a goldfinch. He summarized as gently as possible the facts surrounding the discovery of Anna Marie's body.

Mrs. Montoya crossed herself. Her lips trembled slightly. "Was her body burned in the fire?"

"No," Kerney answered. The couple was silent for a time.

"Did you see her?" George Montoya asked. The years had aged Montoya. His hair was thin, the skin under his chin above his Adam's apple was loose, and his eyes were glazed.

"No," Kerney said.

"How did she die?"

"A blow to the head," Kerney answered.

"Murdered," Mr. Montoya said hesitantly, as though the word could beget the act.

"We believe so. Can you think of any reason for her to travel with someone to Lincoln County?"

Mr. Montoya shook his head. "She had no friends or relatives there."

"Perhaps she knew a person from the area," Kerney said. "A classmate from graduate school, an old Santa Fe friend who'd relocated."

"Anna Marie never mentioned anyone like that," Lorraine Montoya said.

"Did she ever spend time there on business or vacation?" Kerney asked.

"I can't recall that she did," George added, looking at

38

his wife for confirmation.

"It's possible," Mrs. Montoya replied. "But it may have not been important enough for her to mention."

"So, a weekend jaunt out of town or a business meeting she'd attended might not come up in conversation."

Mrs. Montoya nodded solemnly. "We felt blessed that she lived close by to us, and we saw her frequently. But she didn't tell us everything about her day-to-day activities."

"No old boyfriend from that neck of the woods?"

Mr. Montoya slowly shook his head. "She would have told us about somebody that important to her. Why are you asking these questions?"

"I know it's hard right now. Based on the facts we have, I'm inclined to believe your daughter knew her killer. She disappeared for no apparent reason, her car was abandoned, and her body was hidden near a very busy state road a hundred and fifty miles away. If it had been a random act by a stranger, the chances are likely Anna Marie's body would have been discovered soon after the crime, much closer to home."

"Someone she knew killed her?" Mrs. Montoya asked, her voice shaky. "How can that be? Everybody liked Anna Marie."

"It could have been someone she knew slightly," Kerney said. "A casual business or social acquaintance."

"A stalker?" Mr. Montoya asked.

Kerney nodded. "Perhaps. Or it could have been a premeditated attack carried out for some other reason."

"What reason?" George Montoya asked.

"That I don't know. But I'm troubled by the fact that the perpetrator took Anna Marie so far from Santa Fe. I'm wondering if it has any significance."

"Was our daughter raped?" George Montoya asked, his body tensing in anticipation of Kerney's answer.

To Kerney's mind the indicators strongly suggested sexual homicide. "We don't know that, and probably never will," he replied.

"I saved her wedding dress to put in her casket," Lorraine Montoya said in a whisper.

"When can we bring her home?" George Montoya asked, reaching to squeeze his wife's hand as she cried quietly at his side, her rosary forgotten.

"In a day or two," Kerney replied.

"What will you do now?" Montoya asked.

"Try to find your daughter's killer."

"Someone she knew, you said."

"Possibly," Kerney said.

George Montoya's eyes clouded and his voice dropped to a whisper. "For years I hear her footsteps on the front step, hear her voice, see her in the kitchen talking with her mother and sister, thinking that when the phone rang she was calling."

"I am so sorry to bring you this news," Kerney said.

"It is best for us to know," George Montoya replied. "We must tell our son and daughter."

"I'll need to speak to them." Kerney rose and gave Mr. Montoya his business card. "Are they both still living in town?"

"Yes."

"I'll try not to make it too difficult. When would be a good time to call them?"

"Perhaps tomorrow."

"Tomorrow, then."

George Montoya searched Kerney's face. "This never ends." His voice cracked and he turned away to comfort his wife and hide his tears.

Kerney let himself out and closed the screen door. As he crossed the porch he heard Mr. Montoya's heart-wrenching sob.

In Albuquerque Clayton went searching for information about Humphrey from people who knew him. Like most rural New Mexicans Clayton thought nothing about making a four-hundred-mile round trip into the city with the family to shop, take in an afternoon movie, and have a meal, so except for some detours skirting the perennial warm-weather road-and-highway construction, finding his way around town was no big deal. A meeting with Humphrey's VA caseworker led him to a state-operated alcohol treatment center in the south valley just outside the city limits.

On about a five-acre campus, the facility consisted of a modern, single-story inpatient center with two old pitched-roof former military barracks at the back of the lot and a modular office building off to one side. Big cottonwoods that were budding out shaded an already green lawn.

In a reception and staff area inside the treatment building Clayton was directed to Austin Bodean, the supervising counselor. Bodean was a tall, skinny, middle-aged man with two tufts of hair above large ears on an otherwise bald head. His office walls were filled with plaques that proclaimed various twelve-step philosophies and framed certificates of seminars attended and continuing education credits earned.

Clayton identified himself and told Bodean about Humphrey's murder.

"That's terrible," Bodean said. "He didn't have long to live, you know."

"Cancer," Clayton said. "Shouldn't he have been

41

hospitalized?"

"He wasn't end-stage yet, according to our doctor. But the boozing didn't help, especially since he was taking pain killers as needed. I was hoping he'd get himself clean and sober—get his life in order, so to speak, before it ended. But the last time he was here, he didn't seem to give a damn. I guess that's understandable."

"When was that?"

Bodean consulted a day planner. "Six weeks to the day. Joe had seven admissions here during the last four or five years. A couple of times he discharged himself before completing the rehab program. About the best we could do for him was get him through detoxification. He got kicked out of every halfway house we placed him in for drinking."

"Did he make any friends here?"

"He liked to hang out with a couple of guys."

"Can you give me names and addresses?"

"Sure. One of them is here right now, going through rehab."

"I'd like to talk to him."

"No problem," Bodean said.

"Was Humphrey homeless?"

"No, he was more like a transient. He always stayed at one of the motels on Central Avenue where whores take their tricks."

"He used prostitutes?"

"Yep."

"Any one in particular?"

"That I wouldn't know."

"How did Humphrey get by financially?"

Bodean opened a desk drawer, pulled out a file, and flipped some papers. "He had a VA disability pension

42

that paid him six hundred a month. He used to get welfare until they changed the law. This isn't the Betty Ford Clinic. We get the alcoholics who can't pay, and if they have a few hundred bucks, they'll hide it to avoid paying for treatment."

"Do you think Humphrey was like that?"

"I always wondered how he was able to stay off the streets on six hundred a month. Even at twenty bucks a night, a motel room would eat up his whole check. And he always seemed to have cigarette and Coke money."

"Did he leave any personal belongings here?"

"We don't allow that."

"Did he get close to any of the female patients?"

"We don't allow that, either."

"It never happens?"

Bodean shrugged. "We break it up when it does. But I never saw Joe put moves on any of the female patients. And believe me, I would've heard about it in group therapy if he had."

"Did he have any enemies?"

"Not that I know about. He wasn't a mean drunk, or the argumentative type. He was a quiet boozer."

"Any personal stuff come out in treatment?"

Bodean lifted a shoulder. "The usual: an abusive father who abandoned the family, a mother who drank."

"Personal, not family," Clayton said.

"After a tour in Nam he went to work as a helicopter mechanic. That was his military specialty. Had a busted marriage, no kids, both parents dead, no close ties with his siblings. He started traveling about ten years ago after getting fired because of his drinking. He spent winters in Arizona."

"Did he own a vehicle?"

"An old Mercury," Bodean said as he consulted his

file. "Any client with a car has to park it and turn over the keys while in treatment." He read off the license plate number.

"Can you give me those names and addresses?" Clayton asked.

Bodean pulled more files, read off the information, and got up from his desk chair. "Like I said, one of Joe's buddies, Bennie, is back in treatment. I'll go get him. You can talk here in my office."

"I appreciate that."

Clayton spent twenty minutes with Bennie Olguin, a member of the Isleta Indian pueblo just south of Albuquerque. Stocky and round in the face, Olguin wore a tank-top undershirt that exposed his muscular arms. Clayton learned the name of the motel on Central Avenue where Humphrey stayed when he was in town, got a few more names of fellow drunks Humphrey hung out with, and discovered that Humphrey liked to gamble.

"Did he ever get lucky?" Clayton asked.

Olguin's smile showed broken and missing teeth. "Once, with me, that I know of, down at the casino at Isleta. From the winnings, he paid for a *grande* binge we went on. We were *borracho perdido* for days."

"What did he like to play?"

"Slots and blackjack. I heard he scored a week or so ago up at the new Sandia Pueblo casino. He was *estar may pesudo,* rolling in money. Couple of thousand, I heard."

"Who did you hear it from?"

"Maybe Sparkle told me."

"Does Sparkle have a last name?"

"I don't know it. She's a *puta.* Joey liked to buy her when he had the money."

44

"Where do I find her?"

"She sometimes takes her tricks to the motel where Joey stayed when he was in town."

Clayton named the motel Bodean had mentioned.

"That's it," Olguin said, as he studied Clayton's face. "You're Indian, right?"

"Mescalero Apache," Clayton said.

Olguin grinned. "But maybe some white man snuck into your grandmother's tepee, *que no*?"

"Apaches don't use tepees much anymore, and I bet your mouth gets you into a lot of fights," Clayton said.

Olguin rewarded Clayton's observation with a smile. "Yeah, I like to brawl."

Clayton got a good description of Sparkle from Olguin and staked out the motel. It was one of those old 1950s motor courts along Central Avenue that had fallen onto hard times after Route 66 had been replaced by the interstate. The exterior stucco had been painted white and was peeling badly, holes had been punched in the wall of each guest room to accommodate small air conditioners, and the neon vacancy sign above the office door spelled out either VAC or CAN depending on which letters lit up or blinked off.

The motel sign advertised low rates, free local calls, and of course, air-conditioned comfort.

There were only two cars in the asphalt lot, both parked in front of rooms, both totally broken down. Most of the motel guests Clayton watched as they came and went seemed to be without wheels. By eight o'clock at night, not one tourist had checked in, and the lodgers still out and about on foot were either drunk, stoned, or working up to it. But within the hour business picked up. One by one, four cars parked in front of the office

45

and Clayton watched as guys rented rooms and then went inside with their dates, none of whom matched Sparkle's description.

Sparkle showed up at midnight with an overweight, middle-aged customer in tow who turned out to be a Mexican laborer. Clayton sent the john on his way and talked to Sparkle in front of her motel room. A junkie, she looked to be way older than her twenty-six years. About five two, she had a skinny teenager body that attracted certain men.

"Joey won fifty-six hundred at blackjack," Sparkle told Clayton. "He told me about it the next night when we got together for some fun."

"When was that?"

"Seven days ago."

"Did you see him after that?"

"Yeah, two or three times before he left town," Sparkle said.

"And?"

"He said he wanted to have a big blowout before he got too sick to enjoy himself. He was going down to Mescalero to stay at that Indian resort, gamble, drink, and order room service until the money ran out."

"When did he leave town?"

"I saw him two days ago. He was waiting for Felix to show up to go with him."

"Felix?"

"Yeah, Felix Ulibarri."

"Where can I find Felix?" Clayton asked.

"I don't know where he lives."

"Do you know if he's ever been arrested?" Clayton asked.

"He did six months on a drunk driving conviction. He got out about a month ago."

"Thanks."

"Why are you looking for Joey?" Sparkle asked.

"I'm not," Clayton answered. "I'm looking for his killer."

CHAPTER 3

IT TOOK A WHILE FOR THE NIGHT SUPERVISOR AT THE Bernalillo County lockup to copy Felix Ulibarri's arrest records. Clayton left the detention center with a last-known address, a photograph, and some pertinent information about the man. Over the years, aside from his DWI convictions, Ulibarri, age forty-two, had been jailed for petty crimes and misdemeanors ranging from criminal trespass to shoplifting and disorderly conduct—all typical busts associated with garden-variety chronic alcoholics. He also had one fourth-degree felony assault charge stemming from a domestic disturbance involving a former live-in girlfriend.

Not trusting Sparkle to be the most reliable of informants, Clayton drove to Ulibarri's residence, a single-wide mobile home sandwiched between two small houses on a lane just off Second Street about two miles from downtown. He knocked at the front door unsuccessfully and was about to leave when a porch light flicked on at one of the nearby houses. An elderly woman in a housecoat stepped onto the porch.

"Felix isn't home," she called out in Spanish. "Go away."

Clayton stepped quickly to her, showed his shield, and because his Spanish wasn't the best, introduced himself in English. The woman's name was Francis Ulibarri.

47

"I'm sorry to disturb you so late at night," he said. "But I need to speak to Felix. Are you a relative?"

Mrs. Ulibarri's face was heavily wrinkled and glum looking.

"I'm his grandmother," she said, pulling the housecoat tightly around her body. "What has he done now?"

"Nothing. I have a few questions to ask him about one of his friends."

Sternly Ulibarri shook her head. "I do not allow Felix to bring his friends here. All they do is get *borracho* and then the police come."

"Did Felix mention plans to go out of town with a man named Joseph Humphrey?"

"He tells me nothing. He comes, he goes. Sometimes he works for a paving company on jobs out of town."

"Is he working now?" Clayton asked.

"Maybe, *pero* I think he's *otra vez la burra el trigo*. Back to his old tricks, drinking again."

"Why do you say that?"

"Because he stole money from me like he always does when he wants to get drunk. Fifty dollars."

"When was that?"

She closed her eyes to think. It made her face look even more world-weary. "My memory is *no bueno*. Maybe three, four days ago."

"Is that when you last saw him?"

"*Si*." Ulibarri opened her eyes.

"Does he have a girlfriend?"

"No nice woman would have him."

Clayton persisted. "But is there a woman he spends time with or sees regularly?"

Ulibarri shook her head and answered in Spanish. "He knows only women who are sinful in the eyes of

God."

Clayton translated her words as best he could. "I am sorry your grandson has brought you so much pain," he replied. The comment won him a slight, approving nod. "Do you know the name of the company Felix does work for?"

"JG Paving. He has no phone, so I take their messages."

"Have they called for Felix in the past week?"

"No, *pero* sometimes he calls them looking for work when he needs the money."

"Did anyone else call for Felix in the last week?"

"One man, on the day I last saw him," Mrs. Ulibarri replied. "He said for Felix to meet him at a motel on Central Avenue. I don't remember which one."

"My apologies for having woken you," Clayton said.

Mrs. Ulibarri forced a cheerless smile. "You did not wake me. I am old and sleep little. Soon, I will rest forever in the arms of Jesus."

Clayton left Mrs. Ulibarri and checked with the two nearby Indian casinos to see if Humphrey really had hit it rich at blackjack. The books at the second casino confirmed a fifty-six hundred dollar payout. He got a room at a franchise budget motel near the interstate. In the morning, he'd check with JG Paving, and if Felix wasn't working, head back home to Lincoln County. Humphrey's casino winnings were more than enough motive for murder, and Felix Ulibarri was starting to look like a strong suspect.

Satisfied that his time in the city had been well spent, Clayton set the alarm for an early wake up and went to bed.

In early March, after Kerney had arranged for a tour of

two sections of land for sale in the Galisteo Basin and a meeting with a local architect he'd known for some years, Sara had flown in for the weekend. By the time she'd boarded a plane back to Fort Leavenworth, they'd signed a land purchase agreement, retained the architect's services to design their house, leased a furnished guest house on Upper Canyon Road to live in until the new house was built, and rented a storage unit so Sara could have the family treasures she'd inherited from her grandmother shipped to Santa Fe from her parents' Montana sheep ranch.

Recently made a rich man by way of an unexpected bequest from a dear old family friend, Kerney had the money to spend. With Sara's encouragement, he was slowly learning to enjoy his newfound financial freedom after living for so many years on a cop's salary.

Behind a high wall, the adobe guest house had two bedrooms, two baths, a two-car garage, an expansive great room that served as a living and dining area, and an adjoining kitchen with high-end appliances. At three-thousand square feet, the house was the largest and most expensive place Kerney had ever lived in. It came with a tidy backyard tended by professional gardeners, and a shady portal that included an expensive natural-gas barbecue grill, a bar sink, a built-in refrigerator, and a hot tub.

The main house, a mere seven-thousand square feet, was tucked against a hill with views of the valley below. According to the estate manager, the compound was one of ten residential properties owned by a Wall Street stockbroker.

Raised on a working cattle ranch in southern New Mexico, Kerney had been taught by his parents to rise early and get as much work as possible done before the heat of the desert drove both man and beast to seek shade. The habit was so ingrained that unless job demands forced him to work late, he was always up by five in the morning. Recently he'd been devoting the hour or so of uninterrupted time before he had to leave for the office to various tasks that needed doing to get the house built.

Two weekends ago Sara had flown in on a quick day trip for a Saturday closing on the land. Today he was overnighting the architect's plans to her, along with snapshots he'd taken of the property on a rare day off.

Kerney looked through the photographs. The two sections, a little over twelve hundred acres, were located on a ranch southeast of town that was being sold in large parcels zoned for agricultural use only. The property appealed to them from the moment they first saw it, and learning that the surrounding tracts couldn't be developed for residential use cinched the deal. Additionally, the owners, a couple Kerney knew and liked from his days managing a small gentleman's spread in the basin, would continue to ranch a large swath of land that abutted Kerney's two sections, providing added protection from the urban sprawl that kept creeping south of the city limits.

Four miles in off the highway, Kerney's sections consisted of a combination of canyon land and open pastures. Two wells produced good water, and a ranch road ran past the building site Kerney and Sara had selected for the house. When built, the house would be sheltered by a ridge and face south, overlooking a canyon that opened onto a wide meadow with views of the Ortiz and Sandia Mountains. The ridge behind the house, treed with juniper and Piñon, rose gently to the north, exposing the Sangre de Cristo Mountains, but hiding the city from view. The panorama of the Jemez Mountains stretched across the horizon to the west, where at night the lights of Los Alamos and the nearby commuter town of White Rock glistened.

He packed the photos and the house plans in a mailing tube, sealed it, and turned his attention to the old Montoya case file. He had a lot of ground to cover, not much to go on, and a gut feeling that he'd missed something the first time around.

The thought made him grumpy. He forced himself out the front door, thinking maybe his heart wasn't in the job anymore. He would much rather spend his time building the house, putting together a small ranching operation, and establishing something positive for himself, Sara, and their unborn child. Soon Sara would have an ultrasound test, and with any luck they'd know if she was carrying a boy or a girl. The thought made Kerney smile. Either way, he was ready to be a dad.

After striking out on his attempt to locate Ulibarri through his employer in Albuquerque, Clayton arrived at the Mescalero Apache resort and casino, hoping he would find him there gambling with Humphrey's money, which, not surprisingly, hadn't turned up in the ruins of the fire.

Situated in a high valley a few miles outside the city of Ruidoso, the tribal enterprise was a cash cow that drew year-round vacationers and gamblers from all parts of New Mexico and surrounding states. It offered skiing in the winter and all the usual summer recreation activities, such as golf, boating, trail rides, tennis, and swimming, along with twenty-four-hour gaming at the casino, which was within easy walking distance from the lodge and guest rooms.

The lodge had cedar-shingle siding, a high-pitched roof, and an expansive deck that overlooked the lake and the mountains beyond. Small streams, some coursing over man-made rock beds, others cutting through carefully tended lawns, flowed down the hill in front of the lodge into the lake. Small stands of pine and aspen trees and winding walkways gave the grounds a parklike feel.

Most of the permanent employees were tribal members, and the woman at the reception desk was no exception. Barbara Chato, an old classmate from high school, smiled as Clayton approached.

"You never come here anymore, stranger, now that you've left us," she said.

"I haven't left," Clayton replied. "I just work off the rez."

Barbara shrugged. "That's too bad. Billy Naiche made sergeant last week. I heard you would've gotten the promotion if you hadn't quit the department."

"Good for Billy," Clayton said as he put Felix Ulibarri's photo on the counter. "Have you seen this man?"

Barbara shook her head.

"Can you check and see if a Felix Ulibarri is registered?"

Barbara's fingers clicked away at the computer keyboard while her eyes scanned the monitor. "We don't having anybody by that name staying here."

"Maybe he already checked out."

Barbara punched a few keys. "There's no guest record under that name."

"How about somebody with the same initials?" Clayton asked.

"No."

"Can you check on people who paid in cash when they registered?"

"Give me a minute," Barbara replied as she opened another computer file. "We had two in the last week. A Mr. and Mrs. Herbert Weber from Lubbock, Texas, and a Fred Villanueva from Albuquerque."

"Is Villanueva still here?"

"He left yesterday."

"Does his registration form show any vehicle information?"

"I'll have to get that from the business office," Barbara said, picking up a telephone.

She dialed a number, made her request, and after a few minutes handed a scribbled note to Clayton. He read it and smiled. The vehicle make and license plate number matched that of Humphrey's car.

"Thanks, Barbara."

"Well, at least now you're smiling," Barbara said as Clayton stepped toward the administration wing.

Moses Kaywaykla, chief of security, wasn't in his office, but his secretary called for him on the radio and he arrived within a few minutes. Just an inch shorter than Clayton's five-ten frame, Kaywaykla was dark skinned, and had deep creases on either side of his mouth and deep-set eyes that gave him a crabby, somewhat wary appearance. In fact, Kaywaykla had a reputation in the tribe as a good storyteller. Moses was also particularly admired among the men for his bawdy jokes.

Kaywaykla, Clayton's uncle by marriage, dropped his handheld radio on his desk and nodded a greeting at Clayton. In his late forties, Moses always wore a business suit to work with a pair of expensive cowboy boots. Today the suit was dark brown, the shirt blue

54

with a regimental striped tie, the boots a pair of black alligator Larry Mahans.

"So, are you tired of working for the sheriff yet?" Moses asked.

"Not yet," Clayton replied.

"When you are, come and see me. I'll make you my assistant, pay you good money."

"Maybe after I qualify for a pension," Clayton said.

Moses laughed. "That's a long time for me to wait, nephew."

"If I make you wait long enough, maybe I can have your job," Clayton said with a smile, handing over a photograph. "I'm looking for this man. He was registered as Fred Villanueva. Checked out yesterday. His real name is Felix Ulibarri."

"What did he do?" Moses asked, studying the photograph.

"Maybe murder."

Kaywaykla's eyes narrowed. "I don't like murderers in my casino. It happened in your jurisdiction?"

"Yeah, that burned body we found in the fire outside Carrizozo," Clayton replied. "The victim's name was Humphrey. Ulibarri was one of his drinking buddies and supposedly came down here with him. Humphrey had just won a lot of money up at one of the pueblo casinos near Albuquerque. I'm thinking Ulibarri killed him for the money and went on a gambling spree here."

"You say he left yesterday?" Moses asked, handing back the photograph.

Clayton nodded.

"Let's look at some security videotapes," Moses said, "and then we'll talk to some people."

They viewed videos and found Ulibarri playing poker intermittently over a two-day span and mostly losing. In

55

between long sessions at the card tables he drank in an upstairs café and broke even playing a row of quarter slots. In the last video, which Moses fast-forwarded, he won heavily at poker.

The sight of Ulibarri raking in a hefty stack of chips discouraged Clayton. His suspect was bankrolled again and possibly on the move. Was he heading back to Albuquerque or to one of the other Indian casinos in the state? Was he in Juárez drinking in a brothel?

Moses froze the tape. "Want to know what he cashed out?"

"Yeah," Clayton said. "He seemed to be doing a lot of talking in the last tape. Do you know any of the people at his table?"

"Two of them," Moses replied, pointing out two players on the frame. "Gus Hogan is a serious player. We comp him his room and meals. He comes up from El Paso about once a month. Sometimes he plays at the high-stakes tables, sometimes not. Jasper Nava is local. Everyone calls him JJ. He owns an appliance repair shop in Ruidoso. He's here once a week usually. Comes in with a couple hundred in his pocket and plays until he either loses it or wins. He does pretty well most of the time, but won't move up to any of the high-stakes games."

"What does Hogan do for a living?" Clayton asked.

"Nothing. He's a rich guy. I'll get you his home address and phone number, if you want to talk to him."

"Good deal," Clayton said. "I'd sure like to know who else was at the table when Ulibarri won big."

Moses shrugged. "Maybe the dealers know who they are."

They walked from the lodge to the casino on a pathway that led them past the swimming pool, tennis

56

courts, boathouse, and the restaurant that overlooked the golf course. It was too cool and early in the year for swimming, and the tennis courts were empty, but several foursomes were out on the greens.

At the casino Clayton learned that Ulibarri had walked away from his last poker game with seventeen thousand dollars. Two of the dealers who had had Ulibarri at their tables were on duty. They remembered Ulibarri when Clayton showed them his photograph, but didn't know any of the other players by name. None had been regulars.

He got the names, phone numbers, and shift schedules for the three other dealers, said good-bye to Moses, and drove to the sheriff's department in Carrizozo, where he put together an advisory bulletin. It read:

WANTED FOR QUESTIONING
FELIX ULIBARRI
FOR THE MURDER OF JOSEPH J. HUMPHREY

Subject is Hispanic male, age 43, DOB 3/03/59, height 5'8", weight 148 lbs, brown eyes, brown hair, clean shaven, with a knife scar on right forearm approximately 2 inches below the elbow, approximately 3 inches in length. Recent photograph attached.

Subject is known to frequent casinos and is likely to be driving victim's vehicle, a 1979 Mercury Cougar, two-door coupe, dark blue in color bearing New Mexico license 782 KCG. Subject's driver's license has been revoked for repeated

*DWI convictions. See attached arrest record.
Subject's permanent address is 4 Camino Azul,
Albuquerque, NM. Ulibarri is an alcoholic and is
known to associate with prostitutes.*

*Subject last seen yesterday at the casino on the
Mescalero Apache reservation, is presumably
traveling alone, and may be currently using the
alias of Fred Villanueva. Subject is known to
have gambling winnings of $17,000 and could
possibly be at or planning to visit other casinos
in the region.*

*Victim was killed with a knife, type unknown. If
located, detain Ulibarri for questioning, secure
all evidence, and immediately contact the officer
below at the Lincoln County Sheriff's
Department, Carrizozo, NM.*

Clayton spent the next hour faxing the documents to
every law-enforcement agency, casino, and gaming
establishment in New Mexico, west Texas, and Arizona.
As he finished up, Paul Hewitt came into the room and
read the advisory.

"You're making some progress," Hewitt said.

"Some," Clayton replied.

"Is Ulibarri a solid suspect?"

"I think so."

"What's your next move?"

"Ulibarri mostly played poker while he was at the
casino and won big," Clayton replied. "We need to talk
to a few more off-duty poker dealers to learn if he got
friendly or talkative with any other customers. Sergeant
Quinones and Deputy Dillingham are following up that

58

angle, plus trying to contact two possible informants. I wanted to get the advisory out ASAP in case Ulibarri has already hit the road."

"Makes sense," Hewitt said. "Have you got reports ready for me to read?"

"Not yet," Clayton said. "I'll leave them on your desk before I go home tonight."

Hewitt clapped Clayton on the shoulder. "That'll be soon enough. Good job, Deputy."

Clayton shrugged off the compliment. "I haven't made an arrest yet, Sheriff. Is anything happening with the Montoya case?"

"Not as far as I know. Just stay focused on what you're doing. I'll keep you informed if I hear from Chief Kerney."

Clayton nodded, gave the dispatcher a copy of the bulletin to enter in the national and state crime information data banks, and started in on his reports.

Kerney picked up the paper on his way out the front door and glanced at the front page, which featured the discovery of Montoya's body. The headline read:

MURDERED BODY OF LOCAL WOMAN FOUND

The body of Anna Marie Montoya, reported missing from Santa Fe over eleven years ago, was discovered in the basement of a burned-out building after a recent fire in Lincoln County. According to Deputy Police Chief Larry Otero, autopsy results of the remains indicate a strong possibility that Montoya was murdered. "We're treating it as a homicide," Otero said, "and cooperating with

59

Lincoln County law-enforcement officials in a joint investigation."

He quickly read through the rest of the story, which gave the facts of Montoya's disappearance, and glanced at the sidebar articles. One summarized information about six other women who'd been reported missing from the Santa Fe area over the last decade and never found, and the other quoted the spokesperson of a women's criminal justice coalition, who took the department to task for "not caring enough to provide sufficient resources and personnel to locate these missing women and end the unnecessary suffering of families and friends."

Yeah, right, Kerney grumped silently as he closed the door of his unmarked unit and tossed the paper on the passenger seat. He forced down his irritation. Unsolved missing-person cases, especially those involving women and children, always sparked criticism of law enforcement. Kerney understood people's fears that they would never see their loved ones again, fears that were all too frequently and tragically realized. But it irked him when civilians thought that cops didn't care about the mothers, wives, and children who'd gone missing, never to be found.

At the office, he shut his door and started working the list of Anna Marie Montoya's old friends, colleagues, ex-employers, and graduate student classmates. As he'd suspected, many had moved on, changed jobs or residences, or were no longer living in Sante Fe. He spoke to a few, left phone messages for others, and got leads on a couple of the people who'd moved out of state.

Larry Otero, his second in command, popped in

briefly to get approval to hire a new civilian crime scene tech. Kerney signed off on the paperwork. With slightly more than two months in his present position, Otero had been cautiously feeling his way in his new job.

Kerney's decision to appoint Larry had been challenged by the city manager, who for political reasons had tried to torpedo Otero's career shortly before Kerney became chief. He'd placated the city manager by putting Otero in the job on a sixty-day trial period. He'd said nothing to Larry about it, and now the probationary time was up.

"Did we screen, test, interview, and conduct a background investigation on this candidate?" Kerney asked, handing Otero the signed personnel action form.

Larry looked nonplused. "Of course. We do it with every new hire. It's procedure."

"My point exactly," Kerney said. "I'd like to review applications and meet prospective employees once they've been selected. But unless either of us sees a problem, in the future just sign these things yourself."

He leaned back and gave Otero a smile. "From now on, think of your job this way: When I'm not here, you're the chief. When I'm sick or on vacation, you're the chief. When I don't want to be found, bothered, or I'm out of town on business, you're the chief. Do you see where I'm going with this?"

Otero smiled back. "I do. What happens when I get my ass in a sling?"

"Then I'm the chief," Kerney said with a laugh, "and I get the privilege of taking full responsibility for all the screwups, including yours and mine."

"So, it's full speed ahead," Otero said.

"Yeah, your honeymoon is over," Kerney replied.

"I can handle that," Larry said. "How's the Montoya

61

case going?"

"I could probably put thirty people on it with the same results," Kerney replied.

"Nothing?"

"Zilch, but there's still a lot of ground to cover," Kerney said.

He waved Otero out the door, made a few more phone calls, and left to visit with Anna Marie's brother and sister, who'd agreed to meet him at their parents' house.

Cars parked along the narrow lane forced Kerney to leave his unit at the corner. A somber group of visitors filled the small porch and spilled onto the lawn in front of the Montoya residence. Kerney approached slowly, wondering what he'd gotten himself into. His uniform drew some questioning looks as he walked up the pathway, and a few people deliberately turned away. Anna Marie's brother waited for him at the door.

"I've come at a bad time," Kerney said, looking into the crowded front room.

"We can talk in my mother's craft studio," Walter Montoya said shortly, "although I don't see what good it will do. My sister's waiting for us there."

Platters of food filled the coffee table, and empty plastic cups littered the lamp tables bracketing the couch. A framed photograph of Anna Marie, surrounded by lit candles, was centered on top of the television. Mr. and Mrs. Montoya sat on the couch in the company of a priest. Kerney paused and paid his respects as friends and family watched.

"I won't take much of your time," Kerney said, after stepping away from Anna Marie's parents.

"Does that mean you have no leads?" Walter Montoya replied, loud enough to hush a couple standing nearby.

"Let's talk privately," Kerney said, touching the man's arm to quiet him down.

Walter pulled his arm back and led Kerney to a small bedroom that had been converted into Mrs. Montoya's studio, where Carmela, Anna Marie's sister, waited. A long work table with folding legs held neat stacks of fabric, swaths of canvas, and a sewing machine. Within easy reach of a second-hand secretarial chair was a clear plastic four-drawer cart on rollers, filled with yarns, spools of thread, scissors, and embroidery needles.

Both siblings were in their late thirties. Walter, the older by a year, now sported a receding hairline and a mustache that showed a touch of gray. Carmela, who had been married when Anna Marie disappeared, no longer wore a wedding ring. Slim and tense, she shook Kerney's hand reluctantly.

"To have so many show so much sympathy and support must be very heartwarming to you and your parents," Kerney said.

His attempt to be conciliatory fell flat. Carmela nodded tensely as though an invisible wire inside her neck had been pulled, and said nothing.

"When will you find the person who killed her?" Walter asked, dismissing Kerney's words.

"I don't know."

"That's not good enough, Chief Kerney," he snapped.

"Let me tell you what we're doing," Kerney said. He took them through the investigative drill, noting how a lack of evidence and the absence of a targeted suspect made for slow going.

"We've heard those same rationalizations from your department for eleven years," Walter said when Kerney finished. He pointed a stern finger at the window, where in the backyard a bare-branched apple tree had yet to announce the arrival of spring. "My sister's killer is out there a free man, and you've done nothing to catch him."

"Don't lose hope," Kerney said, skirting the criticism. He took out a pocket notebook. "I have a list of people we originally interviewed who have left Santa Fe. It would be a big help to me if you or your sister might know where some of them are currently residing."

"What good will that do?" Walter demanded.

Kerney ignored the remark and read off the list. Carmela gave him the locations of two out-of-state people in a flat voice that didn't quite mask her anger.

"Anyone else?" Kerney asked, glancing at Walter.

He shook his head. "But some man called me at home one night about two months ago, asking if I was Anna Marie's brother. He said he'd just moved back to the area and wanted to get in touch with her."

"Did he give his name?"

"I don't remember it, but it was an Anglo name and he called himself doctor."

"Did he say what kind of doctor he was?"

"No."

"Did you ask him how he knew Anna Marie?"

"I didn't ask, but he said he'd once been her coworker."

"How did he take the news of Anna Marie's disappearance?"

"He sounded shocked and caught off guard."

From the notebook Kerney rattled off the complete witness list.

Walter shook his head. "None of those names ring a bell."

"With a little legwork I should be able to locate him,"

Kerney said.

"I'd like to say something to you before you go, Chief Kerney," Carmela said, her tone brimming with hostility.

"Yes?"

"Our parents are polite, old-fashioned people who believe in being gracious to everybody. However, my brother and I see the world a bit differently. We're perfectly willing to talk to members of the city council if you fail to make significant progress."

She nodded her head at the closed door. "And many of the people who have gathered here today are more than willing to join with us."

"I understand your frustration," Kerney said, stepping to the door.

"No, you don't," she said. "You haven't a clue."

Clayton got home just in time to tuck Wendell and Hannah into bed and give them good-night kisses. He sat with Grace at the kitchen table, ate the meal she'd kept warm for him in the oven, and told her about the Humphrey murder investigation and how it had stalled.

"I was hoping Ulibarri might have done some talking with one of the dealers or the poker players about his plans. We learned nothing."

"You sound frustrated."

"I am, but not about that. It was a long shot to begin with."

"What's bothering you?"

"Today, the sheriff gave me a big pat on the back and told me I was making good progress."

"Well, you are," Grace said. "From what you said you have a strong suspect."

Clayton took a bite of green beans and shook his

65

head. "Any reasonably competent officer would have zeroed in on Ulibarri. The way I see it, Hewitt was just flattering me. Sort of a be-nice-to-the-Indian kind of thing. I hate that kind of stuff."

Grace cocked her head. "Really?"

"What does that mean?" Clayton asked, pushing the empty plate to one side.

She was silent for a long moment. "I sometimes wonder if one of the reasons you married me was because I'm full-blooded Apache."

Clayton gave her a startled look. "That's crazy."

"In high school you never dated a mixed-blood, and when we were in college together you never went out with an Anglo or Hispanic girl."

"I was seeing you in college," Clayton answered.

"Not all the time," Grace said.

"We broke up a couple of times and I just didn't date, that's all."

"Once, we stopped dating for almost a year," Grace said, "and you never had anything good to say about Anglo boys who were my friends."

"That was just jealousy."

"Was it?"

"What are you saying?"

"Secretly, I think you resent the fact that you have an Anglo father, so you try to be two-hundred-percent Apache."

"I'm not like that," Clayton said.

"And now that you've met your father face-to-face, you've gotten worse. You think that anything an Anglo says that strikes you the wrong way has got to be prejudicial or racist."

"That's not true."

"Really? Sheriff Hewitt pays you a compliment and

66

you can't even accept it graciously. What is that all about?"

Clayton lowered his eyes.

"I'm not saying all this to hurt your feelings," Grace said, reaching across the table for Clayton's hand.

"I know," Clayton said with a sigh. "I was short with Kerney on the phone yesterday. He accused me of trying to push his buttons. Said he expected me to treat him with civility in professional matters."

"Well?"

"He's right, I guess."

"What are you going to do about it?"

Clayton smiled. "Think about stuff."

"That's a start."

"But you did say one thing that's wrong," he said, squeezing her hand.

"What's that?"

"I married you because you're smart, beautiful, and I fell in love with you."

Grace took his hand, kissed it, and placed it against her cheek. "I know that."

Clayton's pager beeped. He read the message, reached for the phone, dialed, and identified himself. As he listened, his eyes shifted away from Grace and his expression turned sour.

"I'll be there in a few," he said shortly, punching the off button and dropping the phone on the table.

"Is something wrong?" Grace asked.

"That was Moses," Clayton said. "One of his security officers just reported finding Humphrey's car in the parking lot behind the towers at the resort with an expired guest permit. I have to go."

"That should be good news, shouldn't it?" Grace said, responding to Clayton's tone.

"It would be, if I hadn't been so stupid," Clayton replied. "I didn't even think to look for the vehicle when I was at the resort. I just assumed Ulibarri drove away in it when he checked out."

He snatched his car keys, gave Grace a quick kiss, and hurried out the door.

CHAPTER 4

WHILE GRACE AND THE CHILDREN SLEPT CLAYTON rose early, ate a quick breakfast, and went to meet the state police crime scene tech assigned to conduct an evidence search of Humphrey's car. Clayton had made the request the night before, after having the Cougar towed from the resort to the state police impound lot in Alamogordo.

On the drive from his house he reminded himself to try to be friendlier to people.

The technician, Artie Gundersen, a retired San Diego police officer, was working on the Cougar when Clayton arrived. In his late forties, Gundersen was an outdoor enthusiast who had moved to New Mexico so he could hunt, fish, and camp without sharing the forests, streams, and wilderness with thirty million other Californians.

Sandy-haired, blue-eyed, lean, tanned, and fit, Gundersen looked like an aging surfer. Clayton forced a smile as he walked up to him. It felt phony.

"I just finished a visual inspection," Gundersen said. "The owner was a pig. There's gotta be ten years' worth of fast-food garbage and trash on the floorboards."

Clayton glanced at the open trunk. "What's back there?"

"It's stuffed with paper sacks filled with dirty clothes, cardboard boxes of what looks like pure junk and who knows what else."

"What kind of junk?"

"A broken Walkman, some trashed cassette tapes, some tools—stuff like that. We'll take a closer look in a little while." Gundersen pulled a pair of plastic gloves from his back pocket and gave them to Clayton. "Let's start with the passenger compartment. I'll take the driver's side. Stop whenever you find something that piques your interest and tell me what you've got. Then bag it and tag it. And don't smudge any surfaces with your gloves that might yield prints."

Although it rankled to be cautioned like some rookie cop, Clayton took Gundersen's direction without comment. He forced another smile and nodded.

"What do you hope to find?" Gundersen asked.

"Anything that puts my suspect in the vehicle would help, but finding the murder weapon would be nice. The victim was killed with a knife."

Gundersen shrugged. "You never know. Maybe we'll get lucky."

Two hours later, the two men sat in Gundersen's office and agreed they'd gotten fairly lucky after all. The pocket of a wadded-up threadbare windbreaker had yielded an old pay stub made out to Felix Ulibarri, and a plastic bag from a Ruidoso western-wear store, stuffed into the map holder on the driver's door, held a cash receipt for men's clothing and a pair of new cowboy boots dated the day after Humphrey's murder. Ulibarri had dropped seventeen hundred dollars of the stolen money on new duds.

The best evidence was the dried bloodstain on the rear seat cushion along with some good fingerprints that

69

Gundersen was comparing to Ulibarri's print record, which he'd called up on the computer.

"It's a match," Gundersen said, pointing to a scar on a thumbprint. "If the DNA bloodstain test confirms it's your victim's, I'd say you've got strong evidence that links Ulibarri to the crime."

"The autopsy report said that Humphrey was killed with a single stab wound to the heart by a blade sharpened on one edge," Clayton replied. "There was very heavy internal bleeding in the thoracic cavity. I'm thinking Ulibarri knifed Humphrey while he was asleep or passed out on the rear seat."

"That's possible, given how small the bloodstain on the seat cushion is," Gundersen replied. "If I were you, I'd go for an arrest affidavit that puts your suspect at the scene of the crime."

"I can quote you?" Clayton asked.

"Sure thing, chief."

He doesn't mean anything by chief, Clayton thought as he started to tense up. *It's just an expression.* He waited a beat before responding. "Thanks for all your help."

Gundersen smiled. "Hey, you made it easy for me."

Clayton left Gundersen and on his way to the office stopped at the western-wear store in Ruidoso. It was an upscale establishment that featured custom-made cowboy shirts, expensive boots, fringed leather jackets, high-end designer jeans, and handmade silver rodeo-style, Texas-size belt buckles.

He showed Ulibarri's picture and the cash receipt to the clerk, a middle-aged woman with curly blond-highlighted hair that brushed her shoulders.

"Of course, I remember him," the woman said. "When he first came in, I thought he'd wandered into the wrong store."

"Why was that?" Clayton asked, pushing down the thought that the clerk had profiled Ulibarri as a shoplifter because of his ethnicity.

"He was really scruffy," the woman replied. "But he had a wad of cash he said he'd won at the casino."

"He flashed money?"

"When he paid, he peeled off hundred-dollar bills. He left wearing his new boots."

"Did he take his old ones with him?"

"They were cheap work boots," the woman said with a shake of her head. "You'll probably find them outside in the trash bin behind the store. It gets emptied tomorrow."

Clayton went dumpster diving and found the boots. The right one had a dark stain on a toe that looked like dried blood.

In his unit he made radio contact with Sonia Raney, the state police patrol officer on duty, and asked if she was heading to the district headquarters anytime soon. He got an affirmative reply, and asked if she'd carry some evidence to Gundersen.

"Roger that," Raney said. "Give me a twenty and I'll meet up with you."

Clayton told her where he was, and within five minutes Ulibarri's boots were in the trunk of Raney's unit on the way to Alamogordo. He arrived at the office to find Sheriff Hewitt waiting.

"Dispatch tells me you located Humphrey's car last night," Hewitt said.

As far as Clayton could tell, there was no censure in the sheriff's voice. "One of Moses Kaywaykla's security people spotted it in the resort parking lot," he said. "I didn't even think to look for it there."

"The best mistakes we make are the ones we learn from," Hewitt said with a small chuckle. "How did the vehicle search go?"

"I've got more than enough to ask for a murder-one arrest warrant," Clayton said. He quickly filled Hewitt in.

"Very good. Do the affidavit, update your advisory bulletin, and get me a progress report when you can. I'll call the DA and tell him you're going to need his sign-off and a judge's approval right away. Now that we know Ulibarri isn't driving Humphrey's car, how do you think he's traveling?"

"Don't know." Clayton replied. "But I'm going to call around to every car dealer and rental company in Ruidoso as soon as I get the warrant signed."

"Good idea," Hewitt said. "What if Ulibarri isn't traveling?"

"I've thought about that, and I've asked Sergeant Quinones and Von Dillingham to start phoning area motel and hotels, ASAP."

"Work it hard," Hewitt said, waving Clayton out of his office.

Kerney started a new day still looking for the "doctor" who had called Walter Montoya asking for Anna Marie. Yesterday, he'd checked with the licensing boards for physicians, psychologists, counselors, chiropractors, optometrists, and practitioners of Chinese medicine. The few names he got wound up as dead ends.

After making no progress at the state nursing board, he put in a quick appearance at the office and then paid a visit to the state department of education, asking about any recent appointments of a male PhD in area school districts. He scored another zero.

72

He moved on to the local colleges, hoping perhaps a midyear faculty vacancy or an administrative position had been filled by someone matching the scanty information Walter Montoya had provided. That failed, so he went back to the office and expanded his search by phone, calling colleges in Albuquerque and some nearby area branch campuses, on the chance his unknown party commuted to work from Santa Fe, as more and more people did these days. The hunt fizzled out quickly.

The more Kerney worked to find the mystery caller, the more he began to realize that he still had a lot of ground to cover. The number of specialties, professions, and disciplines offering doctoral degrees had mushroomed over the last thirty years. There seemed to be PhD programs for virtually every occupation. Academia had apparently become a head-count growth industry, much like the private prisons that were springing up all over the country.

He called churches looking for newly installed reverend doctors, local high-tech think tanks asking about recently hired scientists, and state and local civil service personnel offices, hoping to locate any PhDs who were newly employed in the public sector. Zip, zilch, zero, *nada*.

He dropped the phone in the cradle and grunted in frustration as Helen Muiz, his office manager, walked in.

"My, my," Helen said. "Should I warn the troops that you'll be short-tempered and testy today?"

"You are cursed with a wicked sense of humor, Mrs. Muiz," Kerney said with a laugh.

In her fifties, Helen was a grandmother who didn't look like one. Always well dressed, today Helen wore tan slacks and a red silk top. Years ago she'd served as Kerney's secretary when he was chief of detectives. He was delighted to have her working with him once again.

"I like to think of it as a survival skill," Helen said, "made necessary by working in a male-dominated, testosterone-charged environment. That issue aside, Mr. Walter Montoya is waiting to see you. He says it's about his sister."

"Send him in," Kerney said.

Montoya entered, looking a bit sheepish. "First, I'd like to apologize about yesterday."

Kerney stepped from behind his desk and raised a hand to cut him off. "There's no need. I wish the world was more perfect, Mr. Montoya, so that nobody had to go through what you and your family have experienced."

Montoya nodded and gave Kerney an opened envelope. "This came in yesterday's mail at my parents' house."

Kerney read the return address. He'd spent hours trying to come up with the information that had just been dropped in the palm of his hand. He waved the envelope at Montoya and smiled. "I take it this is from the man who called looking for your sister?"

"Yes."

Kerney nodded. It got him one step closer to talking with someone who might have new information. "This could be very helpful."

Montoya shrugged, paused, and spoke slowly, the words coming with difficulty. "Or not, I suppose, given what few facts you have to work with."

"If this doesn't pan out," Kerney said, tapping the envelope with a finger, "we won't stop looking for your sister's killer," Kerney said. "I promise you that."

"I believe you," Montoya said. "Still, I want to apologize for our behavior yesterday."

"That's not necessary. It's perfectly natural to get frustrated when a police investigation stalls, no matter what the circumstances."

"Blaming you or your department serves no purpose. My sister and I talked; we won't cause you any problems."

"I appreciate that."

Montoya solemnly shook hands and departed. Kerney knew the sudden resurgence of goodwill might well be fleeting. The need to finger-point and blame could easily return. He'd seen it happen time and again with family survivors, who could go from feelings of numbing anguish to blistering outrage within a matter of minutes.

He read the return address and the enclosed sympathy note, called information, and got a new residential listing for Kent Osterman in Los Alamos. He dialed the number, identified himself to the woman who answered, explained the reason for his call, and learned that Osterman was at work. The number she gave him at the Los Alamos National Laboratory yielded Osterman's voice mail.

He hung up without leaving a message. On his way out of the administrative suite he paused at Helen's desk and told her where he was going.

"Did you know more people with PhD degrees live in Los Alamos, per capita, than anywhere else in the country?" she said.

Kerney nodded. "And most of them are pursuing peace in our time by designing new, improved weapons of mass destruction. Doesn't that give you a warm, fuzzy feeling?"

"That's the other thing about working with cops," Helen said with a laugh.

"What?"

"You're all so cynical."

"Only about people," Kerney replied.

Los Alamos was coming back from a major forty-thousand-acre forest fire that had burned down hundreds of homes and scorched the adjacent national forest with heat so intense that large swaths of ground were barren of growth. On ridgelines random exclamation points of blackened timber stood as silent reminders of the catastrophe. During the summer months, monsoon rains eroded canyon slopes, buckled roads, broke sewage lines, flooded streets, and seeped into basements.

But with the damage and destruction confined to several heavily forested residential areas, the urban core of the city still looked tidy. High in the Jemez Mountains on a narrow plateau, it was thirty-five miles from Santa Fe. For all practical purposes, it was a corporate town with one industry, a national research laboratory created by the legacy of the atomic bomb. No matter how the chamber of commerce or the town fathers tried to soften the image, Los Alamos remained a place of scientists, spies, and secrets.

He passed through the town center and parked in Technical Area Three, a cluster of buildings including a four-story, flat-roofed, concrete structure that housed the lab's administrative offices.

Signs were everywhere, directing foot traffic to the J. Robert Oppenheimer Study Center, which served as a staff library, a badge office, which Kerney found to be an interesting euphemism for a guard station, and a building that contained the personnel offices and an employee cafeteria. A number of the other buildings in the complex were off-limits, but the personnel department could be visited without going through the security checkpoint.

Halfhearted attempts had been made to landscape the complex with sloping walkways, some trees, and a few planters, but the look was purely industrial and utilitarian, and mostly dismal. Aesthetics did not seem to be a high priority to those building the modern engines of war.

Outside the personnel building, racks held a number of newspapers, some clearly antinuclear in point of view. A small, empty water fountain near the entrance was splattered with bird droppings. The lobby displayed the various presentation bowls and platters that employees would receive on completion of significant years of service.

In the cafeteria the dress code for the patrons on their coffee breaks ran from casual to sloppy, with a lot of mismatched outfits, especially among the men, who seemed to favor top-of-the-line running shoes, plaid shirts, and light-colored Dockers. Kerney felt overdressed in his civvies, which consisted of black jeans, boots, a shirt, tie, and a sport coat.

At the personnel office Kerney explained to three different people that his request to speak to Dr. Kent Osterman had nothing to do with either national security or Osterman's status as an upstanding, law-abiding citizen. Finally, the last person in the hierarchy, a woman with big teeth and a frozen smile, arranged for Kerney to meet with Osterman in the cafeteria.

Escorted by the woman with the frozen smile, Osterman made his appearance in ten minutes. Kerney introduced himself and guided him to a corner table away from chatty clusters of employees.

Forty or so, Osterman had worry lines that creased his forehead, serious brown eyes, and blond, baby-fine hair that covered the tips of his ears.

"You're here to ask me about Anna Marie," Osterman said, sliding onto a chair. "I was so shocked to learn about her disappearance, and now to know she's been murdered." His expression turned into an unhappy grimace.

"How well did you know her?" Kerney kept his eyes fixed on Osterman, looking for any sign of uneasiness or deception.

"We were undergraduates together at the university. Both of us took our degrees in psychology. That was twenty years ago."

"Is your specialty still psychology?" Kerney asked.

"No, I discovered that I didn't have the patience or personality to work with people with emotional or mental problems. I switched to hard science in graduate school and took my advanced degrees in physics."

"When did you last see Anna Marie?"

"We worked as field interviewers on a research project the summer after we graduated. I left New Mexico when the job ended and spent a year taking the math and science prerequisites I needed to switch my field of study to physics."

"Were you romantically involved with Anna Marie?"

"No, we were just friendly. I really didn't get to know her very well until we worked together that summer."

"Tell me about the research project," Kerney said.

"It was a social psych study to assess the cultural causes of alcoholism among Hispanic males. Anna and I conducted interviews to gather raw data about family, employment, and educational histories, drug and alcohol

78

use patterns, and criminal behavior. We spent a lot of time in jails and area treatment programs. It got Anna Marie interested in social work as a career."

"Who ran the project?"

"The primary investigator was a professor named Jeremiah Perrett. I always wondered if he ever published the findings. I never saw it in any of the psych journals. After a while I lost interest and stopped looking."

"Did Anna Marie have any personal problems that summer?"

"No, but both of us thought Perrett was a bit of a flake."

"Why is that?" Kerney asked.

"He kept changing the data-gathering instruments we used in the interviews. You can't draw any significant conclusions unless you have reliable and consistent information to work with." Osterman forced a chuckle. "Maybe that's why he never published."

Kerney smiled at Osterman's humorous attempt. "Did you keep in touch with Perrett?"

"No. He wasn't one of my favorite instructors. At the time, he was thirty-something and tenured, so he may still be at the university."

"Was Anna Marie romantically involved with Perrett?"

Osterman chuckled again. "That's a laugh. He's gay. Or at least he was then."

"Why did you try to contact Anna Marie?" Kerney asked.

"Just to reconnect," Osterman said. "I lost track of a lot of people after I left New Mexico. I thought it would be fun to catch up with old classmates."

"Did you reconnect with anyone else?" Kerney asked.

"A few people," Osterman replied, his eyes widening a bit. "Are you thinking I'm a suspect?"

Based on his conduct, Kerney didn't think Osterman was a murderer. But he'd learned never to rely on first impressions. "Would you mind giving me their names?"

"I'll write them down for you," Osterman said, a touch of coolness creeping into his voice. He reached for a pen in his shirt pocket, scribbled on a napkin, and pushed it toward Kerney. "The first three live in Albuquerque, the others in Santa Fe. I don't have their phone numbers handy, but they're listed in the directory."

Kerney looked at the five names. They were all new to him. "How many of these people knew Anna Marie?"

"As far as I know, just Cassie," Osterman said, pointing to the first name on the list.

"Is Bedlow her maiden name?"

"No, it was Norvell back in college."

Kerney folded the napkin and put it in his shirt pocket. "I may need to speak to you again."

"If you must, please call me at home," Osterman said, rising from his chair. "I'm new here, and I'd rather not have to deal with the police at work. It doesn't create a good impression."

"I assured the people in personnel that you are not under any suspicion," Kerney replied.

"That doesn't stop office gossip," Osterman replied, "and you haven't reassured me."

"Thanks for taking the time to talk," Kerney said.

Osterman nodded curtly and left in a hurry. Kerney followed suit, not feeling overly optimistic that he was making any progress, but pleased to have some new ground to cover. He'd start with trying to locate and talk to Jeremiah Perrett.

When Clayton struck out on picking up Ulibarri's trail through a canvass of car dealerships and rental companies, he made the rounds of the few available public transportation services, which were limited to a shuttle service to El Paso, one taxicab company, a bus station, and the regional airport served by a small puddle-jumping airline. Ulibarri hadn't used any of them. So he was still in the area or he'd gotten a ride out of town.

Back at the office, Clayton worked alongside Quinones and Dillingham, calling what seemed to be an endless list of places where Ulibarri could be staying. As a tourist and vacation destination, Ruidoso boasted lodging options ranging from tent and RV campgrounds for the budget-minded to swanky resorts for the well-heeled. In between there were motels, hotels, cabins, privately owned houses and condos, bed-and-breakfast operations, and apartments available for short-term and long-term rental. Beyond the town limits but within reasonable driving distances were villages and towns with even more possibilities.

It was drudge work that frequently meant leaving messages on answering machines at property management and realty companies, or getting no response whatsoever from the mom-and-pop cabin-rental operators who only took reservations during certain hours of the day. After lunch, Paul Hewitt jumped in to help with the calls and sent Clayton out to start making the rounds of places that couldn't be reached by telephone.

There were cabins off the main roads in canyons sheltered by tall pines, cabins perched above the river, hillside cabins on stilts, cabins that hadn't yet opened

81

for the season, and cabins sprinkled along and behind the main roads through the city. He stopped at property management firms, tracked down real estate people on their mobile phones, and met with resident condo and town-house managers.

After several hours, with most of his list checked off, Clayton called in. Dispatch passed along more lodging establishments Hewitt, Quinones, and Dillingham had been unable to reach by phone. One of them, Casey's Cozy Cabins, was close by Clayton's location.

At the bottom of a hill two blocks behind the main tourist strip, six rental units bordered a circular gravel driveway just off a paved street. Each cabin had a stone chimney; a covered porch; a shingled, pitched roof; and weathered wood siding. Old evergreen trees shaded the structures, and barbecue grills on steel posts were planted in front of every porch. All the parking spaces in front of the cabins were empty.

Clayton cruised by, parked on the shoulder of the road, and walked up to the compound. A hand-carved sign hanging from the porch on the cabin closest to the pavement announced the name of the business. On the porch railing were pots filled with ratty-looking artificial flowers.

Clayton knocked at the door and an older man, probably in his early sixties, opened up. He had a pasty gray complexion, watery eyes, and a heavily veined, pudgy nose.

"Are you Casey?" Clayton asked, showing his shield.

The man eyed Clayton suspiciously, stepped outside, and quickly closed his front door. "He died five years ago. I bought the place from his widow and never got around to changing the name. What can I do for you?"

Before the door closed, Clayton caught a glimpse of

several poker tables in the front room. Tribal gaming operations had wiped out a lot of the illegal poker parlors in Ruidoso, but not all of them. Some players still preferred private big stakes games, where none of the winnings went to the tax man.

"Who are you?" Clayton asked.

"Do we have a problem?" the man responded with a tinge of an east coast accent.

"Let's see some ID."

"Name's Harry Staggs," the man said, reaching for his wallet. He held it out to Clayton. "I run a quiet, family place here, deputy."

"I'm sure you do," Clayton said. "Take your driver's license out of the wallet and hand it to me, please."

Staggs did as he was told. Clayton copied down the information and handed back the license.

"What's this about?" Staggs asked.

"Do you have any guests?"

Staggs shrugged. "Three cabins are rented, but I don't think anyone is here right now."

"How about this man?" Clayton asked, holding up Ulibarri's photograph.

Staggs nodded in the direction of the cabins on the right side of the porch. "Yeah, he's in cabin three, but like I said, nobody's here right now."

"You're sure of that?" Clayton asked, stepping to one side so he could keep the cabin in view.

"Well, I haven't seen him all day, so I'm guessing he's out."

"Did he check in alone?"

"Yeah."

"Nobody was with him?"

"A man and a woman dropped him off, but they stayed in the car."

"Are you sure he doesn't have company?"

"No, I'm not. I rent cabins. As long as my guests don't cause trouble or do damage, it doesn't much matter to me what they do or who visits them."

"Did you get the names of the companions who dropped him off?"

"There was no need," Staggs said. "They waited while he registered, then he got his bag out of the car, and the people left."

"Do you know either of them?"

"It was dark and I didn't get a good look," Staggs replied. "I just saw them sitting in the front seat."

"But you could tell it was a man and a woman."

"Yeah."

"Describe the vehicle."

"Late model Lincoln. Dark color. Maybe blue or black. I didn't pay any attention to the license plate."

"Let's step inside," Clayton said.

"You got no business in my home," Staggs said, a worried look crossing his face.

"The guest in cabin three is a murder suspect," Clayton said, "and I need to use your phone. Either let me inside or I'll arrest you for refusing to assist an officer."

Grudgingly Staggs opened the front door. Inside Clayton asked Staggs a few questions about cabin three and found out all the rental units were identical in layout. Standing at the side of the window with cabin three in view, he called Hewitt, gave him the news, and asked him to request SWAT assistance from the Ruidoso Police Department.

"You've got it," Hewitt said. "Give me specifics for deployment."

"Cabin three is the target. It's in the center of the

84

circular driveway, backed up against a hill. There's good cover if SWAT comes in from the rear. The only windows are one on each side of the cabin and a living-room window near the front door. There's a raised front porch that's high enough to conceal a crouching man."

"No other exits?" Hewitt asked.

"Affirmative."

"Are you under cover?"

"Affirmative."

"I'm rolling. So are Quinones and Dillingham. Stay put and don't take action until SWAT arrives and sets up, unless you have to."

"Ten-four," Clayton said. "I'll be on my handheld." He hung up and looked around the room. It contained a fully stocked, built-in bar, two large poker tables, an assortment of straight-back chairs, a sagging daybed, and a sideboard that contained boxes of poker chips and stacks of unopened playing cards. "Are all the cabins furnished like this one?" he asked.

Staggs said he liked to have his pals over once in a while for a friendly card game.

Clayton pointed at the poker table that gave a clear view out the window. "Sit down."

Staggs sat. Clayton read him his rights as he pushed him forward in the chair and handcuffed him behind the back.

"I want to call my lawyer," Staggs said.

"That will have to wait. What time did the game break up last night?"

"I want to call my lawyer now."

"Did the people who dropped Ulibarri off sit in on last night's game?"

"I'm not talking," Staggs answered.

Clayton resumed his position at the window, switched

his handheld radio to the Ruidoso PD frequency, waited, and listened. In twenty minutes SWAT arrived. He made contact with the SWAT commander and talked the team down the hill and into position. There was no discernible movement in cabin three.

Hewitt made contact by radio, reported his arrival, and gave his location. Quinones and Dillingham followed suit.

"SWAT goes in first," Hewitt said. "Sheriff personnel hold your positions."

From their units, Dillingham and Quinones acknowledged the order.

"Roger that," Clayton replied.

The SWAT commander cut in. "We're ready."

"It's your move," Hewitt said.

Clayton watched it go down. Sharpshooters covered the windows. Three men hit the front door, two on either side, as one smashed it open at the lock set with a battering ram. They went in high and low, automatic weapons at the ready, while Clayton held his breath. Finally the radio hissed.

"Clear," the SWAT commander said, "but you might want to come and take a look-see."

"What have you got?" Clayton asked.

"Looks like one very dead murder suspect," the SWAT commander replied.

Clayton left Staggs in the company of Deputy Dillingham and joined up with Paul Hewitt outside cabin three. Together with Sergeant Quinones they inspected the crime scene. Naked to the waist and barefooted, Ulibarri was on the floor in a sitting position propped against one of two unmade double beds. The new belt with the sterling silver rodeo-style buckle was

86

undone at his waist, his jeans were unzipped, and his feet were bare. His fancy new boots were next to his body with a pair of socks draped over the toes. There were visible bruise marks at his throat suggesting death by strangulation.

"Dammit," Clayton said.

Hewitt stopped scanning the room, glanced at Clayton, and noted the disappointed look on his face. "Let's see what evidence the crime scene techs turn up before you start grousing."

"I wanted an arrest and conviction out of this," Clayton said.

"Like the sheriff said, maybe we can still clear the Humphrey murder," Quinones replied.

"That's not the same thing," Clayton said.

"We can worry about that later," Hewitt said, with a nod at the corpse. "Right now we've got another fresh homicide to work."

"You're not turning it over to the city cops?" Quinones asked.

"Nope," Hewitt said. "The police chief won't like it, but screw him. I'm the chief law enforcement officer in this county and this is in my jurisdiction."

"How do you want the team to operate?" Quinones asked.

Given his mistakes and Quinones's rank, Clayton fully expected Hewitt to bounce him and put the sergeant in charge.

"Let's leave things as they are," Hewitt answered. "Deputy Istee will continue as lead investigator."

"Makes sense to me," Quinones said.

Clayton hid his relief by staring at the corpse and avoiding eye contact with the sheriff. "We need to talk to Harry Staggs," he said. "Maybe he knows what got

Ulibarri killed."

"Let's do that," Hewitt said to Clayton as he turned to leave the crime scene. "By the way, the stain on Ulibarri's boot is the same type found in Humphrey's car. If the DNA confirms a match to Humphrey, as far as I'm concerned you've cleared a homicide."

Before leaving Los Alamos, Kerney made phone calls from his unit. Several years ago Professor Perrett had transferred from his teaching position to administer a chemical and alcohol dependency research project affiliated with the university. Kerney made an appointment with Perrett's secretary and then dialed the orthopedic surgeon in Albuquerque who had reconstructed his shattered right knee after it had been blown apart in a shootout with a drug dealer. He persuaded the office receptionist to slot him in for a ten-minute doctor's visit late in the afternoon.

In spite of weight work to keep his legs muscles strong and his daily routine of slow jogging, the knee had been hurting like hell over the past month, and Kerney's limp was getting more pronounced with each passing day. It was time to see what could be done, if anything, to fix it.

The recently constructed bypass around Santa Fe, built to avoid trucking nuclear waste from Los Alamos through the city, shortened his driving time to Albuquerque. The new Indian casino just outside of Albuquerque, a massive, glitzy pueblo-style complex, loomed up as the traffic slowed to a mere ten miles above the reduced speed limit. Across from the casino the tribe's buffalo herd grazed behind a fence anchored by railroad-tie posts that covered acres of ground. It made for a startling contrast of old Indian traditions and

88

new Native American enterprise.

The administrative offices for the chemical treatment research program were located in an area of the city known as Martineztown, a predominantly low-income, Hispanic neighborhood. The nondescript building, sandwiched between the train tracks and the interstate, reflected the university's politically correct decision to place community services in the barrio to avoid criticism of an ivory-tower mentality.

A few minutes early, Kerney spent his time waiting for Perrett reading a brochure that detailed the scope and mission of the center. It received major funding from a variety of government agencies and private foundations and had half a dozen ongoing projects to develop and test new treatment approaches to hard-core addiction with an emphasis on minority populations. Kerney was halfway through a second brochure when the secretary buzzed him in to Dr. Perrett's office.

Jeremiah Perrett was a man of late middle age who obviously put time and energy into remaining fit. His biceps filled the sleeves of his collarless shirt, and he had a well-developed upper torso. He kept what hair he had cut short, and his blue eyes, partially hidden behind a pair of fashionable glasses, signaled a no-nonsense outlook on life.

If he was gay, as Osterman said, it didn't show in either his mannerisms or appearance. But living in Santa Fe, Kerney was used to meeting gay men of all ages who proved that homosexuals were by no means all swishy queens.

Perrett stood up, reached across the desk, gave Kerney a hearty handshake, and sat back down. "My secretary said this is about Anna Marie Montoya."

The office furnishings were far too nice to have been

bought with grant or public money. No bean counter would have allowed such indulgences. Kerney eased into a comfortable wicker lounge chair with leather cushions. The expensive walnut desk was twice normal size, and Perrett's desk chair was a high-end model that likely sold for eight or nine hundred dollars. The wall art consisted of tasteful, nicely framed posters of old Broadway musicals. Clearly, Perrett had furnished the office with his own funds.

"Are you aware that Anna Marie disappeared some years ago and her remains have just recently been discovered?" Kerney asked.

Perrett nodded. "Yes, of course. Very tragic."

"How well did you know her?"

"Fairly well. I became her advisor when she transferred from university studies to major in psychology. She was a good student with an intuitive talent for working with people. She held promise as a researcher, but she enjoyed direct client involvement more than pure science."

"Yet she worked for you on a research project in northern New Mexico."

Perrett nodded. "She took my senior research seminar and I recruited her to be a field worker the summer after she graduated. She was bilingual. Native Spanish speaking, in fact. A very desirable asset, since we were working to develop a culturally unbiased intake assessment tool for Spanish-speaking alcohol and substance abusers."

"That must have been difficult to accomplish," Kerney said, hoping that focusing on Perrett's professional interests would him loosen up a bit.

Perrett's eyebrows arched slightly in surprise. "Yes, very frustrating. Do you have some knowledge of research methodology?"

Kerney smiled. "Not really. What I know consists only of dim memories from an undergraduate psych course I took years ago. Did you get the results you hoped for?"

Perrett smiled, showing his pearly whites and a hint of smug satisfaction. "Indeed, we did. The assessment instrument we developed is now used in Hispanic alcohol and chemical dependency treatment programs throughout the country."

His reaction, and a framed photograph on the credenza behind the desk of a former first lady presenting him with an award, confirmed to Kerney that Perrett was a man who took great satisfaction in his accomplishments.

Kerney stroked him. "That must be very gratifying."

Perrett gave a modest shrug and said nothing.

Kerney turned the conversation back to Anna Marie and asked if she'd ever come to him with any personal problems.

"None of a serious nature, as I recall."

"What do you remember?"

Perrett reflected for a moment. "Best not to trust to my memory," he said, rising from his chair. He opened an antique oak filing cabinet and sorted through a drawer. "Anna Marie used me as a reference when she applied to graduate school, so it's quite likely I still have my advisor notes attached to my copy of the letter of recommendation."

He returned to his chair with a folder in hand and thumbed through it. "Yes, here it is. She had met a young man, early in her senior year, who she was attracted to but not sure about."

"Another student?" Kerney asked.

91

"She didn't identify him as such," Perrett said, scanning his notes.

"Did she give you a name?" Kerney asked.

"If she did, I didn't write it down."

"What were her concerns about him?"

"A fear that he was just interested in sex."

"Nothing more than that?"

"For a young, heterosexual Hispanic woman raised as a Catholic that would not be a minor issue."

"Was she sleeping with him?" Kerney asked.

"Considering it," Perrett said, setting the folder aside.

"Did she ever tell you what decision she made?"

Perrett shook his head.

"What can you tell me about the young man?" Kerney asked.

"He had money and lived off campus. Other than that, nothing. Perhaps one her former roommates could tell you more."

Kerney left, thinking the fresh information about a hitherto-unknown boyfriend at least gave him another new thread to follow. He didn't know how far it would take him, but it felt like a potential bright spot in an otherwise stalled-out cold case.

He shook off the brief snippet of optimism, called information for Cassie Bedlow's number, got an address, and headed toward the northeast heights.

CHAPTER 5

THE ATTORNEY HARRY STAGGS HAD CALLED WAS Warren Tredwell, a former prosecutor who advertised his services on a billboard along the busiest highway into Ruidoso. The sign promised to secure justice for all who called his toll-free number. A tall man with the frame of a long-distance runner, Tredwell had a bushy mustache and dark, intense eyes. His suspicious glare and pursed lips didn't match up at all with the affable smile that greeted motorists passing by the billboard.

Clayton uncuffed Staggs and waited outside with Paul Hewitt while Tredwell consulted privately with his client. The Ruidoso SWAT team was long gone, and Artie Gundersen's crime scene techs were gathering evidence in Ulibarri's cabin. After a heated exchange between Hewitt and the Ruidoso police chief, the city detectives who'd arrived on the scene had been sent packing. Quinones and Dillingham were busy interviewing the two remaining Cozy Cabins guests, who'd returned to find a full-bore homicide investigation underway.

After a long wait Tredwell stepped outside shaking his head, looking somewhat amused. "Listen," he said, giving Hewitt a hearty pat on the back, "forget about this bullshit arrest and my client will talk to you."

"I can't do that," Clayton said, before Hewitt could respond. "The law clearly states that a suspect can't be unarrested."

"It's your call, Sheriff," Tredwell said, ignoring Clayton and smiling at Hewitt. "But no judge will let it stand. Mr. Staggs was in his own home and your deputy had no exigent circumstances to make the arrest."

"There's plain-view evidence that Staggs was running an illegal gambling operation," Clayton replied.

Tredwell shook his head. "My client explained to you that he often has friends over for a companionable game of poker. There's nothing illegal in that. Having playing cards and poker chips for recreational purposes is hardly probable cause to make an arrest."

"What's the bottom line here, Tredwell?" Paul Hewitt asked.

"Mr. Staggs feels his reputation has been damaged and his civil rights have been violated," Tredwell said, spreading his arms out in supplication to an invisible jury. "Look at what happened: Mr. Staggs, a good citizen, agrees to cooperate with the police and gets arrested for his trouble. All because Deputy Istee jumped to an erroneous conclusion."

"Hardly," Clayton said.

"Will he tell us what he knows, if we agree to drop the matter?" Hewitt asked.

"Yes, with the proviso that you don't pursue any illegal gambling charges against him."

"What else is he willing to do?"

"Mr. Staggs feels it is time for him to move on. You've damaged his reputation among his friends. He no longer feels comfortable living here."

"When?" Clayton asked.

"As soon as possible," Tredwell replied.

"With no more friendly card games until he goes?" Hewitt asked.

Tredwell nodded.

"So how do we unarrest him?"

"At the time Deputy Istee detained my client, he had what appeared to be a potentially dangerous situation involving a murder suspect. Mr. Staggs is quite willing to think that your deputy restrained him solely to keep him from harm's way."

"Yeah, that's why I cuffed him and read him his rights," Clayton snapped.

Tredwell shook his head sadly. "You made a false arrest, Deputy. I've advised my client that he has a strong civil rights case, should he choose to pursue it.

We can either meet at some later date in court, or act today in a cooperative spirit."

Tredwell gave Hewitt his best billboard smile. "Lincoln County would have to pony up out of the public coffers if we won the suit, which I believe we would. I doubt voters would like seeing their taxes going to pay Mr. Staggs for Deputy Istee's mistake."

"Deputy Istee was only protecting Mr. Staggs from a dangerous situation," Paul Hewitt said without hesitation.

"Very good," Tredwell said, turning away. "I'll let my client know we've reached an understanding."

Clayton stared silently at Tredwell's back until he disappeared inside. Never in his years as a cop had he been accused of making a false arrest. "I screwed up, big time," he said, unwilling to look Hewitt in the eye.

Tredwell appeared in the doorway and beckoned them to come in.

"You aren't the first cop to make a bad arrest," Hewitt said as he started toward the porch. "Don't let it eat at you."

"Do you think Tredwell could win a civil rights suit?" Clayton asked as he caught up with Hewitt.

"Oh, yeah."

Cassie Bedlow lived in a fashionable foothills neighborhood near a popular national forest picnic grounds at the bottom of the west slope of the Sandia Mountains. The large house was sited to give views of the West Mesa, where Albuquerque's sprawl petered out and five extinct volcanos rose up from the high desert plateau.

There was no answer at the front door, so Kerney talked to some neighbors and learned that Cassie

Bedlow lived alone, kept to herself, had no children, and owned the Bedlow Modeling and Talent Agency. He called the business and got a telephone answering service. The operator gave him the agency's street address and noted that Ms. Bedlow was not expected back in her office until morning.

The agency, located on a side street near the university, was closed when Kerney got there. A sign on the glass door announced that a new modeling class would be starting in two weeks. At the contemporary art gallery next door, a one-man show was in progress. The artist specialized in paintings reminiscent of Marc Chagall. But unlike Chagall, who often portrayed men, women, and angels floating above villages and landscapes, the artist on display went in for flying automobiles, dishwashers, and other major appliances, all with gossamer wings.

Kerney spoke to the owner, a thirty-something male with dyed blond hair. The man told him Cassie had taken her current crop of budding fashion models out of town to do a show and a location fashion shoot, but he didn't know where.

"How many models went with her?" Kerney asked.

"Eight or ten," the man replied. "That's usually the number of students she enrolls in each class."

"Men and women?"

"Oh, yes," the man answered. "But most of them are girls."

"Does she have any employees?"

"Not really. There's a freelance photographer she uses for portfolio and location work. Other than that, she runs the business by herself."

"Is she successful in getting her models professional work?" Kerney asked, his eye wandering to a large

96

canvas that showed a flying television set with rabbit ears hovering above the Golden Gate Bridge.

"I'd say she's very successful. A lot of the local ad agencies use her students, she has all the major department store contracts for fashion events, and she's in demand as a casting agent for extras and walk-ons when film companies come to town."

"Sounds like a thriving enterprise."

"Yes, I'd say so." The man walked to the picture of the floating TV. "You seemed drawn to ÔAscending the Airways to Heaven.' If you look closely at the distorted picture on the television screen, you can see a weeping Jesus. Miligori's paintings are allegorical statements of the religious fervor of crass consumer consumption in contemporary Western society."

"I can see that," Kerney said.

"Aren't they marvelous?"

"Remarkable," Kerney said, playing it safe. The comment won him an agreeing smile.

Kerney left after allowing the art dealer to give him a brochure on the Miligori exhibit. Outside on the sidewalk, he used his cell phone to call the APD vice unit. The supervisor told Kerney the Bedlow Modeling and Talent Agency wasn't a vice unit target.

"Have any complaints been filed against Bedlow or have any arrests for solicitation been made that involve the agency?" Kerney asked.

"Nary a one," the officer responded laconically. "But it's always good to get a heads up on any new escort services. They come and they go. Are you suspicious of something, Chief?"

"Not yet," Kerney replied.

"Have you got hookers' names or aliases I can run through my data bank?"

Nary a one ran through Kerney's mind. Instead he said, "No."

"Well, Bedlow looks clean from our end, but you never know. Now if it was Honey Pot Escorts you were asking about, that would be a different story."

"Sounds like a classy outfit," Kerney said.

"HIV city, Chief. We call it the get-laid-and-die hooker service. Dial one-eight-hundred dead sex."

Harry Staggs sat on the daybed with a smug look on his face. He glanced at Clayton, gestured at Tredwell, and then addressed Paul Hewitt. "My lawyer says you and Tonto agreed to my terms."

Clayton stiffened in anger. Hewitt stepped in front of the deputy. "There's no need to be disrespectful," he said.

"It's just a word," Staggs said offhandedly, sucking in cigarette smoke. "I don't mean nothing by it. We've got a deal?"

"If you cooperate," Hewitt replied.

"You're just investigating a murder here," Staggs replied, stubbing out the cigarette. "Nothing else, right?"

"That's the deal," Clayton said. He took a tape recorder out of his briefcase, placed it on a poker table, and told Staggs where to sit.

Hewitt and Tredwell joined them at the table. Clayton punched the record button and said, "When I ask you a question, answer it verbally."

"Okay," Staggs said.

Clayton noted the reason for the interview, the persons present, and the time, date, and place. He gave Staggs his full attention, hoping Tredwell and the sheriff wouldn't interrupt him too much.

"Did Ulibarri play poker here last night?" he asked, studying Staggs's face, which remained expressionless.

Staggs caught himself nodding. "Yes."

"Did he win or lose?"

"He came in the game with ten thousand, the house minimum, and cashed out at twenty-five thousand. I counted the chips myself."

Staggs maintained his bland air. Clayton figured he had his poker face on, which made sense given his occupation. "What time did he leave the game?"

"It broke up at five in the morning. That's when everybody left."

"How many players?" Clayton asked.

"Six, including me," Staggs replied. "Ulibarri and the other two guys that were staying here went back to their cabins. Everybody else took off."

"Did you see them leave?"

"Yeah, I stood on the porch and waved bye-bye."

"Don't be a wiseass," Clayton said. "Did you see them leave?"

"No."

"Give me names."

Staggs named the players staying at the cabins.

"What about the other two guys?"

"They both flew in for the game. Ned Halloran came in from Phoenix and Luis Rojas from El Paso. Both have private planes."

"Where are they staying?" Clayton asked.

"I didn't ask, but they probably didn't hang around town."

"You got phone numbers for them?"

"Yeah." Staggs got up, found an address book in a lamp-table drawer, read off numbers, and stuffed the address book in a back pocket.

99

"How well do you know the players who were here last night?" Clayton said, pointing to the chair Staggs had vacated.

Staggs sat back down. "Everybody except Ulibarri are regulars. They been coming since I opened five years ago."

"Do they always play together?"

Staggs laughed. "It don't work that way. Players are in the game for the stakes, not friendship. Only the game matters."

"Have you had any problems with any of them in the past?"

Staggs snorted. "Never. You cause trouble here, you don't come back. End of story."

"So, no problems?"

"Nope."

"Who lost big?" Clayton asked.

"Luis Rojas. He dropped forty grand."

"Was Ulibarri the big winner?"

"Nope, Ned Halloran was."

"How did you do?"

Staggs reached for a cigarette and lit it. "With my house percentage, I made a few bucks." He shot Tredwell a look.

"That's a good enough answer," Tredwell said.

"Did Ulibarri ever play here before?"

"No."

"You let strangers—people you don't know—sit in on illegal, high-stakes games?" Hewitt asked.

Staggs gave Hewitt a baleful glance. "He found his way here and had the cash. That's all it takes to get into a game."

"He didn't find his way here by himself," Clayton said. "You told me earlier a man and woman dropped him off."

"Same thing," Staggs said, tugging an earlobe.

It was the first sign of nervousness, Clayton noted.

"I also told you that I didn't recognize them," Staggs added.

"Isn't that risky business?" Clayton asked. "Ulibarri shows up with no references, dropped off by strangers. What if he had been a cop?"

Staggs snorted at the idea. "No way. The local cops have never been a problem. They got their heads up their asses."

Hewitt leaned forward and scratched his forehead. "I don't get it, Staggs. Three complete strangers show up and that's okay with you?"

Staggs rubbed his nose, which suggested a lie was coming. "It's not that hard to find out where the action is. People talk to people, especially about where the good games are. That's how a reputation gets built."

"Simple as that?" Clayton said.

Staggs crossed his arms in front of his chest. "Sometimes."

Clayton read the body language and knew Staggs was still lying. He pushed the issue. "Ulibarri just shows up, brought by strangers."

Staggs pulled at his earlobe again. "I already said that."

"An unknown man and woman?"

Staggs shifted sideways in his chair. "How many times do I have to answer that question?"

"Until you stop bullshitting us," Clayton said. He glanced at Paul Hewitt, who hit the stop button on the tape recorder.

"How much cash do you have in the house?" Hewitt asked.

"You don't have to answer that," Tredwell said, quickly facing Hewitt. "What's the relevance of the question?"

"We didn't find any money in Ulibarri's cabin," Hewitt said. "People get killed for a lot less than twenty-five thousand, so robbery may be the motive."

"We have a deal to treat my client as a cooperating witness," Tredwell said.

"That deal is about illegal gambling, not murder," Hewitt replied, smiling at Staggs. "I bet the crime scene techs have just lifted your client's fingerprints from Ulibarri's cabin."

"He owns the place," Tredwell said. "You'll find his prints everywhere."

"That's probably true, but the district attorney and a judge might be convinced those fingerprints place him at the scene of a homicide. What if the court issued a search warrant? I wonder what we'd find." Hewitt shook his head sadly at Staggs. "Maybe a lot of cash, maybe twenty-five thousand or more."

"You're way off base, Sheriff," Tredwell said.

"Staggs only gets a free ride for operating an illegal gambling parlor."

"What do you want?" Tredwell asked with tight lips.

"Real cooperation," Hewitt replied. "The names of the man and woman who brought Ulibarri to the game will do for starters."

"Give us a few minutes." Tredwell rose and took Staggs into the bedroom.

Hewitt caught the unspoken question in Clayton's eyes and grinned. "*Never* let a lawyer bully you without a payback," he whispered, "even when they're in the right."

The door opened and Tredwell came out first,

followed by a sulky-looking Staggs.

Clayton waited for the men to sit at the table before turning on the tape recorder. "Who were the man and the woman with Ulibarri?" he asked.

"The guy's name is Johnny Jackson," Staggs replied. "He runs an escort service. High-class talent only. Very expensive. The woman was probably a hooker."

"What else do you know about him?" Clayton asked.

"That's about it," Staggs said, shifting his eyes away from Clayton.

"He's local?" Clayton asked.

"That, I don't know. I hear he's got a private plane and flies his talent all over the southwest."

"How do you contact him?"

"I don't."

"Why did he bring Ulibarri to your game?"

"I didn't ask."

"How long have you known Jackson?"

"I just know who he is, that's all."

"You've never met him?"

"I've seen him around, but we've never talked."

"What else have you heard about him?"

"He's got some fancy place in the area where very special clients can hook up with his girls."

"Does Jackson supply women for your gambling buddies?" Hewitt asked.

Tredwell jumped in before Staggs could reply. "My client is not a party to Mr. Jackson's alleged criminal activities."

"People come here for the game, not pussy," Staggs replied.

"Is that a no?" Clayton asked.

"Yeah, that's a no."

"Describe Jackson," Clayton said.

103

Staggs fidgeted, but didn't answer.

Clayton rephrased. "What does he look like?"

Staggs gulped air before responding. "He's a small guy, thin. Maybe five six or seven. Curly black hair he keeps cut short. Nice dresser. Always smiling. Dark eyes. I don't remember what color. Women think he's good-looking."

"Any distinguishing features?"

Staggs thought for a minute and pointed to his right cheek. "He's got a small mole here."

"You pointed to your right cheek," Clayton said.

"Yeah, a mole on his right cheek."

"How old?"

"Forty, maybe, would be my guess. He looks younger."

"And the car he was driving?"

"It's a Lincoln, dark blue, four door."

"Have you seen him driving anything else?" Clayton asked.

Staggs fumbled a cigarette pack out of a shirt pocket and lit another cancer stick. "He always drives a Lincoln, as far as I know." He blew a cloud of smoke straight at Clayton. "I've seen him around town in it."

Clayton pulled his head back, coughed, and waved the smoke away.

Through the front window Hewitt saw Sergeant Quinones waiting impatiently on the porch. "A few more questions and then we'll take a break," he said while Clayton kept coughing. "Where have you run into Jackson?"

"I've seen him at the casino and the racetrack."

"If you don't know him and have had no dealings with him, why were you protecting him?"

"I didn't want any trouble."

104

Hewitt wondered whether Staggs was talking about trouble from cops, or trouble from Johnny Jackson. "Have you ever been to this private place where Jackson's girls entertain special clients?"

"Nope, that's way out of my class."

"What do you know about it?" Hewitt asked.

"Just that it's like a swanky mountain resort or lodge somewhere in the area. Very secluded. Look, Ulibarri's winnings would be like chump change to Jackson. He'd have no reason to kill him."

"Tell me about these special clients he entertains."

"Rich guys, guys with important jobs, guys in the public eye, guys looking for a little fun away from the wife, where they won't be recognized," Staggs said with a furtive glance at the door, as if he were expecting thugs to bust in and break his legs.

"Do you know any of these rich guys?" Hewitt asked.

Staggs snorted in reply, puffed, and blew smoke through his nose. "Those kind of people don't socialize with me."

Hewitt stopped the recorder and pushed himself out of the chair. "Okay, we'll take a short break." He looked down at Staggs speculatively. "Why are you scared of Jackson?"

Staggs bit his lip. "Who says I'm scared?"

Outside, Sergeant Quinones showed Hewitt and Clayton a bagged-and-tagged plastic bottle of prescription pain killers with Humphrey's name typed on the pharmacy label. The prescription had been filled two days before Humphrey's murder.

"This was in Ulibarri's shirt pocket," Quinones said.

Clayton almost smiled. The bottle was the best possible kind of evidence: it linked killer to victim. Instead, he nodded. "Did you and Dillingham get

105

anything from your interviews?"

"Yeah," Quinones answered. "Now we're going to check the stories out."

Kerney's ten-minute appointment with his orthopedic surgeon lasted half an hour. After examining his knee, asking a lot of questions about his exercise regime, and making Kerney hop, squat, and duckwalk, the doctor announced that the plastic that served as cartilage in the artificial joint had most likely failed, causing increased muscle pain and Kerney's pronounced limp. He gave Kerney a script to make an appointment for a Magnetic Resonance Imaging test, known as an MRI, to confirm the diagnosis, and then showed him the model of a new, FDA-approved, longer-lasting artificial knee that would give him greater flexibility.

It would mean another surgery to implant the artificial joint, and another round of postoperative physical therapy and rehabilitation. But it would mean no more pain, no more limp, and greater mobility.

The only question in Kerney's mind was when to do it, before or after the baby arrived? Before might be better, if he had any reasonable expectation of ever playing on the floor with his child.

The doctor strongly suggested that Kerney take up swimming in lieu of jogging, which would lessen damage to the plastic that served to cushion movement of the steel implant. He wasn't much of a water person. His swimming experiences consisted of hot-weather dips in stock tanks when he was a kid growing up on a ranch, and occasional teenage forays in swimming pools where he could splash around safely without publicly embarrassing himself.

On a weekend outing, Sara had coaxed him into a

hotel pool and then laughed and teased him after he'd awkwardly plowed his way through two short laps. She swam fluidly, dove gracefully, floated effortlessly, and loved the water. Perhaps he should call the architect and tell him to add plans for a swimming pool in the courtyard area behind the house.

He resisted the idea. In the high deserts of New Mexico, which included Santa Fe, water was a precious commodity. As a boy growing up in the arid Tularosa Basin, he'd watched his father constantly worry about drought, and had worked by his side replacing buried pipelines, rebuilding catchment basins, and mending windmills to insure the stock stayed watered. The idea of using thousands of gallons of water a year for a swimming pool went against the grain.

Kerney switched mental gears. The doctor had told him a new knee could wear out just as quickly if he kept jogging on it, and that water exercise was a far better way to keep the leg in shape. If he could lose the limp, which he hated, then he wouldn't look and feel like one of the walking wounded.

Maybe the pool was a medical necessity, not a wasteful, unnecessary luxury. He thought it over and decided that even if it was a rationalization, it was a damn good one.

He dawdled over a light meal at one of the restaurants along a four-lane city street that led to the foothills before driving to Cassie Bedlow's house. Lights were on inside and his knock at the door was answered by a somewhat frumpy, motherly looking woman.

"Ms. Norvell?" he asked, displaying his shield.

"I'm Cassie Bedlow," she answered, looking a bit nonplused. "Is there a problem in the neighborhood?"

"No, I'd like to ask you about Anna Marie Montoya."

Bedlow's expression turned grave. "Please come in. I read that her body had been found, and that the police were calling it a murder. After all these years, how sad."

The word elegant came to mind as Kerney crossed the threshold into a small entrance hall that led to the step-down living room. Two matching easy chairs covered in ivory-colored fabric sat at opposite ends of a large copper-top coffee table. The oak floor was stained a rich brown that contrasted nicely with a neutral gray area rug. The sofa was a soft peach, positioned to give a view of a carved stone fireplace with casement windows on either side. Two expensive traveling bags were on the floor in an archway that most likely led to a bedroom suite. From all appearances, Bedlow made a very good living operating her modeling and talent agency.

She sat with Kerney and answered his questions without hesitation. She'd known Anna Marie in college, but not well, and had no idea who Montoya had dated during her senior year. She knew no one who fit the rich playboy profile Jeremiah Perrett had described as Anna Marie's love interest. Kent Osterman had been Bedlow's college boyfriend for a while, back when she was anorexic, forty pounds lighter, and didn't have to highlight her hair to cover the gray.

"Was Kent interested in Anna Marie?" Kerney asked.

Bedlow shook her head. "Kent liked his girlfriends blond, skinny, and fun-loving."

"How did Osterman locate you?" Kerney asked.

Bedlow didn't understand the question. "Excuse me?"

"He knew you before you were married, when you were still Cassie Norvell."

"Oh, that. He gets the alumni magazine. I was featured in an issue last year. A piece about women graduates who became entrepreneurs."

"I've heard your agency is very successful."

Bedlow smiled prettily. "I've been blessed in that regard, but it's been a lot of hard work."

"Are you still married?" Kerney asked.

Bedlow laughed. "Not for a very long time."

Kerney said good night, left Cassie Bedlow to her unpacking, and drove to Santa Fe thinking he'd been wise not to get optimistic about his new lead, which seemed to be fizzling out quickly. Tomorrow, he'd contact the remaining names on Osterman's list by phone and see where that took him.

The light on the answering machine blinked at him when he got home. He played back a message from Sara asking him to call and not to worry about the time, because she'd be up late studying.

He dialed her number and she answered immediately. "What's up?" he asked.

"I just wanted to hear your sexy voice," Sara replied.

"You sound sleepy."

"I am. My eyes are crossed and I can't read another page."

"What are you reading?"

"A monograph by an archaeologist who researched the battle site at the Little Bighorn. He suggests that contrary to popular belief, Custer didn't blindly go up against overwhelming odds. He made all the correct orthodox, tactical field maneuvers and still got his butt kicked. So much for thinking inside the box. Why are you home so late?"

"Just working. I saw my orthopedic surgeon today."

"And?"

He told her about the newly developed artificial knee, how it would perform, and the idea of building a

109

swimming pool at the new house to use for exercise.

"But I'm thinking maybe a lap pool would be better," Kerney said. "It would use less water."

"No way, Kerney," Sara replied.

"Why not?"

"Because I can't teach both you and our child to swim in a lap pool, and I want something all of us can enjoy. Get that knee fixed and I'll have you ready to compete in a Senior Olympics swimming event within a year."

"You say the sweetest things."

Sara giggled. "I know it. Make sure the pool is heated, so we can use it year-round."

"I didn't think of that. When should I schedule the surgery?"

"At the latest, before your son learns to walk, so you can keep up with him. Preferably sooner."

"Son?" Kerney asked, caught completely off guard.

"That's what I said. The ultrasound confirmed it today."

Kerney sucked in a deep breath and let it out slowly.

"Is that all you can say?" Sara asked.

"I'm flabbergasted. I'm grinning from ear to ear. I don't know what to say, except let's try for a daughter next time."

"One of each would be great, wouldn't it? But slow down, Kerney. Let me get through one pregnancy at a time. Besides, we might find that one child is all we can handle. Just ask the architect to revise the plans to include the swimming pool. I want to make sure that it's perfectly sited."

"I'll call him in the morning."

"Say good night."

Kerney did as told and went to bed thinking of what it

would be like to raise a son, and actually get to be a father.

Finished with a review of all the evidence and information that had been gathered during the day, Clayton and Paul Hewitt lapsed into silence. Except for an on-duty dispatcher, the men were alone in the offices. It was deflating when all of the known suspects in a homicide investigation had airtight alibis, and that seemed to be the situation.

Luis Rojas and Ned Halloran, the two men who'd flown to the game in private planes, had arrived home before Ulibarri had been killed, and their whereabouts had been accounted for by no fewer than three independent sources each, including airport personnel in Phoenix and El Paso and business associates.

One of the guests at Casey's Cozy Cabins admitted to taking Ulibarri to the Ruidoso Downs Racetrack about ten in the morning and said they'd played video poker at the track casino for several hours. The second guest showed up to play the ponies just before televised off-track betting from California began. Surveillance tapes showed that both men were still at the track long after Ulibarri left to go back to his cabin to get himself murdered.

Neither man professed to know where Ulibarri had gone or what he'd planned to do after leaving the racetrack casino.

Tredwell had agreed to let his client account for his activities during the time of the murder. Staggs had taken his car in for warranty service at the dealership, where the discovery of a leaky oil pan made it necessary to keep the vehicle for several hours beyond the scheduled appointment. Staggs had waited until it became apparent that parts would have to be ordered and the car kept overnight, getting a ride home from the lot boy. The parts manager, service manager, mechanic, and the lot boy all put Staggs at the car dealership before, during, and after Ulibarri's estimated time of death.

"All we've got is a staged crime scene," Clayton finally said, looking at the photograph of Ulibarri's body with his belt undone, his pants unzipped, and his cowboy boots placed neatly together on the floor. "Telling us what?"

"Don't know," Hewitt said, rubbing an eye. "Maybe it's not a message meant for us. Maybe it's not even staged. Tomorrow, let's see what we can learn about Johnny Jackson."

Clayton nodded. "I'll also contact the FBI to see if any similarly staged homicides have been reported."

"Yeah," Hewitt said.

"Yeah," Clayton echoed, his mind blank, his body weary.

A quiet, dark house greeted Clayton upon his arrival home. In the living room he removed his weapon, ejected the magazine, and locked both in the gun cabinet where he kept his hunting rifles. He heard Grace shush him, turned around, and found her sitting in the recliner with Hannah cradled in her arms, fast asleep. She shook her head to warn him not to talk, and carried Hannah to her bedroom.

Seeing Hannah out of bed so late at night worried Clayton; she was usually a sound sleeper.

"It's just a cold and a small cough," Grace said when she returned.

Clayton nodded and sank into the recliner.

"I feel like I haven't seen you in days," Grace said, turning on a table lamp.

"The ways things are going, it probably would've been better if I had just stayed home," Clayton said.

"Problems?"

"Mistakes," Clayton replied. "Too many of them, and all mine."

He told her about Tredwell's threat to sue him for the false arrest of Harry Staggs. "Paul Hewitt even went so far as to say he thought Tredwell could probably win the suit," he added.

"Was that the extent of his comments?" Grace asked, as she sat on Clayton's lap and pulled his arm around her waist.

"Yeah."

"That doesn't sound like very harsh criticism."

"Maybe not, but I bet he has second thoughts about hiring me."

"Now you're jumping to a conclusion."

"Not only did he pull me out of the fire with Tredwell, but he showed me a thing or two about interrogating a witness. Hewitt's sharp."

"Don't be so hard on yourself," Grace said, looking into his tired eyes.

Hannah started coughing before Clayton could respond. Grace got up quickly, checked on Hannah for a few minutes, and returned to find Clayton with his boots pulled off, fast asleep in the recliner.

She covered him with a blanket, turned out the light, and went to bed, fretting about her husband. He seemed so down lately, which wasn't like him at all.

CHAPTER 6

HOMICIDES IN LINCOLN COUNTY WERE RARE, SO WHEN Paul Hewitt arrived early at his office he fully expected major print coverage about the Ulibarri case. But he wasn't prepared to have it be front page news in the morning papers from El Paso to Albuquerque, Las Cruces to Roswell. Headlines read:

MURDER SUSPECT KILLED

TOP COPS QUARREL IN LINCOLN CITY

ILLEGAL GAMBLING DEN UNCOVERED IN RUIDOSO

SUSPECTED KILLER SLAIN AT ILLICIT POKER PARLOR

RUIDOSO SWAT TEAM FINDS MURDERED FUGITIVE

GAMBLING DEN OPERATOR GOES FREE

There were sidebar articles about the Anna Marie Montoya and Joseph John Humphrey cases, and a story that summarized Ruidoso's well-deserved reputation during the Prohibition era as a wide-open bootlegging, speakeasy, and gambling town.

Although the quotes were anonymous, Hewitt figured the leak about Harry Staggs and his decision to keep the city cops out of the investigation came from the Ruidoso police chief. The man had been privately denigrating the sheriff's department for years, and resented Hewitt's role as the county's chief law-enforcement officer.

Fuming, he closed his office door, turned on a small portable television, and surfed the network channels for the early morning local news breaks. All of them featured the story at the top of the telecast, with video of the cabin where Ulibarri had been killed.

Tredwell called, pissed and wanting an explanation about how the story hit the papers. Hewitt told Tredwell he didn't control the news media and to direct his outrage at the Ruidoso police chief. The district attorney called, pissed and wanting a meeting so Hewitt could explain why he'd cut a deal with a felony suspect's attorney on his own authority.

Two county commissioners called to tell Hewitt the Ruidoso mayor was talking about asking for a grand jury probe of the sheriff's department. Reporters called wanting interviews. Hewitt put them off.

The only good news was Artie Gundersen's telephone report that the bloodstain on Ulibarri's boot, which Clayton had fished out of the dumpster behind the western-wear store, was a match to Humphrey's, as were the traces of blood on the knife found in cabin three. Additionally, Ulibarri's latents were all over the blade handle, and the murder weapon conformed nicely to the entry wound in Humphrey's chest.

Hewitt called the reporters back and issued a statement: forensic analysis of the evidence gathered by lead investigator Deputy Clayton Istee and state police crime technicians proved beyond a reasonable doubt that Ulibarri was Humphrey's killer, and the case had been closed. He gave specifics, brushed aside questions about the ongoing Montoya and Ulibarri investigations, hung up, and wrote a quick note for Clayton Istee telling him about Gundersen's findings.

He wondered what was bothering Clayton Istee. Over the last several days, he'd seemed wary and constrained in his dealings with others, including Dillingham and Quinones. Were his slipups troubling him? There were all kinds of judgment errors that could occur during a major felony investigation, and no cop was immune to them. But getting bogged down by becoming overly cautious or trying to be perfect could quickly derail an investigation, especially a homicide case where time was of the essence.

He decided to keep a close eye on his deputy, and went off to meet with the DA, wondering how hard it would be to get his butt out of the crack it was in. Fortunately, the DA was an old friend, a hunting buddy, and a member of the same political party. They actively supported each other in their races for office in every election. If necessary, he would call in every personal and political chit he possessed to make the problem go away.

The sheriff's note about the blood match on the knife and Ulibarri's boot didn't make Clayton feel any better about himself. If he had thought to search the resort parking lot for Humphrey's car, Ulibarri might still be alive and in custody, charged with murder one.

He started the day doing paperwork and writing reports. Assembling a homicide casebook was no simple task, and he worked hard to make it thorough, thinking he could at least put together a comprehensive file without screwing it up.

He filled out an offense report, his supplemental reports, the investigation worksheets, and a crime scene worksheet, and completed the last of his canvass field notes. He redrew his crime scene sketches, compiled a witness list, labeled and arranged in sequence all crime scene photographs he and the rest of the team had taken, and updated his investigative narrative. He played back the taped interview with Harry Staggs and decided he needed a better, more detailed description of Johnny Jackson.

He called Harry Staggs on the phone and got him to answer specific questions about Johnny Jackson's physical characteristics. He recorded each response Staggs made on a blank piece of paper.

Physical Description of Johnny Jackson
Head—long & round in shape
Eyes—maybe brown, oval, with small pupils
Brows—straight, possibly thin
Nose—narrow, not too large
Mouth & upper lip—small or average
Chin—square, no dimple noted, but possible
Forehead—wide
Hair—black, curly, full, cut short, with short sideburns, & no graying
Facial hair—none
Mole—small, possibly located just below right cheekbone
Build—slim, weight about 140 to 145
Complexion—light skinned & tanned
Other scars, tattoos, marks—none noted
Age—Approx. 40
Height—5'6" to 5'7"

He placed the telephone in the cradle thinking that for somebody who'd repeatedly denied knowing Jackson personally, Staggs either had a remarkable memory for

117

details or was lying through his teeth.

Clayton suspected the latter. He wondered if Staggs was leading him astray with a false description. Maybe the name was phony, too. If he could come up with an eyewitness who put Staggs and Jackson together, socially or otherwise, he might be able to break Staggs down and discover why he seemed so scared of a pimp, even a high-class one.

He worked up a wanted-for-questioning bulletin on Jackson, did the violent-crime analysis report for the FBI, called the Bureau to ask for an expedited comparison to any similar crime scenes, and left the completed paperwork with the sheriff's secretary, who started faxing it right away.

With the more detailed description Staggs had provided, Clayton used a computer program to create a composite likeness of Johnny Jackson's face. He printed it, made copies, gave some to Quinones and Dillingham, and asked them to start looking for Jackson.

Outside, the wind was blowing hard in an angry gray sky and snow clouds masked Carrizo Mountain. The bleak morning completely matched Clayton's gloomy mood.

He headed back to the Mescalero Reservation and the resort to begin his own search for the mysterious Johnny Jackson, thinking that if he turned out to be a figment of Staggs's imagination there would be hell to pay.

Paul Hewitt had a theory about how people became lawyers, and it had to do with the names parents gave their children. Hang a couple of colorful monikers on a newborn and it was a lead pipe cinch that another budding lawyer would eventually be launched into the world. In the DA's case, the name was Roland Hatley

118

Moore, Hat to all his friends.

Hewitt sipped his coffee at a back table in the Dugout Bar & Grill, waiting patiently for Hat to make his appearance. The Dugout opened early for breakfast, which could consist of either the house special of home fries, eggs smothered in green chile with a side of bacon, or a double shot of whiskey for those who drank their meals.

A favorite local hangout, it also drew travelers passing through town. Bison, moose, and elk heads hung on the dark paneled walls, along with framed posters crusted yellow from nicotine smoke. Mismatched tables and chairs filled the dining area, and two pool tables were crammed into a small adjacent space next to some windows.

A see-through partition separated the dining area from the bar, which was festooned with old six-shooters and rifles. Fortunately, none worked, although the butt of one pistol recently had been used to quiet a rowdy customer.

With the town fathers and local real estate agents now touting Carrizozo as an arts and craft community—which it really wasn't—a small group of newcomers had moved in. Most were retired baby boomers or senior citizens, pursuing their hobbies or artistic dreams and making a few bucks from the sale of their work.

Down the street a new restaurant had recently opened where you could get a gourmet sandwich with sprouts, a veggie burrito, a fancy pastry, lemon-flavored bottled water, an all-natural juice drink, or a decaffeinated latte, all while surfing the Internet.

In the year the place had been open, Hewitt had never seen one cowboy, rancher, or blue-collar worker cross the threshold.

119

Hat arrived, spotted Hewitt in the back of the room, and sat himself down at the table.

"What in the hell were you thinking?" he said as he unbuttoned his western-cut sport coat.

"I think you're getting a little thick around the middle, Hat. It's time for you to join the gym I go to in Ruidoso. We can work out together. It opens at six in the morning."

"I'm not even alive at six in the morning," Hat replied, leaning across the table to look Hewitt dead in the eye. "For chrissake, you can't let a felony suspect walk. That's not your prerogative. Do you know how many reporters have called me asking why I wasn't filing charges against Staggs?"

"How many?"

"Too many."

"Got any suggestions?"

"Arrest Staggs, discipline your deputy, and let me deal with Tredwell. Maybe I'll agree to a plea bargain."

"Can't do that. It was a false arrest to begin with. No exigent circumstances, no probable cause. Tredwell threatened a civil rights suit if we refused to cut Staggs loose, so we agreed that Deputy Istee had simply held Staggs in protective custody during a potentially dangerous felony arrest."

"Jesus, you're kidding me. That's not what the news reports said."

"Consider the source."

"You've got to stop squabbling with the Ruidoso police chief."

"I will, as soon as he goes back to Houston, or wherever the hell he came from." Hewitt waited for the waitress to pour Hat a cup of coffee and move off. "Are you gonna help me out here?"

120

"I'm not going to lie for you, Paul."

"I'm not asking you to. Just say that you agree there was insufficient probable cause to warrant an arrest of Staggs by Deputy Istee."

"Why are you protecting this kid?" Hat asked.

"That's not what this is about."

Hat looked at his watch, slugged down his coffee, and stood up. "Get me copies of everything you have on Istee's investigations, plus I want a written statement from you detailing your conversation with Tredwell."

"You'll have it in two hours. Thanks, Hat."

"Don't thank me yet," Hat said as he adjusted his bolo tie. "I'll get back to you."

Relieved by the outcome of the meeting, Hewitt stayed behind and ordered breakfast.

Kerney went to work in his blues and spent the morning trying to concentrate. Pleased by the possibility of what a new artificial knee could mean, Kerney clock-watched as he ran through the paperwork on his desk, calling at the earliest possible moment to schedule the MRI test and then to speak to the architect about the swimming pool.

The architect said he'd get right on it and have a plan done by the end of the day. Kerney gave the architect the go-ahead to have a survey crew spot the corners for the house and hung up.

He visualized the setting. The house would be nestled below the ridge overlooking a red sandstone canyon capped with a thin line of gypsum rock. Large windows would face south down the canyon to a stand of old cottonwood trees and a meadow cut by a sandy arroyo. To the north, behind the ridge, an expanse of pastureland dotted with Piñon and juniper trees undulated toward the foothills and mountains behind Santa Fe.

It would be fun to cut a new driveway from the nearby ranch road to the building site with a grader. Kerney had learned to operate one under the watchful eye of his father. He could probably borrow or rent a neighbor's machine and rebuild the entire ranch road from the highway to the house site by himself. He would crown it, slope it, cut bar ditches for runoff, and pack it down with base course gravel to make it all-weather. It would be a welcome change of pace from his normal routine and give him a feeling that the dream of actually owning a ranch was underway. He could get the job done over a couple of weekends if he planned it right.

In between administrative staff meetings he called the remaining names on Osterman's list and learned none of them had known Anna Marie in college—or so they said. After the last meeting, he walked to Lt. Sal Molina's office and asked for a few minutes. It was time to put his ego aside and let the department work the Montoya case instead of trying to do it all by himself.

Molina, the major felony unit supervisor, nodded and gestured at an empty chair. Kerney filled him in on his stunning lack of progress in the Montoya case.

"I'm kicking it back to your unit," he said, "but I want to stay in the loop."

"We'll start with background checks on Osterman and the people on the list he gave you," Molina replied, "just to see if anything unusual or kinky shows up."

"Do the same with Cassie Bedlow," Kerney said. "And see if you can find out who Montoya roomed with during her college years in Albuquerque."

Molina nodded. "Anything else?"

"Can you free up Detective Piño?"

Ramona Piño was Molina's only female detective. She was petite, cute, perky, and weighed all of a hundred and five pounds. Molina had watched Piño put a straight-arm takedown move on a perp almost twice her size. The perp had been too busy screaming in pain to be embarrassed.

"That's possible," Molina said.

"Send her undercover as a prospective student to Bedlow's modeling and talent agency," Kerney said. "I'd like her to get a feel for Bedlow's operation, and learn what she can about the freelance photographer Bedlow uses."

"You said the APD vice supervisor thought Bedlow was legit," Molina replied.

"Everybody's legit until they get caught," Kerney said, rising to his feet, his knee protesting as he did so. "I may be getting the leg fixed and losing the limp for good."

"Really?" Molina replied. "When?"

"Don't know. Soon, I hope."

Molina laughed. "That's good news for you and bad news for us, Chief."

"Now why would you say something like that?"

Molina thought about all the good things Kerney had accomplished in a very short time: pay raises starting in July, improved officer training, streamlined operating procedures, promotions based on merit, not politics. Department morale was soaring.

"Because nobody can keep up with you as it is."

"Are you turning into a brownnose, Lieutenant?"

Molina snorted. He'd worked with Kerney back in the old days and knew the chief's sense of humor well. "Yeah, that's me all right."

★★★

Action picked up at the slots and tables as the late-morning customers rolled out of bed and into the casino. From the video surveillance room, Moses Kaywaykla watched as Clayton approached the cashiers one by one, asking questions, and passing out something to each employee. He went out on the floor to investigate.

"Nephew," Moses said, steering Clayton away from a roaming security guard, "what are you doing?"

"Looking for this guy," Clayton said, holding up a sketch.

"You should have brought that to me," Moses said sternly.

"Are you pissed?"

"You're starting to act like a gringo. Let's talk upstairs in the café."

Clayton handed Moses the sketch after they were seated at a table. "Do you know him?"

Moses shook his head as he waved off the approaching waitress. "He doesn't look familiar."

"His name is Johnny Jackson. Five six or seven, about a hundred and forty pounds."

Moses studied the sketch more closely to satisfy Clayton's persistence. "He still doesn't look familiar."

Clayton pushed a driver's license photo across the table. "Him?"

"Harry Staggs," Moses said. "He comes in and plays poker occasionally when he's not busy entertaining his friends."

"You knew about his gambling parlor?"

"It was a well-kept secret until the morning paper appeared," Moses replied. "How come you didn't arrest Staggs?"

"For lots of reasons," Clayton replied brusquely.

124

"I'm sorry you put him out of business."

"Why is that?" Clayton asked in surprise.

"Some of the big winners would come here and keep playing after his game ended. We could usually count on a number of them to lose money at our tables."

"You had knowledge of his activities and did nothing?"

"If it doesn't affect Mescalero Apaches, I don't really care what happens off tribal land. Neither did you, until a short time ago."

There was nothing subtle about the criticism. In the Apache world, family came first and foremost, and that included the entire tribe. "Are you going to lecture me, Uncle?"

Moses smiled gently. "Not today. Do you have more questions?"

"This Jackson supposedly runs a stable of hookers at a nearby location, where important, well-known men are discreetly entertained."

Moses shook his head. "That's a new one on me."

"Never heard of it?"

"Never. About the only skin-trade action we get here is an occasional freelance hooker up from El Paso. I run them off as soon as they show up."

"It's that easy?"

"Bimbos are hard to miss."

"Anything like that happen recently?"

"My night shift supervisor thought he'd spotted one a couple of days ago. But she left the casino alone before he could approach her."

"What day, exactly?"

"I think it was the same night your murder victim was here," Moses said.

"Let's find out," Clayton said as he pushed his chair

125

back.

In the video surveillance room, Moses checked the log and confirmed that the woman had been at the casino the same day as Ulibarri. He pulled a tape from the video rack and ran it fast-forward until a blonde with long curly hair and a lot of cleavage moved jerkily across the screen.

"She's new," Moses said as he reversed the tape and hit the remote play button.

They watched as she circled the poker tables, trying to draw interest. Ulibarri, who was at one of the tables, didn't seem to notice until she whispered something in his ear after he'd won another pot. He smiled, nodded, and watched her walk out the door.

"I don't remember seeing this when we first looked at the tapes," Clayton said.

"I think we skipped over it," Moses said.

"Can I borrow the tape?"

"No, but I can have a couple of stills made for you in less than a hour. I'll get you an enlarged profile and full-face head shot. Will that do?"

"Thanks, Uncle."

While Moses delivered the tape to a computer technician and went back to work, Clayton went to see if the lodge employees remembered anybody who looked like Jackson. No one did.

With the grainy but serviceable photos of the blonde in hand, he canvassed the lodge employees again, without success. He hurried to Casey's Cozy Cabins, hoping Harry Staggs could ID the woman as Jackson's companion.

Staggs wasn't home. From the front porch, he called Tredwell on his cell phone and asked the attorney where he could find Staggs.

"I don't baby-sit my clients," Tredwell said.

"He hasn't left town, has he?"

"Not as far as I know."

"You're a big help, Tredwell."

"Please, no thanks are necessary," Tredwell said.

Clayton punched the off button. A light snow was falling. Maybe it would be a wet year. The wildlife needed it. If he'd stayed with the tribal police, he'd be out checking boundary lines, reporting cattle that had strayed either on or off the reservation, posting new signs to replace the ones stolen by tourists, chasing off the occasional trespasser who had wandered onto Indian land by way of the national forest, and maybe breaking up a fight or a domestic squabble.

But he didn't have time to ruminate about the past or feel sorry for himself. If he wasn't going to catch a break, he'd have to make one for himself. How to do that was the question.

In college Detective Ramona Piño had taken a few drama classes and appeared in several student plays. The experience had served her well in police work. During her time on the force, she'd worked an undercover narcotics assignment and posed as a fence for stolen goods, both with success, so she knew the value of convincing performances.

She'd called ahead to schedule an appointment with Cassie Bedlow and now knocked tentatively on the woman's open office door.

Cassie Bedlow smiled at the young woman standing nervously in the doorway. Somewhere in her mid to late twenties, she was no more than five three and was wearing a short skirt that displayed well-toned, nicely formed legs and a knit sweater that indicated shapely

127

breasts in proportion to her body. Her face was classic northern New Mexico Hispanic, with arched eyebrows, large pupils, dark round eyes, small, thin lips, high cheekbones and even features.

"You must be Ramona," Bedlow said, moving from her desk to a tan leather couch. "Come in and sit with me."

Detective Piño caught the calculating, appraising look in Bedlow's eyes. She sat on the couch, her back straight, knees together, hands in her lap and gave Bedlow the once over. There was nothing flashy about the woman. In fact, just the opposite: she was round, wide in the hips, and had a matronly air.

"So, you're interested in modeling," Bedlow said.

"I shouldn't be wasting your time," she said, giving Bedlow a wistful glance.

There was a breathless, little-girl quality to Piño's voice that Bedlow liked a lot. Costumed correctly, with her small size, pretty features, and tiny voice, Piño would draw plenty of attention from men who liked the innocent schoolgirl look.

"Why do you say that?" Bedlow asked.

"I've always wanted to try modeling," Ramona said as she pouted slightly and looked around the office. "But you probably think I'm too old and too tiny to be a model."

A bookcase along a side wall held large photo albums and casting directories. On the top shelf was a chamber of commerce membership plaque and a silver-plated presentation bowl from a community charity fund-raising organization.

"That simply isn't true," Bedlow replied. "I use models of all sizes, ages, and ethnic backgrounds. For example, you'd make an excellent junior-size catalog

128

model. With the right training, you wouldn't lack for work."

Ramona beamed enthusiastically. "Really?"

"Yes, if you're photogenic, and I have no doubt that you are," Bedlow said. "Did you bring any photographs?"

Chagrined, Ramona furrowed her brow. "No, I'm sorry. I didn't think about that."

"Do you have any handy?"

Ramona shook her head. "Not really. I just moved here from Durango, and I left a lot of my personal things behind in storage."

She looked at the wall of framed photographs of attractive young women behind Bedlow's desk. Some were runway shots, but most were studio photos of women with their hands on their hips or their butts stuck out in provocative poses not unlike those in glossy fashion magazines. They pouted, smiled, or looked haughty for the camera.

Ramona's expression brightened. "Maybe I could use one of your photographers. Those are great pictures. I'd be willing to pay, if it isn't too expensive."

"Let's not get ahead of ourselves. Tell me about you."

Ramona sketched her fictitious past: born in Taos, raised in southern Colorado, high school graduate, work experience in boutiques and women's clothing stores, divorced with no children, new to Albuquerque with no friends or relatives close by.

"So, you know something about fashion," Bedlow said. "That's a plus. Now tell me why you'd really like to be a model."

Ramona gave Bedlow a shy glance. "I guess I'm bored. I want to do something exciting, have an adventure, meet interesting people. I got married too young and now that I'm divorced I'd like to have some fun before I get too old. That's one of the reasons I decided to move to Albuquerque."

"Modeling is hard work."

"I've worked hard all my life," Ramona replied.

Bedlow smiled. "Are you working now?"

"I'm looking. I wanted to find out about your agency before I took a job, so I can fit the classes into my schedule if you decide to accept me. How expensive is the program?"

"The classes run for twelve weeks and cost three thousand dollars."

"Oh," Ramona said. "I don't have that kind of money."

Bedlow patted Ramona's knee. "Don't be discouraged, I sometimes offer a tuition loan to a student I think has potential. You would have to sign a contract with the agency and agree to repay your tuition from your earnings after graduation. But with your looks that shouldn't be a problem."

"You'd do that for me?"

"First things first," Bedlow said, rising to gather a brochure, a student application, and an agency contract from her desk. "Let's get you started on enrolling, and have some photographs taken."

Ramona stood and took the forms from Bedlow's hand. "This is so much fun," she said breathlessly. "Can I fill these out while I'm here?"

"If you like."

"I've just moved into an apartment and I don't have a phone yet. Will that be a problem?"

"Not at all."

"Where should I go to get the pictures taken?"

Bedlow gave her a business card for a photographer,

and directions to get to his home studio in a residential area not far away. "He does all my photography work. I'll call and see if he can fit you in today. He'll do some proof sheets, which you can bring back to me this afternoon."

"That would be super," Ramona said, flashing a big smile. "Thank you, thank you."

Bedlow laughed. "We'll talk again soon, later in the day."

Left outside Bedlow's closed office door, Ramona sat on the edge of a carpeted raised platform and looked through the application forms and tuition loan contract. The contract had a clause that required the immediate full repayment of the tuition loan with interest if the student refused to accept any assignment arranged or sponsored by the agency.

It seemed straightforward enough, but Ramona wondered why the clause didn't specify modeling assignments, given the detailed legalese of the rest of the document.

As she was filling out the application a car pulled to the curb and a young blond woman got out. Dressed in tight jeans and a bulky sweater, the blonde was thin and leggy. She took two last puffs on a cigarette, ground it under the toe of a spiked-heel red boot, and pushed her way inside. There was a welt under her eye, a bruise on the chin, and one cheek was puffy and swollen.

The blonde glanced at Ramona and started pacing back and forth. "Is she in?" she asked, her words slightly slurred.

Ramona nodded. "On the phone."

"Shit."

"What happened to you?" Ramona asked, oozing sympathy.

"Boyfriend," the blonde replied after a slight hesitation. "He's history."

"That sucks."

"Tell me about it," the blonde answered, agitated.

"Did he hurt you bad?"

The blonde laughed harshly and pushed up the sleeve of her sweater. There were bruises on her forearm.

"How did it happen?" Ramona asked.

Nervously eying the office door, the blonde shook her head. "I don't want to talk about it," she said, pointing to her face. "It hurts too much."

"Sorry." Ramona returned her attention to the application. The blonde sat on a leather ottoman that had been used as a prop in some of the photographs on Bedlow's wall.

"I'm Ramona," she said when the blonde looked at her.

"Sally."

"Are you a model?"

"Yeah. You gonna take the course?"

Before Ramona could answer, Bedlow appeared, and Sally stood up.

"I gotta see you now," Sally said.

Bedlow's voice dripped honey. "Of course, dear girl. Come in."

Sally flew by Bedlow into the office.

Bedlow smiled sweetly at Ramona. "My photographer can take you right away. Will that do?"

"Oh, yes," Ramona replied. She dropped her voice to a whisper and glanced at Bedlow's office. "That poor girl."

"It's very unfortunate," Bedlow replied. "Come back with the proof sheets after lunch."

"I haven't finished the application," Ramona said,

132

hoping she could stick around and do some eavesdropping.

"Don't worry about it now," Bedlow replied rather shortly, holding open the front door.

"Okay," Ramona said cheerily. "See you in a little while."

She made her exit and memorized the license plate on Sally's car as she passed behind the vehicle.

Raised in Albuquerque, Ramona knew the city well. Bedlow's photographer, Thomas Deacon, worked out of his home in an older neighborhood of postwar Southwestern-style cottages near Carlisle Boulevard. The house stood out as the only one on the street with a neglected front yard. A converted garage with a private side entrance served as the studio.

Deacon met Ramona at the door and gave her the once-over. She did the same to him, keeping an eager smile plastered on her face. He was in his forties, tall, with a straight, narrow nose, a long chin, and wide, down-turned lips. He had long hair pulled back in a ponytail and wore jeans and a lightweight cotton sweater with the sleeves pushed up to his elbows.

He was hard Piño looking in a way that some women found exciting. To he seemed like a middle-aged white guy who needed to be seen as hip, cool, and on the fringe. In Piño's experience, the kind of man who usually turned out to be an emotional adolescent.

"Yeah, come on in," Deacon said.

Ramona caught a whiff of marijuana as she stepped inside the studio. She checked his pupils; they were slightly dilated.

"Proof sheets only, right?" Deacon said.

"Yes," Ramona said brightly. "That's what Ms.

133

Bedlow wants."

Deacon grabbed a camera from a table, turned on some stand lights, and pointed at a white screen at the back of the studio. "Go over there and try to do what I tell you."

He adjusted the lights, circled around her, gave directions, and took a bunch of head shots.

"Do you just do studio work?" Ramona asked, tilting her chin up.

"Hold still," Deacon said, clicking the shutter. "No, I do a lot of location work."

"That must be fun."

Deacon gave her a sarcastic look. "It's work. Loosen up, will you?"

"Sorry," Ramona said. "I bet you get to see a lot of exotic places."

Deacon snorted as he backed away. "Oh, yeah, lots of exotic places. I'm gonna need to take some full-body shots. Lose the skirt and sweater."

Ramona stifled a desire to protest, pulled off her sweater and stepped quickly out of her skirt.

"Not afraid to show your body," Deacon said approvingly, reaching for another camera. "That's good. Bend over and put your hands on your knees."

"Do you do a lot of location work for Ms. Bedlow?" Ramona asked, showing her cleavage.

"All of it," Deacon replied. "Pout for me."

Ramona pouted and Deacon fired off a bunch of frames. He put a straight-back chair in front of the screen. "Sit, spread your legs, and press your arms against your breasts."

"Like this?" Ramona said, assuming the position.

"Yeah. Now, look tough. Can you do that?"

Ramona put on her cop face.

"That's good." Deacon took shots from different positions and angles, and lowered the camera. "Get dressed."

Ramona wanted to jump into her clothes, but held back. She put a hand on her hip. "We're done?"

"Yeah," Deacon said.

"How did I do?"

"Okay," Deacon replied, walking toward a darkroom in a corner of the studio. "You've got a tight little body. But you gotta learn to relax. You'll get used to it. I'll have the proof sheets ready in a few."

Ramona dressed and looked around the studio. A long table held a dozen or so neatly arranged manila folders. She flipped through them and found eight-by-ten glossies of young women, some rather so-so looking, dressed in trendy western-wear outfits—lots of fringe leather jackets, long skirts or designer jeans, Indian jewelry, and custom cowboy boots.

There was a folder featuring Sally, the girl with the bruises. Buxom, blond, tall, and unbattered, she was the most striking model in the group. Her photographs were exterior shots, taken on a patio of what appeared to be either a resort or an expensive private residence. The patio had a Santa Fe feel to it, although the pictures could've been taken at any number of locations throughout the Southwest.

She heard the darkroom door open, turned to see Deacon, and smiled charmingly at him. "These are wonderful photographs. You're very talented. I hope you don't mind my looking at them."

"That's cool," Deacon said.

"Are they recent?" Ramona asked, placing Sally's folder on the table.

"Yeah, I shot them several days ago."

135

"Where?"

"Down at the lodge on the Mescalero Apache Reservation."

Ramona nodded. "It's so beautiful down there."

"Yeah," Deacon said, handing her a manila envelope. "Here you go. Take these to Cassie. You owe me a hundred bucks."

Ramona paid Deacon with five twenties. "Thanks for doing this on such short notice," she said.

"Yeah," Deacon said as he stuffed the bills in his pocket and opened the studio door. "Later."

Before returning to the Bedlow Modeling and Talent Agency, Detective Piño ran the plates on Sally's car and the full-size van that had been parked in front of Deacon's house. The car was registered to Sally Greer and the van to Thomas Deacon.

Piño drove by Sally's place of residence, which turned out to be an apartment complex in the northeast heights. A "Now Renting" banner hanging from the roof of the building fronting the street advertised move-in special rates with a phone number to call.

She dialed up the leasing agent, who gave her a pitch on the special rates and the available amenities, and some information about the tenants. Most were young professionals, consisting of a mix of single persons with roommates, and married couples without children.

Characterizing herself as a single woman planning to live alone, she asked about safety and security, and was told that the tenants were quiet and peaceful.

Piño swung by the nearest city police district office and found no record of recent domestic disturbance calls at Sally Greer's apartment. In fact, according to the patrol supervisor on duty, there had been no problems or crimes reported at the apartment complex in the six months it had been open.

She ran Greer and Deacon through the APD computer system and got no hits on wants, warrants, outstanding traffic violations, or prior arrests.

A few minutes past the lunch hour, Piño arrived at the Bedlow Modeling and Talent Agency to find it locked up tight. She hung around for a half hour and then blew it off. She'd done all that Lieutenant Molina had asked. She decided to go back to Santa Fe, report in, and let the brass decide if they wanted her to take the investigation any farther.

CHAPTER 7

THE REGIONAL AIRPORT SAT ON A MESA OUTSIDE OF Ruidoso a few miles northeast of Fort Stanton, an old army fort. As a child, Clayton had toured the fort with his uncles, to see the place the white eyes had built to wage war against the Mescaleros and confine them to the reservation.

Opened in the 1850s and decommissioned as a military installation just before the turn of the twentieth century, the fort had subsequently become a hospital for the treatment of tuberculosis, an internment facility for German prisoners during World War II, and a rehabilitation center for the developmentally disabled.

Situated near a river lined by ancient oak trees, the main fort consisted of beautiful old military buildings around a grassy quadrangle. Currently it served as a minimum security prison for women, and was probably one of the prettiest lockups in the entire country.

In an unusual way the fort had reverted to its original purpose, with one notable variation: women—not

Apaches—were now imprisoned on the grounds. Clayton wondered if only the Mescaleros appreciated that irony.

At the airport, a facility that served mostly private planes, Clayton quickly made the rounds of everybody on-site, flashing Johnny Jackson's likeness and the grainy photographs of the blonde, and asking questions. He got a possible make on the blonde from an airplane mechanic.

"Maybe it's her," the man said, "but I can't say for certain. I only got a sideways look at her from a distance."

"Tell me about it," Clayton said.

The mechanic shifted his chewing tobacco from one cheek to the other. "The pilot wanted me to check the idle on his starboard engine. Said it sounded a little rough. The blonde—if that was her—stayed outside the maintenance hangar."

"Did the blonde arrive with the pilot?"

"I'm pretty sure she did. He landed, taxied right up to the front of the hangar, and came in to talk to me. Wasn't a minute or two before I saw her standing outside next to the plane. Nobody can get here walking from the terminal that fast."

"Who was the pilot?"

"Luis Rojas. He was right about the engine: it needed adjustment."

"From El Paso?"

The mechanic spit out some tobacco juice into a handkerchief. "Yeah, he flies in here pretty regular. Keeps a car in the parking lot."

"When did Rojas arrive?"

The mechanic rubbed his nose. "A few days ago. Let me pull the invoice."

He leafed through a folder smudged with greasy fingerprints and read off the date. "He rolled in here at about sixteen hundred hours."

If the blonde was the right one, it all jibed. She had been caught on videotape at the casino that very same night.

"Did the woman go with him when he left for El Paso?" Clayton asked.

"Nope, he flew out alone."

"You're sure of that?"

"Absolutely. After he paid, I walked him to his plane and showed him what I'd done. I watched him taxi and take off."

Before leaving the airport grounds, Clayton checked the thirty or so cars in the parking lot for a late-model Lincoln, found two, and ran the plates. Both were registered to prominent, well-known Ruidoso businessmen, neither of whom matched Staggs's description of Johnny Jackson. Jackson and his car were looking more and more like figments of Harry Staggs's imagination.

But the blonde and Luis Rojas were very real. It was time to find Staggs and lean on him harder.

Ramona Piño sat at the small conference table that butted up against Chief Kerney's desk and made her report. She finished to smiles and nods from Kerney and Lieutenant Molina.

"Good job," Sal Molina said.

"Interesting," Kerney said, sliding his chair back from the conference table so he could cross his legs. He dangled a foot over his knee and rubbed his leg to relieve the pain.

He'd changed out of his uniform during the day and

now wore jeans, boots, and a blue shirt that matched the color of his eyes.

Piño found him rather good-looking for an older man. "Should I go back to meet with Cassie Bedlow?" she asked.

"First let's hear what Lieutenant Molina has learned," Kerney replied.

Sal consulted his notes. "The background checks on the people Osterman contacted after he returned to New Mexico weren't helpful, Chief. Of course, we haven't had a chance to dig very deep yet, but I don't see a killer lurking in their midst."

"What about Montoya's college roommates?" Kerney asked.

"She had four. We talked to three of them." Molina listed the women by name. "One lived with her for two years in a dorm until she moved off campus. During her junior and senior years, Montoya shared an apartment with two other students. None reported any love interest on Montoya's part involving a rich kid from Albuquerque."

"Who are we missing?" Kerney asked.

"Belinda Louise Nieto. She roomed with Anna Marie during a summer session."

"When was that?" Kerney asked.

"After Montoya's junior year," Molina replied.

"What do we know about her?"

"Now it gets interesting, Chief. Nieto was Anna Marie's cousin. She attended junior college in California for a year and then transferred to the university in Albuquerque. She was supposed to continue living with Montoya, but she never enrolled in the fall semester. When Montoya's old roommates returned, Nieto had already split."

140

"Where to?"

"Denver, supposedly, but nobody knows for sure."

"There's been no contact between Nieto and her family for over twenty years?" Kerney asked.

"There really isn't any immediate family left," Molina said. "Nieto was born and raised in California. Her father was the younger brother of Montoya's mother. He enlisted in the navy, pulled a tour in San Diego, and stayed there after his discharge. He married an Anglo girl and got a civilian job as a cargo specialist on the base. The marriage broke up when he caught the wife sleeping with a sailor. Guess she couldn't resist a man in uniform. The father got custody and the mother dropped out of sight."

Molina flipped a page. "Allegedly, Nieto had a wild streak, so she was sent to New Mexico by her father in an attempt to settle her down. Everybody thought Anna Marie would be a good influence on her. Three months after Nieto split, her father was killed on the docks while loading supplies on an aircraft carrier. The last time anyone saw her was at her father's funeral in San Diego. Anna Marie's mother said she showed up looking like a floozy."

"Mrs. Montoya is your informant?" Kerney asked.

Molina nodded.

"Tell me what she knew about the girl's wild streak."

"The usual stuff: boys, parties, drinking, staying out late, being rebellious," Molina said, passing Kerney a photograph. "She was quite a looker. That snapshot was taken right after she came to New Mexico. She was nineteen years old."

Kerney agreed with Molina's assessment. The photo showed a slender, very attractive young woman with high cheekbones, long curly dark hair and a well-proportioned figure. He passed it on to Detective Piño.

Piño rolled her eyes. "Five eight at least. God, I hate tall women."

"Why's that?" Molina asked.

"Because I'm not one of them," Piño said, dropping the photo on the tabletop.

"Hang on a minute," Kerney said as he searched his desk for Jeremiah Perrett's office phone number. He found it, dialed, then hit the speaker button, asked for Perrett, and the secretary rang him through.

"One question, Dr. Perrett," he said, "when exactly during Anna Marie's senior year did she talk to you about the young man we discussed?"

"Early in the first semester, as I recall," Perrett answered.

"Could it have been during the summer session?"

"That would depend on whether or not I was teaching that summer."

"Can you check on that?"

The three officers heard a sigh, followed by the sound of a squeaking chair.

"Let me look in my records," Perrett said.

The officers stared at the phone, listening to file drawers opening and papers being turned, before Perrett came back on the line.

"Yes, I did teach that summer," he said, "and Anna Marie was one of my students. We very well could have talked about the boy during that time."

"Thanks," Kerney said.

"Is there anything else, Chief Kerney?"

"That'll do it." He disconnected and looked at Piño and Molina. "Do we have a coincidence here?"

"Maybe more than that," Molina replied.

Kerney nodded. "Let's assume that Nieto arrives as

142

Anna Marie's new roommate, gets right into the party scene, and pulls Anna Marie into it with her."

"Which leads to the appearance of a young man with money who puts the moves on our victim," Detective Piño said.

"A young man none of Anna Marie's friends or roommates know anything about because they were away for the summer," Molina noted.

"We should try to find Belinda Louise Nieto," Kerney said.

"I'll do a public-records search in Colorado," Molina said.

"What about the mysterious rich boy?" Piño asked.

Molina smiled. "Actually, I've got one identified—Cassie Bedlow's older bother. His name is Tyler Norvell. He lived in Albuquerque and went to law school at the same time his sister and Anna Marie were undergraduates. According to several people who knew him, he always had money to burn—not your average struggling grad student.

"He's now a four-term state senator from Lincoln County. Just got reelected last fall. Owns the biggest real estate agency in Ruidoso, a ranch, and he's a partner in a bank."

Kerney's expression brightened. As a state senator, Norvell would routinely come to Santa Fe for legislative sessions and other state business. "When was Norvell first elected?" he asked.

"The November before Montoya disappeared," Molina answered.

"I like that connection. Does his family have money?"

"Unknown," Molina replied. "I haven't gotten that far yet."

"What do you have on Cassie Bedlow?" Kerney asked.

"She seems clean," Molina said.

"Let's stay on her for a while." Kerney swung his gaze to Detective Piño. "Ask APD vice to assist. Maybe they can give you a heads up on what to look for, and how to go about it. Continue to play the eager student with Bedlow, and see what more you can find out about the blonde who got beaten up. She might be a source of information."

Piño nodded and scribbled herself a note. "What about Norvell?"

"I'll take the politician," Kerney said, holding out his hand to Molina. "Give me your fact sheet on him."

Molina passed it over. "On paper, he's a boy scout."

Kerney laughed. "So is every New Mexico politician, on paper."

Clayton joined up with Quinones and Dillingham to compare notes. They sat in a nearly empty diner by the racetrack and talked over coffee as long-haul trucks rattled by on the highway, the engine noise vibrating the plate-glass window.

Dillingham gave his brief report first, which consisted of nothing but goose eggs when it came to finding anything out about Johnny Jackson, then sat back to watch Istee and Quinones follow suit. After Quinones admitted to coming up empty, Clayton trumped them both with the thing about the blonde at the airport with Luis Rojas.

"Well, at least one of us got something," Quinones said.

"It's only a possible ID on the blonde," Clayton said, sliding the freeze-frame photos of the woman across the

144

Formica tabletop. "I still have to confirm it."

"So how come Jackson's so hard to find, and this blonde pops up on the radar screen?" Quinones asked.

"Because Staggs fed me a line of bullshit about Jackson," Clayton answered.

"You're thinking Jackson is Rojas disguised?" Dillingham said.

Clayton nodded. "It's possible, and since the blonde didn't matter to Staggs, he didn't try to cover for her."

"Just another whore," Quinones said.

"Something like that."

"Let's go talk to Staggs," Quinones said suddenly.

"All three of us?" Dillingham asked.

"Why not?" Quinones answered, his eyes on Clayton. "We can overwhelm him with our collective charm."

Clayton wasn't sure if Quinones was simply making a suggestion or pulling rank and taking charge. Was he saying it's time to step aside, boy, you've fucked it up? Or was he just putting out a good idea?

With patient detachment, Quinones waited for a reaction. Since the sergeant hadn't jacked him around for stupidly falling for Staggs's fabrication, Clayton decided it wasn't a slam.

"Me and Dillingham will hold Staggs's hand while you take a crack at him," he said.

Quinones stood up and dropped some change on the table as a tip. "So, off we go to Casey's Cozy Cabins. Since you called this little meeting, you get to buy the coffee."

Clayton peeled off some singles, stuck them under the tab, and followed Quinones and Dillingham out the door.

For two hours they waited vainly for Staggs to show. Dillingham stayed in his unit concealed nearby to block off any retreat in case Staggs drove up and decided to bolt. Clayton and Quinones, who had checked each cabin carefully to make sure no one was about, passed the time in Clayton's unit doing paperwork.

Finished, Quinones dropped his clipboard on the floorboard, put his pen in his shirt pocket and said, "Let's take a look inside."

"That's illegal entry," Clayton replied.

"I'm concerned about Staggs's welfare," Quinones said.

"His car isn't here, the cabin is locked up, and nobody's around."

"All the more reason to worry. Could be that Staggs is a victim of a crime. Maybe somebody beat him up, ripped him off, and stole his car. Maybe he's lying inside badly hurt, in need of our assistance."

"I don't know," Clayton said, staring at the closed window curtains. He didn't need to make another dumb blunder.

"Don't you want to know if Staggs really duped us?" Quinones asked, reaching for the radio microphone.

Clayton laughed and opened the door. "Yeah, I do."

Quinones gave Dillingham a heads up on the plan, followed Clayton to the cabin, kicked in the front door right above the lock set, and went in first. The place was empty, but Staggs had cleaned out his clothes, all his small personal possessions, and whatever cash he had on hand. They found no papers or documents of any value.

While Quinones kept searching Clayton punched the last-number-called buttons on the telephone, jotted down the information and ran it. It came back listed to the El Paso company owned by Luis Rojas. He told Quinones.

"Well, well," Quinones said, "duped we were, so it seems. I'll fill Hewitt in, and let him know you're heading to El Paso."

"Thanks."

"Hey, Clayton."

At the door Clayton paused and looked back. "Yeah, Sarge."

"This is a mother of an investigation. You nail the perp's ass and believe me nobody's gonna sweat the small stuff. Talk to Captain Vincent Calabaza with the El Paso PD before you go to see Rojas. He's an old friend of mine. Maybe he can give you some inside skinny on the guy. I'll let him know you're coming."

Clayton felt himself loosen up. A grin spread across his face as he waved good-bye to Quinones.

Harry Staggs was petrified, almost unable to speak in complete sentences. Sitting in Luis Rojas's living room, he got the story out in spurts, telling him about Ulibarri's murder, the police SWAT team, and his interrogation by the local sheriff and the sidekick Indian deputy.

While Staggs gulped and talked Rojas asked no questions, made no comments, showed no sign of annoyance. He sat on a pale green couch and listened thoughtfully, occasionally lifting his hand to brush an imaginary stray hair away from his forehead.

Seconds ticked off in silence after Staggs concluded his monologue. Desperate for a reaction, he said, "What d'ya think?"

Rojas decided it wasn't a stray hair on his forehead, it was an itch. He scratched it. "Ingenious," he said, "but it would have been better if you'd left the girl out of the story."

"I was thinking on my feet," Staggs replied, "trying to cover for you."

Rojas smiled at the stupid little man who had told the police too much. He stood up and patted his flat stomach. At six two and two hundred pounds, he still had the body of the wide receiver he'd been in college, although he'd lost a step or two over the years. "I appreciate that," he said. "Would you like a drink?"

Staggs nodded and felt some of his apprehension fade. Maybe Rojas wasn't gonna grind him up and feed him to the dogs after all. "Yeah, Scotch, neat."

Rojas poured two drinks at the built-in bar and brought one to Staggs. "The police already know that I was gambling at your place, and that I was in my office at the time of the murder, so there's nothing to worry about."

"Except I'm out of business," Staggs said after he knocked back the Scotch, "and it's gonna take me a while to sell the cabins and get the money I need to relocate permanently and set up shop again. By that time, I'll have lost all my regulars."

"Are you going back to Ruidoso?"

"Not a chance," Staggs replied. "I gave my lawyer a power of attorney to handle the property sale. He says it's best if I don't show my face around there again. The cops would be all over me."

"Can you trust him?" Rojas asked as he poured Staggs another shot.

"As much as you can any lawyer. I get to review and approve any offers before he can close the deal."

"That's smart," Rojas said, returning to the couch. "Did you tell him where you were going today?"

"Nope."

"Why don't you set up shop here, in El Paso? The

Indian casino outside of the city is starting to draw a lot of high rollers. I'm sure many of them would find their way to you, once the word got out."

"Like I said, it takes money."

"Let me help you with a loan. When you sell your property, you can pay me back the principal with no interest."

"We're talking two hundred fifty thousand, minimum."

"I'll still come out ahead," Rojas said with a shrug. "Some of your customers are going to want some female companionship, right?"

Staggs smiled. "Like always."

"So, let's do it."

"That's damn good of you, Mr. Rojas."

Rojas raised his glass. "Then it's settled. Do you need a place to stay?"

"I thought I'd get a motel room for the night."

Rojas shook his head. "That won't do for my newest business partner. I've got a nice house that isn't being used in a good neighborhood in Juárez. You can stay there until you get settled. It's fully furnished and supplied. I'll have Fidel drive you there in your car, so you don't get lost. In the morning, we can talk again to finalize things."

Staggs got a little leery, wondering who the fuck Fidel was. "You don't have to go to any trouble on my account."

"It's no trouble," Rojas said, reaching for the telephone.

He asked Fidel to come to the living room and in less than a minute a well-groomed, smiling, skinny kid no more than twenty years old arrived. Staggs stopped feeling wary. Polite introductions were made, Fidel was given his assignment, and Rojas said good night.

In the car, Staggs asked Fidel if he was from Mexico.

Fidel smiled at the question. "Nope, born and raised in El Paso."

"What do you do for Rojas?" Staggs asked.

"I'm an errand boy, mostly," Fidel replied. "I pick up his laundry, get his cars serviced, take him to the airport when he's flying on a commercial plane—stuff like that. It's only part-time, because I go to college a couple days a week. I've got an apartment over the garage. No rent. It saves me a lot of money."

"Sounds like a good deal," Staggs said.

"It's the best."

"What are you studying?"

"Business administration."

They passed through customs and drove over the Rio Grande into Juárez along a main street teeming with cars. Locals and tourists strolled past gaudy storefronts, neon signs blinked out messages, loud mariachi music blared, and food vendors hawked their specialties on every corner.

Fidel's cell phone rang. He flipped it open and said, "What's up?"

"Kill him," Rojas said.

"That's cool," Fidel said enthusiastically.

"Lose the body, lose the car, and everything in it. Any money he has with him is yours."

"No kidding? That's great. I'll talk to you soon. Bye." He disconnected and smiled at Staggs. "My girlfriend just found out one of our favorite groups is going to be in concert here soon. She's already scored some tickets for us."

"You got a girlfriend, do you?" Staggs said.

"Yeah, a real hot chiquita, and smart as a whip," Fidel

said as he made a turn that would take them toward the Juárez dump. "We'll be there in a few minutes."

Staggs leaned back against the seat and closed his eyes. Everything was going to be just fine.

Back in Albuquerque late in the afternoon, Detective Ramona Piño sat next to Sgt. Jeff Vialpando in front of a computer screen. A supervisor in the Albuquerque PD vice unit, Vialpando talked as he moved the mouse around and clicked on some of his favorite sites stored in memory. They ranged from adult porno sites to escort services to personal ads.

"Computers have changed everything," Vialpando said, "and the day is gonna come when streetwalkers will go the way of dinosaurs. Well, maybe not entirely: there will always be guys looking for action on the streets. But they'll be the real low-end shoppers."

A really gross photo of a man and a woman came up on the screen. "This is what you do all day?" Piño asked. "Cruise the Internet and look at dirty pictures?"

Vialpando chuckled. "Not all day. Not even every day. Some of it's pretty disgusting. A lot of the porno stars are traveling hookers. They come into the city for a month or two, sometimes on a regular basis, rent a furnished pad, and ply their trade. The adult sex sites are a good way to get a make on those girls when we get a tip. A john who feels ripped off will call anonymously, a landlord might complain about a tenant, or a neighbor will report unusual activity at an apartment. We'll go out, take a few photos of the lady in question, or get a name and a good description, and see if she pops up on the Internet as a wet and wild one. Sometimes we get lucky."

He enlarged a photograph of a naked woman on a bed

151

with her legs up in the air giving the camera a come-hither look. "That's Brenda. We got her for soliciting. It was her first bust, so she walked with a fine. But she won't be back in Albuquerque, at least not anytime soon."

"Charming," Piño said.

"Did you know that adult porn sites are the biggest Internet moneymakers, worldwide? What does that tell you about civilization as we know it?"

"There must be a lot of horny sick guys out there," Piño said.

"And women." Vialpando clicked on another favorite, an escort service. "We check escort services all the time. There are some local sites we keep an eye on, but the really big ones are out of state. They offer the full menu: fetishes, S and M, bondage, domination, threesomes, bisexual encounters, and your straightforward heterosexual party girl. Some of these women work part-time, usually away from their home territory. If you've got the cash and are willing to pay, they'll fly in for an overnight or even for a week. It can cost anywhere between a couple of thousand for a night, to fifteen grand or more for a week of intimate companionship."

"That's what I paid for my car," Piño said as she read the bio on Tammy the Temptress, who was twenty-four and was studying for an advanced degree. Tammy was proud to be a courtesan, and loved romantic evenings with generous, virile gentlemen.

"Tammy the T is out of Houston," Vialpando said. "We missed her by a day last time she was here, but we're hoping she comes back soon. The airport cops are keeping a watch out for us. Want to visit her photo gallery?"

"No thanks," Piño replied.

"Next up are the Internet personal ads." Vialpando clicked one up. "There are two types we scan: the blatant come-ons and the intimate encounters. Just about every site has both."

"Why do you look there?" Piño asked.

"The escort services and sex sites are getting more sophisticated in their marketing strategies. They know cop shops are monitoring them. Placing personal ads for individual girls not only gives them another venue, but it also makes our job tougher. There's gotta be millions of women looking for love or whatever through the Internet."

"So, how do you score a hit?" Piño asked.

"You've never cruised the personals?" Vialpando asked.

Piño shook her head.

Vialpando looked her over and smiled. "I guess you don't need to."

Piño had noted the absence of a wedding ring on Vialpando's hand. "Do you?"

"No way," Vialpando said, laughing. "Anyway, you can narrow the field if you've got a make on a subject. Just use the subject's physical description as your preference for what you're looking for in a woman. Height, weight, age, hair and eye color, body size. For location you can search city, state, region, or you can go national or international if you like."

"It's as easy as that?"

"It gets you closer. Then you scan the ads, looking for suggestive content. A lot of them come with pictures. You can forget the ones that are posted with casual snapshots, unless they're just totally shameless. Instead, concentrate on the professional or slightly provocative

153

photos. We put two freelancers out of business last month by mining the personals."

"How did you do that?"

"By responding to their ads. Would you like a hard copy of the Web sites we use the most?"

"That would be a big help. Do you keep tabs on any local smut photographers?"

Vialpando printed out the hard copy, signed off, and shut down the computer. "Give me a name."

"Thomas Deacon."

He reached over, got the sheets off the printer, and handed them to Piño. "I'm not familiar with the gentleman's work."

"How should I proceed with Cassie Bedlow?"

"If she really is a front for a prostitution ring, she'll be looking for girls who are vulnerable—down on their luck, out of a job, hurting for money. Girls that are estranged from their families or far away from home."

"That's good to know. I told her I was divorced, I'd just moved here from Durango, didn't have a job yet, and was pinching my pennies," Piño said.

"Nicely done," Vialpando said with genuine sincerity. "Are you?"

"Am I what? Pinching pennies? What cop doesn't?"

Vialpando laughed. "Are you divorced?"

Piño studied Vialpando. In his early thirties, he was way beyond average looking, with intelligent brown eyes, no receding hairline, and a slightly turned-up nose. She shook her head. "You have to get married to do that, and I'm not. How about you?"

"You know the old saying: become a detective and get a divorce."

"That must have been tough," Piño said.

Vialpando shrugged. "Fortunately, it ended before

154

we'd started a family."

Piño waited a beat for more, like perhaps an invitation to grab a cup of coffee. Nothing came. "Thanks for the tour of the wonderful world of vice," she said.

"Any time," Vialpando said with a laugh. "Will you need backup tomorrow?"

"I don't think so."

"What time are you coming down?"

"I've made an appointment with Bedlow for ten o'clock."

Sergeant Jeff Vialpando smiled shyly. "If you'd like, I'll buy you lunch and you can tell me what you've learned about my backyard."

"That would be very nice," Detective Ramona Piño said demurely.

Clayton didn't like El Paso very much, not even with a pretty sunset in full view on the western horizon. A hundred and twenty miles south of Ruidoso, it was sandwiched between the New Mexico state line and the Mexican border city of Juárez, across the Rio Grande. In spite of new shopping malls, spreading residential subdivisions, and a partially revitalized downtown area, El Paso held no appeal for him. Perhaps it had something to do with geography. It was the westernmost city in Texas, much closer to the New Mexico state capitol in Santa Fe than to white-bread Austin. It was a gateway city, heavily populated by native Hispanics, as well as a growing number of both legal and illegal immigrants from Mexico and Central America. It was a desert city with blistering windstorms, little rain, and brain-deadening hot summers. But most of all, it was an industrialized city, filled with warehouses, freight

155

companies, NAFTA maquiladoras just across the border, wholesale distribution centers, and major drug runners operating out of Juárez.

The interstate and major railroad tracks cut through the city. Endless truck stops, gas stations, and vast, fenced storage yards lined the highways. Squalid barrios on both sides of the border spread way beyond city limits. All of it gave Clayton a dismal feeling.

Captain Vincent Calabaza of the El Paso Police Department headed up an intelligence unit that was part of a multiagency drug interdiction task force. Housed in a new building built with federal funds, the task force consisted of agents from DEA; FBI; Immigration and Naturalization; Alcohol, Tobacco and Firearms; and a host of state and local officers.

A heavyset man in his fifties, Calabaza listened while Clayton asked about Luis Rojas, and ran down the reasons for his inquiry.

"Are we talking about the same Luis Rojas?" Calabaza asked when Clayton finished.

"He owns a trucking company," Clayton said.

"And you think he may be a party to a homicide?" Calabaza asked. "Or running whores in Ruidoso?"

"Is he a friend?" Clayton asked, reading Calabaza's skepticism.

Calabaza snorted a laugh. "I don't travel in such heady social circles, Deputy. Rojas chairs the citizen advisory board for the police department and serves on the mayor's downtown redevelopment committee. If he's dirty, it's a big surprise to us."

"You're that sure?" Clayton asked.

Calabaza opened a desk drawer, removed a file, and gave it to Clayton. "Take a look yourself. Everyone on the citizen advisory board goes through a thorough background investigation before being appointed by the chief."

Clayton read the intelligence report on Rojas. He was single, never married, born and raised in El Paso. Father was a construction worker, mother a hotel maid. Played high school football, made all-state his senior year as a first team wide receiver, attended the University of New Mexico on an athletic scholarship, and graduated with a degree in marketing. Parents deceased, five siblings— two brothers and three sisters. The brothers, two sisters, and a brother-in-law worked for the trucking company Rojas owned. One sister lived in Las Cruces, New Mexico—forty miles north—and currently served on the county commission.

Clayton scanned the financial data. Rojas had an eight-figure personal net worth, and aside from the trucking company, was a one-fifth partner in a privately owned local bank, owned an office building leased by a state agency, and held shares in an investment firm.

"A real rags-to-riches story," he said, studying Rojas's photograph. He didn't come close to matching Harry Staggs's description. Light brown hair, full nose, no mole on the right cheek, wide, full lips.

"That's right," Calabaza replied.

The report documented that Rojas liked to gamble occasionally at the nearby Indian casino and enjoyed piloting his own plane. Interviews with women Rojas had dated revealed nothing out of the ordinary in his personal relationships. The list of Rojas's friends and associates included corporate executives, area politicians, civic leaders, and wealthy patrons of the arts, all of whom gave Rojas high marks as a businessman, friend, and upstanding citizen.

After college and before returning to El Paso, Rojas

had lived in Denver for a number of years working for an advertising agency that was no longer in business. A criminal- and traffic-records check in Colorado had come up empty, as had inquiries to various federal law-enforcement agencies.

Clayton read the narrative report filed by the investigator who'd interviewed Rojas. Rojas had cooperated fully, allowing the officer access to his personal income tax statements and corporate financial records. Everything checked out.

"Do you see anything in that report that's illicit, immoral, illegal, or of dubious character?" Calabaza asked.

"He looks like Mr. Clean," Clayton replied as he wrote down Rojas's home address and closed the file.

"I don't know much about the New Mexico criminal statutes," Calabaza said, "but in Texas, illegal gambling is a Class C misdemeanor that carries a five-hundred-dollar fine. Are you going to file charges?"

"Right now, he's just a possible witness," Clayton answered.

"Well, if you do charge him, let me know. My chief will want his resignation from the citizen advisory board."

"Thanks, Captain," Clayton said.

Calabaza nodded. "Give my best to Oscar Quinones."

Mansion was the only word that came to mind when Clayton arrived at Rojas's house. He'd never seen anything like it. The semicircular driveway was paved with brick, and an attached six-car garage had a second story accessed by an exterior stairway. The entryway, illuminated by soft lights, was a series of arches under a covered portal. Above the portal four double-sash doors

158

opened onto a roofed balcony with a lacy cast-iron railing. The place looked like a Spanish villa.

Motion-sensitive lights came on as Clayton walked up the pathway to the house and Luis Rojas greeted him at the door. Clayton went through the formality of identifying himself and showing his shield.

"By all means, come in, Deputy," Rojas said pleasantly. A couple of inches taller than Clayton, Rojas wore a lightweight crewneck sweater and a pair of casual slacks.

In the living room Rojas directed Clayton to a sitting area in front of a window that looked out on a lighted landscaped interior courtyard with a fountain.

"How can I help you?" he asked.

"Have you seen Harry Staggs today?" Clayton asked.

"No, but he called me to apologize for any trouble he might have caused. I told him he'd done the right thing by talking to the police. After all, a man has been murdered. That's far more serious than getting busted for playing an illegal game of chance. Are you here to arrest me?" Rojas smiled charmingly. "I must tell you my reputation will suffer if you do."

Clayton shook his head. "That's not my intention."

"What a relief," Rojas said with a chuckle, as though it was all a big joke.

"Did Staggs tell you what his plans were?"

"I didn't know Harry had any plans, other than to obey all the gambling laws in New Mexico. He told me you'd shut down his operation."

"We think he's left Ruidoso," Clayton replied.

"I wouldn't have any idea where he might have gone," Rojas said.

"Do you know a man named Johnny Jackson?"

Rojas shook his head. "Sorry, I don't. I'm not very

helpful, am I?"

"Do you know this woman?" Clayton said, holding out the blonde's photograph.

Rojas took it. "She doesn't look familiar."

"You were seen with her at the Ruidoso airport."

Rojas didn't blink. "That's not possible." He rose from his chair. "Excuse me for a minute. I think I can clear up the confusion."

He came back in the company of a strikingly attractive blonde. "Deborah, this is Deputy Sheriff Istee. He wants to ask you a few questions. Deborah is my girlfriend."

Deborah smiled at Clayton with pretty blue eyes, shook his hand, and answered all his questions. Yes, she'd flown to Ruidoso with Rojas. No, she wasn't at the poker game. She'd spent that night at Rojas's vacation home, and stayed over an additional day after Luis had returned to El Paso.

"Did you go anywhere, see anybody, do anything?" Clayton asked.

"I took several hikes by myself," Deborah replied. "But I didn't see anybody. Other than that, I didn't go out at all."

"How did you get back to El Paso?"

"I drove Luis's SUV. That's why I went with him. He's trading it in for a new one, and he asked me if I'd like a few days in the mountains in exchange for doing him a favor. I jumped at the chance to get out of the city and be by myself for a while."

"What kind of vehicle did you get?" Clayton asked Rojas.

"I'm still shopping around," Rojas replied, "although I'm considering a Mercedes. It's a civilian version of a military vehicle used by the German army. Are you familiar with it?"

Clayton had read somewhere that the movie stars who made action flicks and owned ranches in Montana all had them. He'd seen photographs. They were macho adult toys that went for about a hundred thousand dollars. Almost four times his annual salary.

"Yeah, I've seen pictures," Clayton said, concentrating his attention on Deborah. "Are you sure no neighbors saw you at the vacation house?"

"I have no neighbors," Rojas said. "It's very secluded."

"Where is it?"

"I've had a map drawn up for friends," Rojas said, "so they won't get lost when they visit. I'll give you a copy."

He opened an end-table drawer and handed Clayton the map. The retreat was on private land surrounded by national forest, northeast of the village of Alto.

"That's deep in the mountains," Clayton said.

"Which is why I need good transportation to get to it," Rojas said. "Especially in bad weather."

"I bet you do," Clayton said as he folded the map into his shirt pocket and looked at Deborah. "I'll need to see your driver's license, miss."

"What on earth for?" Deborah asked.

"My report."

Deborah smiled. "Of course. I'll get my purse."

She fetched her purse and handed Clayton her license.

"You have your own place?" Clayton asked, noting the address on the license.

"Yes, but I'm here a lot," Deborah said, sliding her arm around Rojas's waist.

He made sure all the license information was current, got a work and home phone number, and closed his

161

notebook. "I doubt that I'll have to bother you again."

"It's been no bother," Deborah said.

"None at all," Rojas said, giving Clayton a hearty handshake. "Good luck with your investigation."

Outside, Clayton walked to his unit thinking how convenient it was that the girlfriend had been on hand to confirm Rojas's story.

CHAPTER 8

SALLY GREER RENTED A FIRST-FLOOR APARTMENT IN A building at the rear of the complex. There was no sign of activity inside, and her assigned parking space with the apartment number stenciled on the curb was empty. Ramona Piño found an inconspicuous spot away from the security night-lights and waited in her vehicle for Greer to make an appearance.

Ramona wasn't sure how she would play it, if and when Greer showed up. Approaching her directly would raise too many questions. She would hang out for a while to see what developed. Besides, the only thing waiting for her back in Santa Fe was the tiny guest house she rented from a retired cop, whose last tenant had been Chief Kerney.

It was nice enough, but lonely. Moving out on her ex-boyfriend had been the smart thing to do. He'd turned into a channel-surfing couch potato, who spent his evenings at home watching cable sport shows, bitched at her for working late on the job, and never seemed to want to do anything fun.

During their last six months together, he'd treated her like a wife, and that wasn't going to happen to her again. She needed a close relationship with someone who cared for her as a friend and lover, who accepted her as an equal, who respected her independence, who appreciated the demands of her job.

She wondered about Sgt. Jeff Vialpando. He was good-looking, seemed bright, had a sense of humor, and didn't put out a macho attitude—all good signs. She put the skids on her thoughts and decided not to dwell on him any further. Lunch tomorrow would give her a better idea if he really had potential as a boyfriend, although dating a cop who lived sixty miles away might be something of a problem.

An hour into Piño's wait, Greer appeared. Within a short time she was back in her car, after changing from tight-fitting jeans and a turtleneck pullover into a short dress with spiked heels.

Piño followed her downtown to a hotel near the convention center. Inside the crowded hotel bar, Greer joined two middle-aged men and a young woman at a table. Piño recognized the other woman from the photographs she'd seen at Thomas Deacon's studio. Neither of the men looked to be particularly likely dates for such attractive young women.

She retreated to the lobby and sat behind a placard on an easel that welcomed a trade association to the hotel. When the foursome appeared Greer was paired off with one of the men, walking arm in arm to the main exit, smiling and chatting. She'd covered her facial bruises with makeup. Piño pegged the man with her to be in his fifties. Balding and portly, he had an eager expression on his face as he laughed at something Greer said.

Piño waited until they were outside before taking a side exit. By the time she turned the corner the foursome was gone, the taillights of a car fast disappearing down the street. As she walked to her vehicle Piño called her older sister, Rebecca, who lived in the city.

"Becky, I need a bed for the night, if it's not an imposition."

"Come on over," Becky said.

"Can I use your computer and borrow some clothes?"

"Sure, I'd even throw in Tim, if you wanted him, but he's out of town on business."

Ramona laughed. Tim was Becky's husband, and the two were about the most perfectly married couple imaginable. "Too bad. One night with me, and you'd be history."

"I'll tell him that when he calls."

"Don't you dare," Ramona said as she pulled away from the curb. "See you in a few."

A year apart in age, the two sisters were often taken for twins. Rebecca, a middle-school social-science teacher, was taller by a quarter of an inch, had thicker eyebrows, a slightly wider mouth, and a more oval face. On the phone to each other at least once a week, there wasn't much catching up to do, so after a cup of tea Ramona explained why she needed to use the computer, and Becky asked if she could watch.

In the home office Ramona worked Jeff Vialpando's favorite list of local Web sites with Becky sitting at her side, looking for a personal ad for Sally Greer. First she cruised the adult personals sites.

"Unbelievable," Becky said abruptly, reading the sexually explicit narratives, many of which were posted with revealing or completely nude photographs that showed everything. "I wonder if our school computers block this kind of smut. This is just porn, for people who don't want to visit the adult sites, isn't it?"

"Ask your students," Ramona replied as she exited a site and called up another. "They would probably know."

She went to the preference screen and entered information closely matching Greer's age and physical characteristics, and scrolled through the ads.

"Are these sites all like this?" Becky asked.

"According to Jeff Vialpando what we're seeing is fairly typical," Ramona said.

"Who is Jeff Vialpando?" Becky asked. She was always interested when Ramona mentioned the name of a new man, especially now that she'd broken up with her live-in boyfriend, whom Becky had never really liked anyway.

"He's an APD vice sergeant," Ramona said.

"And?" Becky asked, searching her sister's face.

Ramona smiled. "And, nothing. At least not yet. We're having lunch tomorrow."

"I'll want to be told everything."

Ramona nodded. "Don't I always?" She switched from the adult personals and started in on the list of love and relationship sites, which were much more mundane and rather like classified personal ads that ran in newspapers. Most consisted of blurbs describing how interesting the women were, and their laundry lists of desired traits in a man. Some wanted friendship only, others were looking for soul mates, and a few sought intimate encounters, cyber sex—whatever that was—or E-mail pen pals.

"It's just an Internet meat market," Becky said with a groan, getting out of her chair.

"Seen enough?"

"More than enough," Becky said. "There's something so sad about it all."

165

"There are desperately lonely and needy people out there," Ramona said.

"I'm going back to the real world," Becky said as she picked up a thick manila folder from the desk. "I've got papers to grade."

Ramona stopped scrolling and gave her sister an apologetic look. "I've stolen your space."

"I'll use the kitchen table."

Becky left, and Ramona returned her attention to the screen. Time passed. Through the open door she heard Becky's footsteps. She turned to find her sister in her pajamas with a toothbrush in her mouth. It brought up the memory of Becky wandering through their parents' house every night just before bedtime, brushing her teeth and being ordered back to the bathroom to complete the job. No parental chiding ever stopped her behavior, and by the time Becky was a teenager their mother had given up trying.

Becky took the toothbrush out of her mouth and said good night. Ramona smiled in response, called up an ad for Sultry Sally, and clicked on the photo icon. A picture of Sally Greer in a scoop top that showed a lot of cleavage appeared on the screen. Ramona read the accompanying narrative.

Hi, I'm Sally. I'm not looking for a serious relationship yet, and I like older men who enjoy the company of a playful, sexy lady. If you enjoy adventurous dates with a woman who isn't afraid to be honest about her desires, e-mail me. You should be intelligent, discreet, affluent, honest about your needs, and willing to show your appreciation for the time I spend with you. I hope to hear from you soon! Oh, by the way, I love to travel!

The ad was new and the photograph looked very much like the work of Thomas Deacon.

Greer had included an Internet address for her personal Web site where visitors could view a photo gallery with new pictures recently posted. Ramona called it up and smiled as two photos she'd seen at Deacon's studio appeared on the screen.

She perused the gallery. There were photos of Greer wearing a summer frock and smiling over her shoulder, on a bed with a long cocktail dress hiked up to show a bit of thigh, and sitting in a chair with legs crossed and a smoky look on her face.

One shot showed Greer and the woman who'd been in the hotel bar with the two men. Both wore short dresses and high heels and stood arm in arm smiling at the camera. The caption read: THIS IS MY FRIEND STACY. WE LOVE TO DOUBLE-DATE!

Ramona printed out copies of everything and stuck them in her briefcase. Jeff Vialpando had written his home phone number on the business card he'd given her. She thought about calling him to ask if he'd be willing to respond to Greer's ad, and decided the hour was late and it could wait until morning.

Pleased with her progress, Ramona shut down the computer, yawned, and undressed in the small guest bedroom. Sally Greer was a working girl, no doubt about it. How that tied into Bedlow's modeling agency—if it did at all—was a question yet to be answered. She fell asleep anticipating her lunch date with Jeff Vialpando.

Clayton got up early and fixed breakfast for Grace and

the kids. They sat around the table making small talk. Using her finger Hannah showed Clayton two different ways to make the letter A, drawing each letter carefully in the air. Very seriously she explained that one was big and the other was little.

"What do those letters do?" Clayton asked.

"Make words," Hannah replied happily.

"Tell me an A word."

"Apache," Hannah said with a broad grin, poking herself in the chest. "That's me."

"You're a very smart girl," Clayton said.

Hannah nodded in agreement. "I have two a's in my name. Little ones."

"Who taught you all this?"

"Mommy," Hannah said. "I'm gonna learn all my letters."

From across the table, Wendell smirked at his sister. "What comes after A?" he asked.

Hannah lifted her chin in Wendell's direction. "You," she answered.

"That's wrong," he said with authority.

"B for boy, boy, boy, boy," Hannah chanted from her high chair as her feet tapped against the underside of the table. "And C is for Daddy's name."

Clayton grinned at Grace. "I think she's going to be as smart as you." Perhaps, when the time came to give Hannah her Apache name, he would ask for her to be called Bright Girl. That would be perfect.

Grace smiled back. "Smarter, I hope. She wanted to wait up for you last night, so she could tell you what she'd learned. I had to make her go to bed."

"Does my mother know of this wonderful achievement?" Clayton asked.

"Hannah told her over the phone last night.

Grandmother was very proud."

Hannah nodded in agreement.

Grace's expression turned thoughtful.

"What is it?" Clayton asked.

"Something your mother told me after Hannah got off the phone. She once asked Kerney what he would have done if he'd known about you from the beginning. He said he felt he'd missed out on something important, and even against her wishes he would have wanted you to know him as your father."

"But that didn't happen," Clayton said evenly.

"Hannah would like to tell her grandfather what she has learned," Grace said.

Hannah nodded her head vigorously.

"Whose idea was that?"

"Your mother's," Grace replied. "But I agree with her completely."

"So, are you going to call him so Hannah can recite her ABCs?" Clayton asked.

"We thought you should do it," Grace replied.

Clayton considered it, or pretended to. "I don't think he wants to talk to me."

"Perhaps," Grace said, "but he might enjoy talking to Hannah and Wendell."

Wendell kept his head down, eyes fixed on his plate. For the motormouth he'd become, he was unusually quiet.

"Would you like to talk to your grandfather?" Clayton asked his son.

"I drew a picture for him," Wendell said with a slight nod.

"Let me see it."

Wendell brought him the drawing. It showed Kerney and Wendell standing together against a backdrop of

169

mountains with the sun high in the sky. Wendell had carefully colored the sun yellow, the sky blue, and the mountains green, and lettered his name and the word grandfather, badly misspelled, under the feet of the crude figures. Both were smiling.

"It's a very nice picture," Clayton said, rubbing his son's head and smiling at Hannah. "We'll call your grandfather tonight, when I get home from work."

Smiles greeted Clayton's announcement as he rose from the table.

Ganged up on by his family, Clayton drove away from home feeling a bit put out. Not at Grace and the kids, but with his mother. Why the change of heart? She'd never wanted him to know his father, and now it was suddenly okay for Kerney to be treated like a grandfather. What was that all about?

He consulted the map Rojas had given him, told dispatch he was in service and where he was going, and made his way up the forest road into the mountains until a locked gate stopped him. He got out, climbed the gate, and walked the steep, curving road. At the last bend a large log cabin with a covered porch came into view.

It was one of those modern cabins made from precut logs, with a pitched green metal roof and two stone chimneys at either end of the building. The cabin sat on an elevated stone foundation overlooking a small meadow and a frozen streambed that meandered out of a narrow mountain ravine. Large windows gave a view of the forest beyond the meadow and the white-capped Sierra Blanca peaks in the distance.

Clayton gauged the size of the cabin and decided it was at least four thousand square feet, minus the covered porch with the redwood railing and massive hand-cut stone steps. It was way more than twice the size of his house in Mescalero.

Yesterday's light snowfall in Ruidoso had left two inches on a deep bed of frozen snow in the mountains. It was the first precipitation since the Ulibarri murder. Clayton scanned the area for more cabins hidden in the trees and saw none. On the north side of the road, where the sun couldn't reach, he knelt and carefully brushed away the fresh snow looking for tire tracks on the hard-packed ice. The last vehicle driven over the frozen surface had tires much wider than a car, pickup truck, or SUV.

He tried several more places with the same results and switched to the south side, brushing a channel across the width of the roadway. Again, only the very wide treads of a heavy vehicle showed.

Clayton stood in the driveway and studied the cabin, wondering if it was the private retreat where Harry Staggs's fictitious Johnny Jackson provided female companionship for important, well-known men.

He decided that if Rojas was the pimp who provided girls for VIPs, he certainly wouldn't have given him a map to the place. The windows were shuttered on the inside so Clayton couldn't get a look. But from all appearances, it seemed to be just a rich man's vacation lodge.

Rojas's girlfriend had mentioned taking several hikes during her stay at the cabin, so at the front porch steps Clayton brushed away the snow, looking for any telltale remnants of boot prints. He did the same at the back door, at a trail head next to a covered wood pile that wandered into the forest, and on the front porch around an expensive hot tub where wind-blown snow had collected. There were bobcat and deer tracks in the snow behind the cabin, and old claw marks from a black

171

bear on the trunk of a nearby tree. But Clayton saw no evidence of any recent human activity. Not even the woodpile had been disturbed.

On the side of the house he found more tire indentations that matched what he'd seen on the road, and clear boot tracks in a man's size led to a propane tank lettered with the supplier's name.

He called the company, spoke to the manager, gave his location, and asked when the tank had last been filled. The manager searched his paperwork and came back with a date that matched exactly the time Rojas's girlfriend said she'd been at the cabin.

"Ask the driver if anyone was here when he made his delivery," Clayton said.

"Let me get him on his cell phone," the manager said.

Clayton waited patiently and smiled to himself when the manager reported that no one had been at the cabin when his driver had filled the tank. It was exactly what he'd expected to hear.

"I need to take a statement from him," Clayton said, checking his watch, figuring his travel time back to Ruidoso on the forest road. "Where can I meet him in the next thirty minutes?"

"Do I have a problem with my driver, Deputy?" the manager asked.

"Not at all," Clayton said as he walked quickly down the road toward the locked gate.

The man told him where to meet the driver. Clayton disconnected and smiled to himself as he climbed the gate. What was that old saying? Sometimes people were just too smart for their own good.

Detective Piño sat quietly in Sergeant Vialpando's office while he examined the hard copy printouts from

Greer's Internet personal ad and Web site. One shelf of a bookcase held a display of baseball caps from various police departments. On Vialpando's desk was a framed photograph of a large, smiling black dog.

The bull-pen area outside the office was nearly empty. Only two detectives were at their desks. Except for paperwork or court appearances, mornings weren't the busiest times for vice cops.

Vialpando looked up from the copies. "Compared to a lot of the crap on the Net, this is pretty classy stuff. Some soft-porn poses, no totally nude pictures, good photography, a sexy, narrative come-on that only hints at sex for hire, and a good-looking woman who wouldn't raise any eyebrows if a guy was seen in public with her. I'd say the whole thing was professionally done to appeal to high-end clients."

"So send her an E-mail and ask her for a date," Ramona said.

"Not yet, unless you're in a hurry," Vialpando said. "We've got reasonable suspicion to believe Greer's a hooker, but no probable cause. I'd rather put surveillance on her for a day or two, document her next date, interrogate her client afterwards, and then bust her when she asks me for money. If I can scare her enough, maybe she'll roll over on her pimp."

"I can wait," Ramona said. "Do you think she has a pimp?"

"From what you've told me, Greer is probably new to the game, so I'm betting somebody fronted the money for the Web site. They don't come cheap, and I doubt Greer built it herself."

"And Thomas Deacon?" Ramona asked.

"You've done me a huge favor identifying him as the photographer. Chances are he makes his bread and butter in the skin trade. He should prove to be a very valuable informant."

"I get first crack at him," Ramona said.

"Of course," Vialpando replied. "Are you ready for your meeting with Bedlow?"

"I am."

He gave her a worried look. "We never send our undercover female vice detectives out alone. Let me put a wire on you, just to be safe. I'll park a block away, record the conversation, and be there in case you need backup."

Given what Ramona had learned about Sally Greer, it was a good idea. She nodded her concurrence.

Vialpando nodded back, relieved. "We can meet for an early lunch afterwards." He named the restaurant, a nice but not expensive eatery in the Nob Hill district just east of the university. "I'll have a lot of questions."

"About the case?"

"Yeah, but mostly about you," Jeff said with an easy smile.

Ramona stood and smoothed down her skirt. "I may have some of my own questions to ask."

Jeff Vialpando glanced at her legs and said, "Like what?"

She touched the framed photo of the smiling black mutt. "I want to know everything about your dog."

Vialpando laughed.

Ramona turned crisply on her heel to hide the flush on her face. "Let's get me wired," she said, as if she weren't already buzzing with the small jolt of electricity that had passed between them.

Yesterday's MRI test and his prior commitment to teach a late afternoon class at the law-enforcement academy had left Kerney with no time to follow up on state senator Tyler Norvell. On his desk he found a file from Sal Molina with an attached note indicating that Detective Piño was still in Albuquerque and hadn't yet reported in.

Molina's public-records check on Belinda Louise Nieto had uncovered some fascinating information. Colorado court records showed that soon after the death of her father, Nieto legally changed her name to Crystal Fox. One year later she became a murder victim in an unsolved homicide still carried as an open case by the Denver Police Department.

Kerney read the investigative narrative provided by the Denver PD. The murder had occurred in the victim's car outside a trendy city nightspot. She'd been shot once in the chest by a small-caliber handgun. Analysis of the powder burns and flash points on the woman's clothing disclosed that the barrel of the weapon had been placed in direct contact with the victim's body.

Witnesses at the nightclub reported that the victim had been in the company of a well-dressed, Hispanic male, approximately thirty years old, of average to slightly above average height. None of the patrons or employees at the club recalled previously seeing the couple, who had arrived at the club separately. The detective noted that most witnesses interviewed at the scene appeared to be high on cocaine "or under the influence of other illegal substances."

Faced with an unknown suspect, the detective assigned to the case had naturally concentrated on the victim. Crystal Fox turned out to be a "personal escort who specialized in entertaining well-heeled out-of-town male visitors to the city."

An address book at the victim's apartment yielded the

175

names of men who'd been entertained by Ms. Fox, many on a regular basis, according to a meticulously up-to-date social calendar discovered among her possessions. The night of the murder she'd had nothing scheduled.

Departments as far away as Los Angeles and New York City had cooperated in the investigation, interviewing every one of Crystal Fox's customers who could be located. None, based on verified alibis, had been in Denver at the time of the murder.

A knock at the open door made Kerney look up. Helen Muiz came in and presented Kerney with the agenda of the appointments he'd asked her to make. Kerney knew each person on the list. All were politically well connected, reasonably trustworthy, and could possibly provide valuable information about Senator Tyler Norvell.

"You'd better get cracking," Helen said. "Your first meeting is downtown in twenty minutes."

"Thanks."

"Whatever happened to your promise to make your own phone calls?" Helen asked.

"Because of your charm and persuasiveness, I knew you'd have better luck getting through to these guys," Kerney said, waving the slip of paper at her.

"Baloney," Helen said.

Kerney laughed. "Don't you mean to say that you respectfully disagree with my statement?"

"No, just baloney will do," Helen replied with a twinkle in her eye.

Kerney knew that look well, so he took the bait. "What is it?"

"Your doctor's office called. The results of your MRI came in. He wants you to call him back so he can schedule surgery. Does this mean no more limp?"

"I hope so."

"Wonderful," Helen said.

Clayton questioned the propane delivery driver carefully and learned it was company policy for the driver to announce his arrival at a customer's home. The man had honked the horn and waited for several minutes before proceeding to fill the tank. No one had appeared during the time he was at the cabin. Since the stop was on his regular route, he'd been furnished a key to the locked gate to gain entry. He delivered every two months. When asked, the driver noted that the tank was over three-quarters full, which probably meant the cabin hadn't been used much during the cold weather.

At the airport Clayton reviewed a list of airplane owners who kept personal vehicles at the parking lot. The list showed make, model, year, and license plate information for each. Rojas hadn't lied about owning an SUV. After cruising the lot without finding the vehicle, Clayton decided that maybe the girlfriend, Deborah, also hadn't lied about driving the SUV to El Paso as a favor to Rojas. But that was about the only truth the woman had told. It got Clayton to start questioning the whole girlfriend-boyfriend thing, again.

He headed toward Carrizozo and the office, using the road that would take him off the mesa and past Fort Stanton. He reached for the radio to call in his destination and ETA just as dispatch advised him that Hewitt, Quinones, and Dillingham were standing by for a meeting. He acknowledged the message, hoping maybe the blond woman seen with Ulibarri at the casino had been located. That might make things go a lot easier.

★★★

From her sister's wardrobe Ramona had selected a gray, midcalf skirt, a half-sleeve charcoal cowl-neck sweater, and black pumps. In Cassie Bedlow's office she sat quietly while the woman reviewed her enrollment application.

"You didn't answer one question," Bedlow said, looking up from the papers.

Ramona shifted her weight and dropped her head. "I didn't want to lie," she said, "so I left it blank."

"Well, have you ever been arrested?" Bedlow asked.

"Is it that important?" Ramona asked.

"I don't expect my students to be perfect, Ramona," Bedlow replied gently. "But I do need to know if you have a criminal record. If you do, it doesn't necessarily disqualify you from enrolling."

"Once," Ramona said in a small voice. "I was arrested once."

"For?"

Ramona stood. "I shouldn't be here, wasting your time."

Bedlow waved her hand, palm down, in a gesture for Ramona to sit. "This isn't an interrogation, and you're not wasting my time, dear. We just need to be honest with each other."

Ramona stayed standing. "You'd give me a tuition loan, even though I've been arrested?"

Bedlow laughed lightly. "I might be willing to take a chance on you. People make mistakes. You didn't murder anyone, did you?"

Ramona reclaimed her seat. "Oh no, I was arrested for possession of cocaine."

"Tell me what happened."

Ramona laid out the story; her ex-husband had been a

178

heavy user who always had her carry his stash. One night while they were going home, he'd been stopped and arrested for driving under the influence.

"We were both pretty high," she added. "They found the cocaine in my purse. Just a little bit. It was my first offense. I pled guilty and paid a fine."

"Were you high on cocaine?"

"Yes," Ramona answered in a tiny voice.

"Do you still use it?"

"No."

"Are you drug free?" Bedlow asked.

"Not completely," Ramona said, looking away from Bedlow. "I sometimes smoke a little weed. I drink, but not a lot, and sometimes I take a sleeping pill at night."

Bedlow smiled sympathetically. "That doesn't make you a major criminal."

"I guess not," Ramona said with a weak smile.

"Have you found a job yet?"

Ramona put on a dejected face. "I've been offered a part-time sales position. But I wouldn't get enough hours to even pay my rent."

"Have you ever worked as a waitress?"

"Before I got married, I did."

"Let's see what we can do," Bedlow said. "I have a friend who owns a club, and he's always looking for pretty girls to work for him. It's an upscale sports bar and restaurant, with an all-girl waitstaff. You'd have to wear scanty shorts and a low-cut halter top, but the girls make great tips."

Ramona perked up and looked animated. "That wouldn't bother me, especially if I could make some good money."

"If I asked, I'm sure he'd be willing to schedule you to work nights so it doesn't interfere with classes."

"That's perfect. I'm a night owl anyway."

Bedlow wrote out the name of the bar, the owner's name, and the address of the establishment. "He's usually there around noon," she said, handing Ramona the information. "I'll give him a call to say you're coming to talk to him."

"Oh, I hope he hires me," Ramona said.

"I think your chances are excellent," Bedlow replied.

"Thank you so much," Ramona said.

Jeff Vialpando was waiting when Ramona got to the Nob Hill eatery. The lunch crowd hadn't arrived yet and the waitstaff was standing around the bar chatting. The place had a rustic, antique feel to it, with lots of dark wood and reproductions of old advertising signs on the walls. He stood up as she approached the table.

"I guess we don't have much time," he said as he pulled out a chair for her.

"Forty-five minutes," Ramona replied, checking her watch.

"You handled Bedlow very well," Jeff said, returning to his seat.

"Thank you. But I thought we were going to talk about your dog."

"That will have to wait for another time," Jeff replied. "While you were with Bedlow, I had one of my detectives search several escort-rating Web sites."

"An escort what?" Ramona asked.

Vialpando smiled. "Your education about vice and the Internet has just begun. Many hookers are rated by their clients on the World Wide Web. Some women even post the testimonials they've received from satisfied customers on their personal Web sites. Sultry Sally has gotten her first grade, and it's a good one."

He handed Ramona a computer printout. It read:

Although new to her profession, Sultry Sally from Albuquerque is a charming, lovely young woman eager to please. She could be a bit more inventive, but takes direction well. Sally is well worth your time and money. I look forward to our next date. Four stars, which is excellent for a girl just starting out.

"This is mind-boggling," Ramona said.

Jeff waited for the busboy to pour water and go away. "It could be fake. Many of the Internet ads and testimonials are. You don't always get what you call up and ask for."

"So that's why some of the sites guarantee that it's an actual picture of the girl."

"Exactly. Truth in advertising, so to speak."

"Now what do we do?" Ramona asked.

"Order lunch," Jeff said as a waiter approached with a basket of freshly baked breads and rolls. "I recommend the cup of soup and the house salad."

Ramona grabbed one of the menus that had been left on the table and scanned it. Nothing jumped out at her. "You're not a meat and potatoes kind of guy?"

"Not at this time of day."

"Soup and salad sounds good," Ramona said, handing the menu off to the waiter.

Vialpando ordered the same. The waiter nodded and left.

"You didn't answer my question," Ramona said. "What's the next move?"

"You still don't have anything solid on Bedlow," Jeff replied.

"Yeah, I know it. But I got this feeling about her. She didn't even raise an eyebrow or give me a motherly lecture about smoking dope and popping sleeping pills when I copped to being a user. It was almost like she was pleased that I wasn't a straight, Goody Two-shoes. Then she laid this job possibility on me. Don't you think that was a little strange?"

"Not if she's reeling you in for something other than a career in fashion modeling," Jeff answered.

"I wonder if that's what happened to Sally Greer," Ramona said.

"Where's the job she turned you on to?"

Ramona gave him the note and his eyes widened. "Jesus, we've been trying to get someone in this place undercover for the past six months. So has narcotics."

"Well, here's your chance," Ramona said as she buttered a roll.

"This could be dangerous," Jeff said, searching Ramona's face. She had remarkably pretty eyes.

"I think I can handle it." Ramona took a bite of the roll. She'd skipped breakfast and her stomach was grumbling for food. "I did two years undercover narcotics. Fill me in."

CHAPTER 9

SINCE KERNEY'S ARRIVAL IN SANTA FE YEARS AGO AS a rookie officer, the city had changed dramatically. Where there used to be open pastureland and dirt roads, there were now trailer parks, residential subdivisions, strip malls, and paved streets. Several working cattle ranches that once bordered the city were either gated communities for the very rich, burgeoning middle-class

182

enclaves for those who sought country living on an acre and a half, or clustered housing tracts on postage-stamp lots for families willing to pay a quarter of a million dollars or more for the convenience of living in town.

Untouched hills that rose up to the national forest in the mountains behind the city had sprouted multimillion-dollar-view homes. Along Cerrillos Road, the ugliest and busiest gateway into the city, a commercial building frenzy was underway with national chain stores, discount stores, motels, supermarkets, and specialty retail outlets rising up from the leveled, graded, paved earth with alarming frequency.

Most of the population growth came from newcomers to the city, a motley assortment of the new rich, old rich, new-age spiritualists and healers, wanna-be artists, movie stars, celebrities of every stripe, trust-funders, ski bums, restless youths of various ages, baby boomers who'd taken early retirement, and true believers of every possible persuasion who were drawn to the magic of Santa Fe. While they all laid claim to the trendy aesthetic life of the city, politics, a favorite local pastime, remained firmly in the hands of Hispanic and Anglo old-timers.

Kerney's sources of information about Tyler Norvell consisted of a retired state legislator, a former chief of staff for an ex-governor, a lobbyist, and a syndicated political columnist. He made the rounds, picking up a bit more information about Norvell from each informant.

After three stops, he knew that Norvell owned an expensive Santa Fe home, which he frequently made available to key legislative leaders when they traveled to Santa Fe on official business. He'd also learned that Norvell was the only senate minority member who consistently got his pork-barrel appropriations passed and signed into law. His success was attributed to a close personal friendship with the senate majority leader and backroom deal making with his colleagues.

Additionally Norvell, who was divorced, frequently threw parties at his Santa Fe house during legislative sessions, using his sister's modeling students as hostesses. Some probing questions about possible indiscretions involving the young women failed to yield any embarrassed pauses or gossip. Norvell's sister, Cassie Bedlow, was always in attendance at the parties and kept a careful eye on the girls.

That didn't mean the informants weren't equivocating. Sex was always the subject people lied about first and foremost.

Interestingly, Kerney's first three contacts had slightly different takes on the source of Norvell's wealth. The lobbyist thought that Norvell had made his money in Colorado as a lawyer, where he'd lived for some years before returning to Lincoln County and getting into real estate. The ex-chief of staff believed Norvell had been a partner in a commercial construction firm that had cashed in on the Denver building boom. The retired legislator thought Norvell had gotten rich through the stock market.

Kerney met with his last contact, Ellsworth Miller, in the press and media room that overlooked the dark senate chambers at the state capital. By law the New Mexico legislature convened only once a year in either thirty- or sixty-day sessions, so the chambers were generally empty. While some critics considered a part-time legislature unprogressive, Kerney liked the idea that the house and senate incumbents couldn't turn public service into a well-paying, full-time sinecure.

Ellsworth Miller touted himself as the dean of New Mexico journalists, which wasn't an exaggeration. In his seventies with fifty years of experience as a reporter, Miller had become a fixture at the capital. He sported a full head of curly, disheveled gray hair that rolled over his shirt collar, and a scruffy beard always in need of a trim. In the twenty years Kerney had known him, the look hadn't changed. But he had aged dramatically. Ellsworth's face was permanently flushed red by drink, and the skin around his neck was loose and flabby.

"Why the interest in Tyler Norvell?" Ellsworth asked in his gravelly voice, after Kerney had explained the focus for the meeting.

"It's supplemental to an investigation," Kerney replied.

"That tells me exactly nothing," Ellsworth said.

"Maybe we can exchange information," Kerney said. "You go first."

"Only if I get an exclusive on the story."

"If there is a story, you'll get it first," Kerney replied.

"Is this part of a criminal investigation?" Ellsworth asked, peering over the rim of his reading glasses.

"It's possibly tied to one," Kerney answered.

Ellsworth put his glasses in his shirt pocket. "Okay, I'll play along. I assume you know the basics: He's divorced, no children, his ex-wife lives out of state, he's rich, votes conservative, and he's well regarded on both sides of the aisle."

"I've got all that."

"I've heard very little dirt or gossip about him. There was word of a DWI that got buried by a former Santa Fe county sheriff some years back, but I never could confirm it."

"Which sheriff?" Kerney asked.

185

"Mike Olivera."

"Did you hear any specifics about the incident?"

"Just that during Norvell's first term in office, he took out a mailbox driving some woman home from a party."

"Who was your source?" Kerney asked.

"A state police officer who stopped to offer the deputy assistance. He said Norvell failed the field sobriety test, but was never booked into jail."

"Did you get an ID on the woman?"

"No."

"Who was the state cop?"

"Nick Salas. He passed the information on to me while he was assigned to security during a legislative session."

"How did Norvell get elected to his first term?"

Ellsworth rubbed his fingers together. "Money and influence. He outspent his opponents three to one in both the primary and the general election. And he got endorsements and personal appearances during the campaign from two old college chums who'd already been elected to the legislature, Silva in the senate and Barrett in the house. All three are still serving."

"Who would know the most about Norvell's college years?"

"Locally? Probably Mark Shuler," Ellsworth answered. "He was the editor of the university newspaper back when Norvell and his buddies were in college and law school together. He runs a political research and polling outfit here in Santa Fe. He's very liberal and very much opposed to Norvell's conservative agenda."

"Where did Norvell get his money?" Kerney asked.

"My understanding is that he was a successful commodities broker in Colorado."

Kerney renewed his promise to give Ellsworth first crack at any story and left, puzzling about why four informants would all have different impressions of how Norvell got rich. As he walked through the empty rotunda he called Sal Molina on his cell phone and asked him to have someone start digging into the source of Norvell's wealth.

Running over the high points in his mind, Clayton left the team meeting Sheriff Hewitt had convened. Because of a significant lack of progress in the case, Quinones and Dillingham were back on patrol duty effective immediately. Clayton was now a homicide task force of one, but at least he wasn't spinning his wheels anymore.

The autopsy and forensic reports had arrived, showing that Ulibarri had a high level of alcohol and pain killers in his bloodstream, which meant he'd most likely been strangled while unconscious. The medicine was identical to Humphrey's prescription.

Indentation marks around the neck suggested the murderer was male. Partial fingerprints had been lifted, enough for a match. But a computer data search had failed to identify a suspect. Blond hairs combed from Ulibarri's groin area confirmed Ulibarri had engaged in sexual intercourse sometime prior to his murder.

Clayton's query to the FBI about other homicides with similar signatures had come back negative. There was nothing in the Violent Criminal Apprehension Program data bank that correlated to other murders with a similar or identical staged placement of the body.

The DA wanted Harry Staggs found and held as a material witness, so with a search warrant in hand, Quinones and Dillingham had scoured every inch of Casey's Cozy Cabins, looking for personal papers and financial records that could give them a line on Staggs's whereabouts. The exercise failed, as did a canvass of area financial institutions, banks, and government offices. Apparently, Staggs was a man who'd worked hard at not leaving behind a paper trail. He'd paid his property taxes, utilities, and living expenses with cash or by money order, and had no known bank accounts or credit cards.

Finding Staggs wasn't going to be easy, but Hewitt had added that task to Clayton's already full plate anyway. With instructions from the sheriff to dig deeper into Luis Rojas and his girlfriend, Clayton was headed back to El Paso. But first, he needed to make a couple of detours.

He stopped first at Warren Tredwell's office in Ruidoso. The lawyer sat behind an old library table that served as his desk. With a foot propped on his knee, brushing his bushy mustache with a finger, he didn't bother with a greeting or make an attempt to be civil. Clayton's aversion to the man rose up like a tight knot in his stomach.

"I honestly don't know where my client is," Tredwell replied in answer to Clayton's question.

"He's wanted for questioning as a material witness," Clayton said.

"I know that," Tredwell said tersely, leaning back in his chair. "I spoke to the DA earlier today about the matter. But I can't inform my client until he contacts me."

"Has he left town permanently?"

"You could assume that," Tredwell replied.

"And why should I assume that?"

"Good question," Tredwell said sarcastically.

"Answer it," Clayton said. He hated the snippy little

word games so many Anglos liked to play. His sharpness with Tredwell earned him a serious look.

"He put his property up for sale and gave me a power of attorney to handle the transaction," Tredwell said.

"How do you contact him?"

"I don't," Tredwell answered. "He said he would call once he got settled."

"And you haven't heard from him?"

"If I had, I would have told the district attorney."

"Where did he go?"

"He didn't say."

"Not even a hint?"

"South," Tredwell replied. "He said he would be traveling south."

There was a casino outside of El Paso and a racetrack nearby, just inside the New Mexico state line. It made sense that Staggs would want to relocate close to the action, where he could set up shop and draw business.

"Did he mention any plans to visit El Paso?" Clayton asked.

"No, he did not."

"How did Staggs pay your fee?" Clayton asked.

"That's none of your business," Tredwell replied.

Clayton smiled. "If he paid in cash, I'm sure you won't forget to report it to the IRS."

"We're done here," Tredwell said, unwinding himself from the chair.

Clayton nodded in agreement, left, and paused to see Grace at work to tell her he would be gone overnight. Her classroom was filled with happy, noisy children who were finger painting on large sheets of newsprint spread out on low tables. From the doorway Clayton caught Grace's eye and motioned for her to approach. The room fell silent as the children watched as Grace

189

came close and gave him a quick kiss on the cheek. Several children giggled. He told her what was up.

"You promised Wendell and Hannah a phone call to Kerney tonight," Grace said.

"It can wait for a day or two."

"That's not fair," Grace replied. "It may not be a big deal to you, but it is to them."

"You can call Kerney. It doesn't have to be me."

"I'd prefer if you did it," Grace said.

"Not tonight," Clayton said with a shake of his head.

"You can't keep running away from the fact that Kerney is your father," Grace said.

"I'm not. Tell him I wanted to call but couldn't."

"Do you mean that?" Grace asked.

"Half and half," Clayton replied with a weak smile. "He's not an easy man to talk to."

"Neither are you," Grace said, squeezing his hand. "I'll call him."

Clayton kissed his wife and left to the sounds of tittering children. He fired up the engine of his unit, thinking his best move, given what he'd learned at Rojas's mountain retreat and from Tredwell, would be to get a handle on the girlfriend and then start looking for Staggs in El Paso.

Ramona Piño got the lowdown on The Players Green Club & Restaurant from Jeff Vialpando. It wasn't an ordinary sports bar. High-class and expensive, it had opened less than a year ago in a new building in the Northeast Heights, and catered to young, affluent singles who lived in the town homes and condominiums close by.

The grand opening had been attended by the mayor, several city councillors, a couple of state legislators, and some important local business leaders.

Within several months narcotics agents were hearing street talk about drug dealing at the club, and vice cops were getting rumors of illegal Las Vegas-style betting on televised athletic events. Weeks of outside surveillance had identified only two known drug dealers who frequented the club on a regular basis. Undercover cops posing as customers saw no evidence of dealing or illegal wagering. About the only incidents of note involved a duo of college-type hookers, just barely of legal age, who worked the bar on the weekends.

Everything pretty much looked on the up-and-up, but rumors and talk persisted, mostly passed on by two reliable white-collar snitches, who'd fingered an ecstasy drug ring of graduate students at the university.

Surreptitious attempts to get an officer hired as an employee failed. Staff turnover was minimal, and the owner, a man named Adam Tully, always seemed able to bring a new waitress on board quickly without advertising or interviewing applicants.

Tails were placed on staff members, and background checks were run as identities were ascertained. All had clean sheets, but interestingly, all were recent arrivals from out of state, particularly Colorado and west Texas.

Tully, a New Mexico native recently returned from Colorado, was listed as the sole owner of Five Players, Incorporated, doing business as The Players Green Club & Restaurant. If he had partners, they were silent.

Tully had no criminal record, and owned another club in Denver operated under the same name, which had been given a clean bill of health by the Denver PD. All his business licenses, corporate reports, and state and local tax filings were current and in order.

Vialpando had described the club's layout. The bar

and dining area were separate from a large room where big-screen televisions were set up in six different viewing areas consisting of comfortable couches, overstuffed chairs, and coffee tables. Only the bar menu and drinks were available to customers in the screening room. Six adjacent rooms with televisions were available for fans who wanted to dine and watch a specific televised event. Those rooms were already booked months in advance. On the weekends, a jazz trio played dance music in the main dining room.

As she drove to the club, Ramona pushed pleasant thoughts about Jeff Vialpando out of her mind and ran over the cover story she'd laid on Cassie Bedlow. Whatever she told Adam Tully had to match what Cassie Bedlow "knew" about her.

Good undercover cops always built fictional personas based on reality. Ramona's previous assignments had taught her the importance of character development. Blending fact with fiction made the role more natural and authentic, easier to pull off. But there couldn't be any gaps or lapses that might give you away.

In fact, Ramona had been both a waitress and a sales clerk in Durango during the year she'd attended college there as a transfer student. She'd returned to the city several times since then, so dredging up recollections and recalling places and streets wasn't much of a stretch. She did it anyway, because you never knew what could trip you up.

She stepped inside the club and let her eyes adjust to the dim lights. The man standing at the end of the bar talking to the hostess matched Vialpando's description of Adam Tully. Five eight, narrow shoulders, a thin frame, with an arched, slightly turned-up nose. Tully smiled as she approached, and Ramona smiled back.

Adam Tully liked what he saw. She was all that Cassie had told him in her phone call and more: great Hispanic features with dark, liquid eyes, a tight, shapely body with a tiny waist, and creamy skin with a golden hue.

"You must be Ramona," Tully said.

"Yes, I am."

Her baby-doll voice ran through him, right down to his cock. If everything panned out, he could work this bitch every night for five, maybe eight years, and make a hell of a lot of money. He knew a Major League baseball player who'd pop fifteen or twenty grand for a week with her, easy, as soon as she started tricking. Plus, a former Colorado congressman who favored the thin, schoolgirl type with nice knockers. Put her in thigh-high stockings, lacy panties, a push-up bra, some candy-apple-red platform mules, and braid her hair, and the guy would get a hard-on just looking at her picture.

"Let's talk," Tully said, leading her to his office, where he eased back in his thousand-dollar ergonomic chair and inspected the woman more closely. Thick dark hair, small bones, comfortable with her body, five three, one-ten at the most, perfect teeth. She took his gaze without flinching. She was used to getting attention from men, wasn't put off by it. That was good.

"Tell me about yourself," Tully said.

Ramona licked her lips and ran out her cover story: Durango and her failed marriage, the need to make a change, dreams of becoming a model, looking to have some fun and excitement. Tully nodded all the way through it.

"Have you waitressed before?"

Ramona named the restaurant in Durango where she'd worked.

"Isn't that in the old downtown Victorian hotel?"

"No, it's by the railroad station. When were you in Durango?"

"Some time ago. I rode my Harley from Denver for the annual motorcycle rally."

"Every September," Ramona said with a nod. "It's a lot of fun."

"Why did you leave the restaurant?"

"My ex-husband didn't like me working nights."

"The jealous type?" Tully asked.

Ramona remembered her ex-boyfriend and made a face. "He thought every man I talked to I wanted to take to bed."

Tully laughed. "Do you smoke dope, get high, use drugs?"

Ramona paused. "Sometimes," she said in her tiniest voice. "But not a lot."

"If I hire you, you can't come to work high."

"Okay," she said seriously. Was she playing it too Goody Two-shoes?

"You see how my girls are required to dress at work. They show a lot of skin, a lot of T and A. Is that a problem for you?"

"I bet they get good tips," Ramona replied with a grin, "and I can use the money. Besides, I don't mind men looking."

"Do you like men?"

"Most of them."

"I have a girl leaving in a week," Tully said. "See Lisa. She's the hostess. She'll give you a tour and an employment application. I'll work your schedule around Cassie's classes. You'll have to take an alcohol beverage server course before you can start. Lisa will set it up."

194

"Thank you, Mr. Tully."

"You'll do just fine," Tully said. He watched Ramona leave, wondering how long it would take to get her strung out and in debt big-time to one of his dealers. He figured maybe two or three months, if he played it right.

Clouds had thickened outside, but not enough to promise rain. The April sun broke through the cover, casting patches of yellow light on the brick walkway that led to the old adobe house near the state capitol where Mark Shuler ran his research and polling company. Shuler was round, had probably been round all his life, but he wasn't fat, although if you only looked at his chubby cheeks you might think so. Add a foot to his solid stocky frame and he'd pass for an NFL linebacker. He pressed his lips together when Kerney mentioned Tyler Norvell.

"I understand you went to college with Norvell," Kerney added.

Shuler closed his office door on the four researchers who worked in office cubicles in a room just behind the reception area. "Why the interest in Norvell?"

"I'm told you don't like him."

"Don't trust him would be a better way to put it."

"Why is that?" Kerney asked.

"Are you going to tell me why you're investigating Norvell?"

"No," Kerney said with an apologetic smile.

"Then it's probably best for me to keep my thoughts to myself," Shuler said. "I make my living in the political world, Chief Kerney, and while it's public knowledge that I'm not a member of Senator Norvell's fan club, I keep my personal opinions to myself."

"I'll do the same with what you tell me," Kerney said.

195

"You went to college with Norvell. What kind of person was he back then?"

Shuler found his way to his desk chair and settled in. "Are you familiar with F. Scott Fitzgerald's work?"

"I read *The Great Gatsby* in college."

"Norvell was like Gatsby, always full of subterfuges, superficially charming, good at keeping up appearances, but basically unscrupulous. He was quick-witted, ambitious, and smart enough to align himself with people who would help him socially. By the time he entered law school, he'd transformed himself from just another college student who was scraping along into a big man on campus."

"How did he do that?" Kerney asked, as he pushed an office chair to the front of Shuler's desk and sat.

"He joined the right clubs, hung out with the right people, especially the popular jocks, and got involved in campus politics—member of the student senate, student rep on an activities planning committee. That kind of thing."

"So, he played the angles," Kerney said. "How was he unscrupulous?"

"Drugs, women, and gambling," Shuler answered. "While the campus cops and narcs were busting the longhairs and student radicals for using, Norvell and his pals were allegedly selling drugs to frat boys, sorority girls, and students living off campus. He supplied women for bachelor parties, took bets on sporting events, even organized spring vacation gambling jaunts to Denver."

"You know all this as fact?" Kerney asked.

"I got some information from an anonymous informant while I was editor of the college newspaper, but I couldn't confirm it. I spent a lot of time trying to

196

corroborate the story through other sources. All I got was second- and third-hand rumors and gossip."

"What stood in your way?"

"I was the longhair liberal running the college newspaper. The enemy, so to speak. Norvell's customers were the kids who saw themselves as the elite. They were well-off, clannish, spoiled brats. Socially, they kept to themselves and partied pretty much out of sight. They'd rent a suite of rooms in a nice hotel, gather at private houses away from the campus, or go out of town for their big bashes."

"How did the anonymous information come to you?" Kerney asked.

"By letter. Two of them."

"Did you happen to save them?"

"You bet I did," Shuler replied. "I kept hoping someone would come forward and give me something tangible that I could verify and print."

"Were they typed or handwritten?" Kerney asked.

"Handwritten."

"I need to see those letters," Kerney said.

"They prove nothing."

"I still need to see them."

Shuler rummaged around in a file cabinet, pulled out a folder, and handed two sheets of paper to Kerney. They were note size, no dates, with writing on one side only. The first letter read:

Tyler Norvell is supplying drugs to a young friend of mine and taking advantage of her. He has parties at his house and gets her high on drugs. She tells me that she sometimes wakes up in the morning in bed at his house with a boy or a man she doesn't know, and can't remember what

197

happened. She says there are lots of girls at his parties who have had the same experiences. I think he and his friends are drugging these girls and then raping them. My friend also tells me that Tyler and his friends take some girls to Denver on weekends once a month and the girls come back with expensive gifts. Something very bad is going on.

If a student who is supposedly a campus leader is doing these kinds of things, I think it should be made public knowledge.

The second letter read:

I wrote you before about the illegal things Tyler Norvell is doing. Now my friend is addicted to cocaine and says that Tyler loves her and wants her to enter a treatment program in Denver, which he will pay for. I think he just wants to get her out of town. She's planning to drop out of school and move to Denver. I've talked to a psychologist and have tried to use his advice to help her, but it hasn't changed her mind about going. Can't you expose this criminal in your paper? All students should know about the terrible things he does.

"When did you receive these letters?" Kerney asked.

Shuler checked his file and read off dates that corresponded with Anna Marie's cousin Belinda Louise Nieto's time in Albuquerque.

"Whoever the person was," Shuler added, "I don't know why they didn't go to the police."

Kerney knew the answer to Shuler's question. There were millions of reasons why people shied away from talking to cops. It didn't matter if they were friends, family, relatives, or total strangers. He'd seen women protect abusers; parents lie on behalf of felonious teenagers; people confirm false alibis for friends; and witnesses deny they'd seen a crime occur. The rationales for either lying to or avoiding the police were endless.

If the author of the letters had been Anna Marie Montoya—and Kerney was virtually convinced that she was—he would never know why she had chosen to deal with her cousin's situation so obliquely. At this point it didn't really matter.

"Who were Norvell's pals in this enterprise?" he asked.

"Luis Rojas, a football jock from El Paso; Adam Tully, a high school buddy from Lincoln County; and Gene Barrett and Leo Silva, both from Albuquerque. Tully was part of the campus brat pack. That's how Norvell and the others got accepted into the clique."

"Barrett and Silva are state legislators, right?"

"That's right," Shuler replied.

"I heard they got behind Norvell's political ambitions big-time after he moved back from Colorado."

"Right again."

"Any old rumors about them?"

"Just what I've already told you," Shuler replied. "They were rarely on campus, except to attend classes. I don't really know how large a role they played in what went on."

"How do they make their money?"

"Silva has a successful law practice, and Barrett owns a management consulting and CPA firm."

"What about Cassie Bedlow, Norvell's sister?"

"I never heard anything bad about her. She had her own circle of friends, mostly sorority types and fine-arts majors."

"And Rojas?"

"A lady's man who cut a wide swath. But not your average dumb jock. Along with Tully, he was Norvell's off-campus roommate. They shared a large house in the North Valley. People thought that maybe some rich alum was subsidizing Rojas. He dressed nice, drove a new car, always had money to spend."

Kerney held up the handwritten notes. "I'm going to need to hold on to these for a while."

"Just as long as I get them back," Shuler said.

Kerney nodded. "Of course. You've been very helpful."

"Maybe I'll read something about this in the newspaper someday," Shuler said with a slight smile.

"Maybe you will."

Kerney found George Montoya outside, planting bare-root rosebushes in a flower bed. He wanted to know why Kerney needed a sample of his Anna Marie's handwriting. Trying not to raise false hopes, Kerney explained that he'd been given some letters which might have been written by Anna Marie. But he wouldn't be sure until he could have her handwriting compared and analyzed.

A bright eagerness lit up Montoya's eyes. "What do these letters say?"

"It won't matter what they say if Anna Marie didn't write them," Kerney replied.

"But you think maybe she did," Montoya said.

"It's worth checking into."

"Why do you tell me so little?"

"Because I want to give you facts when I have them, not unfairly raise your expectations with speculation."

Montoya's eyes shifted away and his shoulders sagged a bit. "We want so much for there to be justice."

"It can happen," Kerney said. "Always believe that."

Montoya nodded, pulled himself together, gave Kerney a weak smile, and gestured at his house. "Come inside and take what you need."

With a handwriting sample and the letters in hand, Kerney met with the state-police-lab documents specialist and asked for a quick turnaround. In Kerney's case, it paid to be a former deputy state police chief. The man said he'd have a preliminary comparison done in an hour.

Kerney spent his time waiting by questioning Nick Salas, a fifteen-year veteran who now served as a lieutenant in the district headquarters housed next door to the Department of Public Safety. Salas remembered the Norvell DWI incident that had been swept under the rug by the sheriff's department.

"How did you hear about it?" Salas asked, cocking an eye at Kerney.

"Ellsworth Miller," Kerney answered.

"You got something going on Norvell, Chief?"

"Maybe."

Salas laughed. "What do you need to know?"

"Date, time, place, name of the woman with Norvell—if you've got it—name of the deputy who made the DWI stop."

Salas snorted. "You think I can remember all of that?"

"No, but I bet you've got the information stashed somewhere. You're one of the biggest pack rats in the

201

department."

Salas grinned and got up from his desk. "That's affirmative, Chief. Like I tell the rookies, hold on to everything. You never know when you might need stuff you once thought was useless. Give me a few minutes to search through my old paperwork."

Salas was back in fifteen minutes with a dog-eared pocket notebook in hand. He rattled off the day, time, and place. "The deputy was Ron Underwood. He's still with the sheriff's department. He got bumped up to patrol sergeant about the same time I made lieutenant. We tipped a few together at the FOP to celebrate. I've been catching his radio traffic lately so he's back on day shift. I didn't ID the woman."

"Did you see Norvell?" Kerney asked.

"Yeah. I watched Underwood put him through field sobriety tests. He was almost falling-down drunk."

"Thanks, Nick."

"No problem," Salas said, reaching for the phone. "Where are you going from here, Chief?"

"I should be back in my office in thirty minutes."

"I'll give Underwood a call. Maybe he can dig out his report and get it to you today."

"That would be a big help," Kerney said.

Kerney returned to the crime lab to wait for the document specialist's report, and spent his time chatting with the officers and civilian staff who passed him in the small waiting area. During his tenure as deputy state police chief, he'd worked with all of them, so even though he cooled his heels longer than expected, he enjoyed catching up and making small talk.

Stan Kalsen, the document specialist, a burly man with a raspy voice, finally appeared and led him back to his office.

"Sorry to make you wait," Stan said as he spread out the documents, which had been placed in clear plastic sleeves. "I took a quick look at slant, connection, formation of letters, size of letters, punctuation, and embellishments on the questioned documents." He pointed out each element he'd reviewed with a pair of tweezers. "Comparing the two samples, I'd say they were written by the same individual. If you can get the subject to write out the complete texts of the documents again, I'll probably be able to make an unqualified judgment to that effect."

"I can't do that," Kerney replied. "The subject was murdered."

Kalsen nodded. "I thought so. The note written to her mother was signed Anna Marie, so I figured it had to do with the Montoya homicide. I took photographs of the anonymous documents under oblique light to pull up any indentations on the paper. That's what slowed me down. Take a look at this one."

Kalsen held up a photograph of the second unsigned note. Down at the bottom were the indentations of Anna Marie's signature. "It's identical to the standard you gave me," he said.

For the first time, Kerney had a bonafide suspect. Surely, as a newly elected state senator, Tyler Norvell might have had reason to silence a woman who had knowledge of his prior criminal activities. But proving that would be a whole different matter.

Still the information made Kerney smile. "Excellent," he said. "Thanks, Stan."

"Anytime, Chief."

His cell phone rang as he left the lab. Helen Muiz reported that Detective Piño was on her way back to Santa Fe with an APD vice sergeant in tow, Sal Molina had just returned to the office looking to speak with him, and a sheriff's sergeant had dropped off an envelope for him.

"I'm on my way," Kerney said. "Anything else?"

"As always, we're in complete disarray without you," Helen said. She hung up before Kerney could think of a comeback.

CHAPTER 10

TO SAVE MONEY, A NEW POLICE HEADQUARTERS HAD been built some years before on city-owned land near the outskirts of Santa Fe, which of course made it inconvenient for everybody except south-side and some west-side residents.

During the prior administration, two community policing substations—one in a closet-sized space in the downtown library, the other in a building that looked like a large tool shed in a city park—had been established.

Kerney had shut them both down. The city needed a real substation to serve the north and east sides, not cops on duty standing behind a counter fielding chamber-of-commerce type questions, Monday through Friday, nine to five.

He was hoping that if the city ever got around to demolishing the old downtown high school gym next to city hall—it now served as a woefully inadequate convention center—he could put a real substation on the site in at least part of the space. That would alleviate the cramped conditions at headquarters and reduce patrol response times on the east and north sides of the city.

Kerney doubted it would happen on his watch, but

he'd started the planning process anyway in hopes that the concept would survive and eventually come to fruition.

In the first-floor headquarters conference room, he met with Sal Molina, Ramona Piño, and Jeff Vialpando, the APD sergeant, and Helen Muiz, who was present to take notes. Detective Piño summarized the information she'd gained about Cassie Bedlow, Sally Greer, Thomas Deacon, and Adam Tully.

Vialpando explained why Tully's club was a target of investigation, and made a pitch to let him use Piño on a temporary undercover assignment. Kerney tabled the request until later in the meeting.

Molina added some preliminary information about Norvell's Colorado business dealings. Then Kerney went over what he'd learned from Mark Shuler and the anonymous letters.

"Maybe we've got a hard target," Molina said.

"Maybe that and a whole lot more," Kerney said. "Let's back up and outline everything we now know." He moved to the easel at the end of the table and flipped open a newsprint pad. He wrote:

NORVELL & TULLY—BOTH FROM LINCOLN COUNTY, WHERE MONTOYA'S BODY FOUND.

COLLEGE YEARS—NORVELL AND TULLY RUN GIRLS. SELL DRUGS, ECT.

MONTOYA ACCUSES NORVELL OF DRUGGING & SEDUCING COUSIN FOR SEX TRADE PURPOSES.

NORVELL & TULLY BOTH MOVE TO DENVER AFTER COLLEGE. TULLY OPENS PLAYERS CLUB,

NORVELL STARTS A MEDIA ESCORT AND
SECURITY SERVICE.

MONTOYA KILLED AFTER NORVELL RETURNS TO
NM & IS ELECTED TO STATE SENATE.

Kerney stopped writing and turned to Sal Molina.
"Fill us in a bit more on Norvell's Colorado years."

"Like I said, Norvell's company supplied cars and
drivers for celebrities who were in town for concerts,
book signings, media events, and movie and television
productions. He also provided private security for them,
as well as for concert promoters and film companies
shooting on location."

Molina pulled a piece of paper out of a file. "It was
incorporated in Colorado as Five Partners Enterprises,
solely owned by Norvell. That's all I have, so far."

"That doesn't sound like a way to make a fortune,"
Kerney said.

"But the company name is interesting," Ramona said.
"Tully's business in Albuquerque is incorporated as
Five Players."

"A coincidence, I'm sure," Kerney said.

"Add one more," Jeff Vialpando said. "Cassie
Bedlow's agency is on the books as Five Stars
Enterprises."

"Hold on," Sal Molina said as he quickly flipped
through his notes from the Denver PD. "Here it is.
Belinda Louise Nieto was murdered outside The Players
Club in Denver."

"Surely, it's just an unrelated circumstance," Kerney
said, writing it down.

MONTOYA'S COUSIN KILLED OUTSIDE DENVER

CLUB OWNED BY TULLY.

"Three different companies incorporated as Five Players, Five Stars, and Five Partners," Kerney said. He tore off the sheet of newsprint and taped it to the wall. "Tully, Bedlow, and Norvell. Who are the other two?"

"Silva and Barrett attended Tully's grand opening in Albuquerque," Vialpando said.

"Okay, they're possibles," Kerney said.

"And what about Luis Rojas, the ex-college jock?" Ramona asked.

"We know nothing about him yet," Kerney said, shifting his gaze to Helen Muiz. "Let's start a things-to-do list, Helen. Personal and business background checks on Silva and Barrett. Locate Rojas and do the same."

He returned to his chair while the officers stared at the list on the wall.

"If Norvell killed Montoya to keep her from exposing him, you've got motive, Chief," Vialpando said. "But what about opportunity? Can you place him in Santa Fe at the time of the murder?"

"Or at Tully's Denver club, the night Belinda Nieto was killed?" Ramona added.

"That's two more things to do," Kerney said, nodding at Helen, who was already writing them down.

"I'll ask Denver PD for their crime-scene witness list," Molina said.

"I'll check Norvell's travel reimbursement records with the state," Kerney said. "Can you free up a detective to run down information on Barrett's and Silva's businesses?" he asked Molina.

"Can do," Molina replied, "and I'll cover Luis Rojas."

"Okay," Kerney said. "From what Detective Piño and

Sergeant Vialpando have said, I'm inclined to assume that Norvell, Tully, and Bedlow have been operating a vice ring for the last twenty years. It's likely they have at least two more partners. We've got potential informants in the Greer woman and the photographer, Deacon."

Kerney stared at Piño and Vialpando. "How do you two want to proceed with them?" he asked.

"I've made a date with Greer for tonight through her Web site," Vialpando said. "We've got a room booked at an expensive hotel. We'll videotape the transaction, bust her, and see where it takes us."

"Don't have too much fun before the bust," Ramona said.

Vialpando leaned close to Piño and gave her a big smile. "I wouldn't think of it."

Ramona grinned back.

"And Deacon?" Kerney asked, interrupting the byplay.

"He's mine," Ramona said, turning off her smile. "I called and asked him to make some enlargements of the pictures he took. I'm picking them up this evening. Maybe he'll be stoned enough to let down his guard."

"I'd like to see those pictures," Vialpando said.

"Not a chance," Ramona replied.

"Can you give Detective Piño backup at Deacon's?" Kerney asked Vialpando.

"It's already arranged."

"Very good," Kerney said.

"I'd like to use Detective Piño undercover at Tully's club, Chief," Vialpando said.

"I haven't forgotten your request, Sergeant, and I'm willing to go along with it, if needed. You've been very helpful to us, and I appreciate it. But let's see how far we get before Ramona has to start her new job."

Kerney pushed his chair back. "I want reports from everybody ASAP. I'll be at home tonight. Call me there."

All except Helen Muiz left the room. She stood up, handed Kerney the to-do list, and said, "I think those two young people like each other."

"I noticed that," Kerney replied.

"Well I hope they do a better job hiding it when they're undercover."

Helen left the room laughing.

Getting lost in El Paso put Clayton in a foul mood. What looked so easy to get to on a street map wound up being a series of false starts, wrong turns, and wasted time parked at the side of roads trying to figure out where in the hell he was. He did a lot better at finding his way in the mountains and forests on the rez than in the concrete and asphalt of cities.

Finally, he made it to the Upper Valley, a suburban strip of land on the west side of El Paso that bordered the Rio Grande. He drove through wide streets lined with shade trees, passing newer two-story homes, looking for the right turnoff. Here and there along the road were old farmhouses, some irrigation canals, and patches of agricultural land that had not yet given way to the sprawl.

Deborah Shea, the girlfriend who'd been so conveniently present at Rojas's house, no longer lived at the address listed on her driver's license. Clayton got the story from the current owner, an older, retired army major who actually thought cops were the good guys. He pulled out a mortgage settlement statement which showed that the seller of the house had been Big Five

Trucking, Inc., Rojas's company.

"I don't know this woman you're looking for," the man said. "The house was vacant when we bought it."

Clayton checked the closing date for the sale of the house against the issue date he'd recorded from Shea's driver's license. She'd used the address to renew her license six months after the new owner had moved in.

Clayton wondered if Deborah Shea had ever even lived in the house, and went looking for neighbors who might know. According to one woman, a homeowner on the same street, the house had been built six years ago and a Hispanic family lived there prior to the retired army major moving in.

"Were there any other occupants?" Clayton asked, trying not to stare at the woman's tinted and wildly curled hairdo that probably cost a hundred bucks a pop every time she went to the beauty parlor. He'd never known Apache women to do such strange things to their hair, and it had nothing to do with money.

The woman, whose husband ran a maquiladora in Juárez, shook her head. "No, it was just Tony, Martha, and the children."

"How well did you know them?" Clayton asked.

"They were nice people who always came to the annual neighborhood potluck parties. The children were polite and well behaved. Other than that, they didn't do a lot of socializing. The kids kept them too busy."

Clayton rephrased his question: "What do you know about them?"

"Tony worked for a trucking company. He had a management position of some sort."

"Big Five Trucking?"

"Yes, I think that's it. Martha was a stay-at-home mom."

Clayton thanked the woman, left, and kept looking for Deborah Shea. She wasn't listed in the phone book or in the several recent city directories he examined at a branch library. He tried a long shot at a motor vehicle office, hoping that Shea had reported an address change, and struck out.

"Can you search your database of licensed drivers by address?" Clayton asked the office manager.

"You bet," the manager said, turning to his keyboard. "How far back do you want to go?"

"Six years."

The man pulled up the data on his computer screen and printed out the information. The retired army officer, his wife, former occupants Tony and Martha Duran, and Deborah Shea topped the list. But another eight people, all young females, had also used the address to get licenses at one time or another.

"What is this address, an apartment or something?" the manager asked. "A group home? A sorority house?"

"None of the above," Clayton replied. "It's a single-family house."

"That's unreal. What's going on?"

"I'm not sure," Clayton said, handing the list back to the manager. "Can I have hard copies of the license information for each of those drivers?"

"Sure thing."

Clayton took the information to the El Paso police headquarters and got a desk officer to cross-check all the names with computerized arrest records. Two of the women had rap sheets of one count each, for soliciting. The officer escorted Clayton to a vice-squad cop and introduced him as Detective Brewer. He was an older, soft-bellied man with a passive face who wore a shirt with a cigarette-ash burn in the pocket. His breath stank

211

of nicotine.

Brewer pulled the offense reports on the women. Both had been busted at an El Paso hotel.

"What were the case dispositions?" Clayton asked.

It took a minute for Brewer to ferret out the notations. "Both paid fines," he said.

"Where can I find them?" Clayton asked.

"Hell if I know," Brewer said. "They haven't been seen in town for over a year, maybe two. Whores move around a lot these days, one city to the next."

"What about their pimps?"

"There's nothing in the files about that."

Brewer didn't seem particularly eager to help, and his attitude bothered Clayton. He stuck Deborah Shea's motor vehicle photograph under the man's nose. "Do you know this woman?"

Brewer shook his head.

"How about Luis Rojas?"

"I don't know any Luis Rojas who's working girls in El Paso," the detective said.

One by one, Clayton fed Brewer all the driver's license photographs to review.

"Except for the two whores, I don't know any of these women," Brewer said, handing them back.

Although he didn't mean it, Clayton said, "Thanks."

Brewer nodded, watched the Indian cop leave, and dialed a private number. "Tell Mr. Rojas I need to talk to him," he said to the kid who answered the phone.

"Call back at six," Fidel said. "He'll be here then."

The deputy's report on the Norvell DWI stop identified the passenger in the car as Helen Pearson, and gave a rural route address. The phone book carried no listing, so Kerney called the post office and learned that

Pearson now had a postal box. The application listed her permanent residence on a road off the Old Santa Fe Trail, just outside the city limits. It was a high-end neighborhood with big houses on large hillside view lots.

Kerney drove to the address. No one answered his knock at the main house, but two cars were parked in front of a large detached studio. A sign over the door read BUCKAROO DESIGNS.

Inside, two Hispanic women were working at sewing machines, and an Anglo woman was pinning pattern paper to some fabric at a large work table in the center of the room. Racks of custom cowboy shirts, embroidered blue jeans, western-style dresses, and fringed jackets were lined up along a back wall. Bolts of fabric were neatly arranged on floor-to-ceiling shelves. Scraps of cloth littered the floor.

The Anglo woman looked up, set aside a pincushion, and crossed the room. About forty, she had brown hair cut short, delicate features, and wore no makeup other than lipstick. The face of a film actress flashed across Kerney's mind, but he couldn't put a name to it.

"Helen Pearson?" he asked.

"That's me," the woman replied cheerily.

Kerney showed Pearson his shield and her smile faded. "What is it?"

"I've a few questions about Tyler Norvell."

Pearson broke off eye contact and her voice rose. "What kind of questions?"

"You do know him?" Kerney asked, keeping an agreeable look on his face.

"Past tense," Pearson said. "I haven't seen him in many years."

The palpable tension in Pearson's body made Kerney

want to probe more. But the shut-down look in her eyes argued against it. He moved off subject. "This is quite the enterprise you've got going," he said, looking around the studio. "How long have you been in business?"

"Eight years," Pearson said, still frowning.

Pearson wore a plain gold band on the ring finger of her left hand. "Do you run the business with your husband?" Kerney asked.

She glanced at the ring as though it had betrayed her. "No, he's a landscape architect."

On a bulletin board behind a nearby desk were crayon drawings signed by Melissa and Stephen. "Do you have children?" Kerney asked.

Pearson's tension rose again. Her hand fluttered to her neck and her eyes looked frightened. "Why are you asking me all these things?"

"How long have you been married?" Kerney asked.

"Stop it," Pearson hissed. She turned away to glance at the two women. "Why are you questioning me like this?" she whispered.

"Would you be more comfortable if we talked outside?"

Pearson nodded stiffly, her eyes dark with worry. She walked through the open door and led Kerney a good distance away from the studio.

Pearson had reacted to Kerney's innocuous questions in a way that made him believe she was hiding something. A straight-out lie just might shake it loose. "I know you worked for Norvell," he said.

"What do you mean?"

"Do I really need to be more graphic? I'll put it another way: Norvell pimped for you."

Pearson trembled, hugged herself, and said nothing.

214

Kerney stepped in closer. Pearson backed up. "It looks like you've built a new life for yourself," he said. "Talking to me doesn't have to ruin it."

She laughed, harshly, shallowly. "Oh, so you're the good cop, right?"

"Or the bad cop," Kerney replied, "depending on how you want to play it."

"What would the bad cop do?" she asked, struggling for composure.

"You have a husband, children, a thriving business, a reputation, new friends . . ."

Pearson finished Kerney's thought. "Do I want them to know I was once a whore, a hooker, a prostitute?" The words spilled out of her.

"Something like that."

She caved, lost her poise, buried her head in her hands. Kerney stayed back and let her cry. She forced herself to straighten up, composed her face, and spread her arms wide, as if to embrace the hilltop house, the views of the mountains in the distance, her reinvented, respectable life.

"If I hadn't done what I did, I would have none of this," Pearson said. "Can you understand that?"

Kerney nodded.

"How can you possibly protect me?"

"When the time comes, I'll ask the DA to have you appear before a grand jury. Your testimony will be sealed and never made public."

Kerney knew he might be making a false promise, and while he didn't want to cause Pearson any pain, getting to Norvell was much more important than preserving the woman's secret.

"It's your call," he said.

Pearson's slight nod of agreement gave Kerney no

215

sense of satisfaction. She had the look of a small animal about to be eaten by a predator.

"Come inside the house," she said.

It took an hour for Pearson to tell her story. Part confession, part rationalization, it spanned the years just before Norvell's return to New Mexico and his election to his first term in office. Pearson had been the number-one girl in Norvell's Denver stable; the most expensive, the most in demand, the one with the most repeat customers.

She had made money, spent money, gotten high, lived the good life: designer clothes, weeks at luxury resorts with wealthy men, extravagant gifts, world travel. She explained what it had meant to a girl from a dysfunctional family who'd felt worthless and stupid.

She told him how watching Norvell's older girls get dumped as they lost their bloom made her realize she had to do something with her life before it was too late. How coming to Santa Fe on working weekends to be with clients, she found a place where she thought it would be possible to turn things around.

Kerney didn't interrupt. He heard her out as she talked about breaking away from Norvell, moving to Santa Fe, going into therapy, apprenticing with a clothing designer, opening her business, meeting her future husband, starting a family. Finally, she stopped, exhausted by the outpouring. But her eyes looked clearer, less troubled.

Kerney decided not to press too much for specifics. That would come later in an in-depth interview. He brought up Adam Tully and Luis Rojas and got confirmation that both were Norvell's partners. He learned that Rojas lived in El Paso. She had no knowledge of Cassie Bedlow, Gene Barrett, or Leo

Silva.

"We'll need to meet again," he said. "You can pick the time and place, but it must be soon."

"How did you find me?" Pearson asked.

"Luck," Kerney replied.

"Here at the house is best, in the mornings after eight. My husband goes to work and drops the children off at preschool on his way."

"Tomorrow, then," Kerney said. "I think we can wrap things up in one session."

Pearson's eyes bored into Kerney with the hardness of a con who'd been trumped. "You suckered me with this bullshit about the grand jury, didn't you?"

"Not necessarily," Kerney replied. "I'll try to work something out on your behalf."

She snorted in disbelief. The sound stripped away the last shred of her sophisticated veneer. "Yeah, right. Son of a bitch. Have you got a cigarette?"

"I don't smoke."

"Neither do I."

"If you change your mind about tomorrow, our deal is off."

"No kidding," Pearson said.

Outside, the glare of sunlight bounced off the roofs of the houses in the valley below, washed out the roughness of the mountains beyond, and pulled most of the color from the sky. Kerney drove away from Helen Pearson thinking that the siren call of Santa Fe had always drawn searchers, dreamers, nonconformists, and oddballs looking to transform their lives. Why not a hooker? Considering everything, Pearson had done a damn good job of it.

His cell phone rang. At Kerney's request, the fiscal officer who kept the records of legislators' travel and

217

per diem reimbursement payments had searched Senator Norvell's old files. Norvell had attended a three-day meeting of a joint-house finance committee in Santa Fe that coincided with the date Anna Marie Montoya had disappeared.

Kerney now had motive *and* opportunity, but he needed more. He decided a trip to Lincoln County would be worthwhile. That was where Montoya's body had been found and where Norvell and his buddy, Adam Tully, had grown up. The connection between the two was too strong to dismiss.

He checked the time. The architect was waiting for him at the building site with a survey crew, and Sara was standing by at Fort Leavenworth for his call. This was the day the site for the house would be spotted and staked. It was the last chance before the contractor broke ground to make sure everything was as it should be. He would talk Sara through it as the survey crew and the architect laid out the footprint for the house.

He wondered if Sara would reinvent herself once the baby came and the house was finished. Could she give up her career and be satisfied with the role of wife and mother? It was all still undecided.

He called the architect, said he was on the way, and pressed the accelerator.

There had been something not quite right about Clayton's meeting with Detective Brewer. After a few worthless hours of trying to get a handle on Harry Staggs, Clayton ate a quick meal at a family-style diner and tried to sort it out. For starters, Brewer hadn't shown any interest in Clayton's investigation, hadn't asked any questions about what a deputy sheriff from Lincoln County was doing down in El Paso seeking information about local prostitutes.

Was that because he simply didn't care, or because he already knew about it? If he knew, how did he know? Had the El Paso police captain who'd given Rojas a clean bill of health passed the word to the troops about him nosing around?

Brewer had held on to the paperwork, showing Clayton none of it, instead reading little excerpts. Was there something he didn't want Clayton to see? Clayton doubted that offense reports of solicitation for the purposes of engaging in prostitution held much in the way of sensitive or confidential information a brother officer would be reluctant to share. Or maybe they did.

Clayton had two bits of information, the names and photographs of the prostitutes. He looked at the women's pictures. Both were young and very attractive. Not what Clayton considered to be typical streetwalkers, although he'd only actually met one: Sparkle, the hooker who'd fingered Ulibarri in Albuquerque.

He decided to spend some time visiting the best El Paso had to offer in the way of expensive hotels. There were only a few, if the yellow pages were anything to go by. Maybe he could to find out if Brewer had been holding something back.

After three stops with no results, he made his way downtown, which had one nice hotel near the plaza. The area looked like an urban redevelopment project that had gone down the tubes when the money ran out. Around the spruced-up plaza were old commercial and retail buildings in need of attention. One, which had obviously been a flagship department store, sat empty. Two public works buildings, a public library, and an art museum were nearby. Behind the plaza several Victorian homes sat forlornly on a small hill surrounded

219

by vacant lots. There was no life to the place, few people, and Clayton didn't see many customers inside an eatery steps away from the hotel.

Modern in design, the hotel towered over the district in startling contrast to the bleak, shabby-looking street that cut a straight line to the Rio Grande and the Mexican border.

Inside, the lobby was empty. At the reception desk, Clayton asked for the hotel security chief, and was soon greeted by a slender man in a suit and tie who introduced himself as Bob Rigby.

"Yeah, I know these two," Rigby said as he looked at the photos of Victoria and Sandy, the two hookers.

"Have you seen them lately?"

"Yeah, a couple of weeks ago they were here in the restaurant dining with two of our guests. Then they went up to their rooms."

"You're sure of that?"

Rigby nodded. "I'm sure. Those two are in the hotel three, maybe four times a month, sometimes more. I know why they're here, but I'm not a cop. Whatever guests do in their rooms doesn't matter to me, as long as they don't cause a commotion, trash the place, skip out on their bill, or steal the towels."

"What about the cops?" Clayton asked.

"They don't care either, unless they get a complaint. We try to avoid that, if possible."

"Bad for business, I suppose," Clayton said, wondering what else Detective Brewer might have lied about. He handed Rigby the rest of the photographs of the women he'd collected at the motor vehicle office.

"All of them have been here at one time or another," Rigby said. "All of them are working girls."

"Including this one?" Clayton asked, pointing to

220

Deborah Shea's photo.

Rigby nodded. "But I haven't seen her in quite a while."

"Do you know who these women work for?"

"That, I don't know."

Pumped by what he'd learned, Clayton left Rigby and drove past Rojas's house. In daylight it was even more impressive, probably a million-dollar property, which for El Paso was about as pricey as it got.

He cruised the neighborhood, trying to think of his next move. He still needed to locate Deborah Shea, but he wanted to do it without tipping off Rojas. All the houses—there weren't very many along the paved street—looked down on El Paso over a wide stretch of open desert. At both ends of the road, signs of a private security company were posted, citing twenty-four-hour armed patrol.

That gave Clayton an idea. A security patrol vehicle had passed him when he'd been on his way to talk to Rojas. Maybe someone at the company could shed some light on who came and went at the residence. Maybe they even had a record of who lived on the property with Rojas.

After finding an address in the phone book at the closest convenience store, consulting his map, and getting lost again, he finally reached the business, which had a small suite of offices in a building across from an adult bookstore.

The owner inspected Clayton's credentials, said that he was an ex-deputy sheriff himself, talked a little cop stuff, and pulled the file on Rojas.

"We've never had any problems at the Rojas place," he said.

Aside from Rojas, two residents were listed: a

221

personal assistant and a live-in housekeeper. Clayton wrote down the names. An attached frequent-visitor list carried the names of what looked to be Rojas's friends and business associates. Shea's name was included, along with a description and license plate number of the car she drove.

"Do your people check on unfamiliar vehicles traveling through the neighborhood?" Clayton asked.

"All the time," the man replied. "It's policy."

"Can I look through your patrol logs?"

"How far back do you want to go?" the man replied.

"A week will do it."

The man pulled the logs and let Clayton use his office, a small, tidy space next to a room where a uniformed security officer manned a radio. He sucked in his breath and whistled when he saw the entry for Harry Staggs's car and license plate number. Then he checked the date, sat back in the chair, and smiled at the ceiling.

Staggs had been with Rojas just hours before Clayton had arrived to be fed a line of bullshit by Rojas and Shea.

A small copying machine stood on a rolling cart next to a file cabinet. Clayton checked with the owner for permission, and made a copy of the log and the frequent-visitor list, mulling over his next step. It was too soon to confront Rojas. He decided to stake him out instead. Maybe Deborah Shea would show, or someone else equally interesting.

He thought about the lay of the land in front of Rojas's house. There wasn't much that provided concealment, but he could make do. On the rez he'd stalked poachers through open fields, caught trespassers in vast meadows, and busted out-of-season hunters above the timberline. He had everything he needed in his unit to stay warm and comfortable when night came

222

and it got cold.

The prospect of the surveillance pleased Clayton far more than the thought of spending the night in an El Paso motel. He checked the wall clock. There were two hours left before dusk. If he hurried, there was enough time to locate a place to conceal his unit at the bottom of the hill below Rojas's house, hike up it, and pick a spot to hunker down.

The architect and the survey crew left just before sunset. Kerney stayed on at the building site watching touches of color fringe the few stray clouds, shadows deepen in the canyon, and the mountains fade into gray ghostly shapes. He stood behind the stakes that defined the placement of what would one day be his living room, imagining the house completed—the ceiling overhead, the plastered adobe walls, the tiled floor, the picture window looking beyond the portal to the canyon and the mountains. All of it on twelve hundred and eighty acres of ranch land just a few miles off a highway, yet far enough away to be private and secluded.

The night was quiet. Hills a mile or so to the east blocked any traffic noise, and the air was still. He thought about his parents, now long dead, who had lost their ranch. He thought about Sara, who'd left her family's ranch in Montana to attend West Point. He thought about his best friend, Dale Jennings, who'd never done anything but ranch, and vowed that he wouldn't trade one day of it to live any other way.

Kerney understood Dale's feelings. There was a pride that came from being a steward of the land, a satisfaction that came from hard physical work outside in the natural world, and a richness of spirit that came from the beauty that surrounded you.

223

Once, the idea that he could ever have anything close to this land had only been a dream, totally out of reach. Now it was coming true.

It wasn't a big spread and would never be economically self-sustaining. Maybe he could break even with it. If not, it was his, free and clear, with enough money left over from his inheritance after all the bills were paid to provide a comfortable life for his family and pass it on to his son, and maybe someday a daughter.

Kerney cracked a smile in the darkness. The land was beautiful but the native grasses were hardly sufficient for raising livestock. Still, he wanted to put some animals on it, and had decided to raise horses, primarily for pleasure, selling a few every now and then. Perhaps, when he retired, he'd get into breeding, but there was a lot he had to learn. Modern ranching had become a science, and he was way behind the curve on what he needed to know.

Did he have any horses? Yeah, one. A mustang named Soldier he'd bought at auction and turned into a good cutting horse. Dale was keeping Soldier on his ranch until the time came for Kerney to claim him. That time was coming fast.

Sara had been bugging him to give the ranch a name. Today on the phone, after he'd talked her through the final house siting, she'd teased him about it. Everything he'd suggested she dismissed as insipid. He had orders to come up with something good, perhaps even creative.

What did he have? Right now, he owned two sections of land and a horse.

That was it: The One Horse Ranch.

He made his way down the rocky dirt road thinking he really did need to rebuild it. He would call around to see if he could scour up a grader soon.

CHAPTER 11

THE TELEPHONE CALL FROM WENDELL AND HANNAH caught Kerney by surprise. Hannah recited the letters of the alphabet she'd learned along with her numbers, which she rattled off into the double digits. As the pièce de résistance she informed Kerney that she could write out her name. Kerney said he was amazed and that Hannah was a very, very smart girl.

"I know," Hannah said, handing the phone off to Wendell.

Wendell described the picture he'd drawn for Kerney and asked if it would be all right to have his mother mail it to him. Kerney said that he would love to have it. He would keep it in his office at police headquarters.

"I'm gonna be a policeman, just like you and my dad," Wendell said.

The pleasure in the children's voices made Kerney realize that no matter what stood between him and Clayton, to Hannah and Wendell he was their grandfather, and they seemed to like it. He wondered where the idea for the phone call had come from. He didn't think Clayton was behind it, so that left Grace, or Clayton's mother. He settled on Grace as the instigator.

Grace came on the line and Kerney asked about Clayton.

"He would have called himself," she said, "but he's out of town."

"Give him my best, and tell him I'll be coming down there soon."

"Stop by the house while you're here," Grace said. "Wendell and Hannah would love to see you."

225

"I'll do that," Kerney said. "Thank you for calling, Grace. It made my day."

"From the smiles on your grandchildren's faces, I'd say the feeling was mutual."

The phone rang immediately after Kerney disconnected. He picked up to find Sara on the line.

"Sara, I just . . ."

"Don't talk, Kerney, listen. I'm pissed at you and this whole situation. I think you just want me only for sex, or for carrying your child, or for occasional companionship when I can fly in on one of your rare free weekends."

Kerney's cheerfulness evaporated. "What are you talking about?"

"I should have been there today for the house siting, not hearing about it on the other end of a phone call. I should have been there because it's supposed to be our house. I don't think you give a damn about me. You've just got this fantasy going about a wife, a family, and a ranch, not necessarily in that order."

"That's crazy. I thought you said you couldn't get away between now and graduation."

"Of course I can't get away," Sara snapped. "That's not what I'm talking about. You could have waited. What's one month? Shit! I hate to curse. Shit, shit, shit."

"Why didn't you tell me this before?"

"I shouldn't have had to. It should have been clear in your mind that it was something we needed to do together."

"I've just been trying to move things along."

"Why? So it can all come together perfectly according to some master plan? The house gets built, the pregnant wife appears, the baby gets born."

Stunned by the criticism, Kerney tried again to

226

explain. "I just wanted have everything ready for you and the baby."

"The place you're renting is more than adequate for us."

"You're being wrongheaded about this."

"Wrongheaded? If I'm so wrongheaded why do you even bother to know me?"

Kerney heard the phone go dead. He dropped the receiver and stared at it, pulled his hand back from it. Now, he was pissed—beyond belief pissed. He was a jerk, a dummy, an unfeeling, inconsiderate SOB. A bum for wanting to make Sara happy.

Where had all this come from? A few hours ago she was laughing on the phone, talking excitedly about the house plans, consulting the architectural drawings he'd sent her, and asking questions.

The phone rang and Kerney picked up.

"Do you want to talk?" Sara asked.

He could hear her crying. "Yes, of course." A long silence followed, punctuated by Sara's sniffling. "Are you still angry?" he asked.

"I'm hurt, not angry."

Kerney's indignation abated. "I had no intention to hurt you."

"I know that. But sometimes you get so single-minded I want to give you a swift kick."

"I think you just have."

"I guess I did."

"Are you all right?" Kerney asked.

"No, I'm hormonal, pregnant, lonely, exhausted, and wondering what's in store for us."

"A good life together," Kerney said, trying for something upbeat.

"Yeah, the rare times we're together."

227

"We still have to work that out."

"Yes, we do. If you want me to raise this child on my own, tell me now."

Her words hit Kerney like a sucker punch. "Hold on a minute."

"Do you?"

"Never, dammit." He heard her intake of breath followed by another silence.

"Okay."

"What do you want?" he asked.

"I'd like to reach out and touch you in my bed tonight. Oh, never mind. I have to go. Good night."

"Sara, don't hang up this way."

"I'll be fine."

"I'm not sure I will," Kerney said.

"I wouldn't embarrass myself by crying at you over the telephone if I didn't love you. My nose is running, my eyes are red, and I need a big hug."

"Do you want me to fly in this weekend?"

"No, I won't have a spare moment."

"Okay."

"Just say good night," Sara said.

"How about if I say I love you, instead?" Kerney countered.

"That will do nicely."

"I love you."

"Me too," Sara replied.

He held the dead phone in his hand until a recorded message urged him to hang up. Then he poured whiskey into a glass and stood on the patio staring at the hill behind the house in the darkness. He felt angry, hurt, above all misunderstood. Suddenly, he was dissatisfied with himself, with everything.

He sipped the whiskey. The quarter moon and the

star-filled sky couldn't hold his interest. The stiff cold breeze against his face felt insignificant even though he started to shiver. The whiskey burned his throat.

Was he really so unfeeling? Pigheaded? Inconsiderate? How could Sara ever think that he would want her to raise their child alone? Was she sending him a message? Had she decided to keep her commission and stay on active duty after her maternity leave?

Confused, Kerney went inside and tried to get his head straight, although he didn't hold out much hope that it would happen easily.

Thomas Deacon was a little high and a little horny. He sat close to Ramona on a couch in his living room, occasionally letting his leg touch her knee as she looked at the enlargements she'd asked him to make. His leering smile made her want to slam his face into the hardwood floor.

The room was decorated with mismatched furniture, cheap throw rugs, and shelves made from concrete blocks and boards, which held a large number of videotapes within easy reach of a VCR and big-screen television. There wasn't a book in sight.

"You've got a good start on a portfolio," Deacon said. "But it's only a start. We need to get you in some evening wear, swim suits, lingerie, and do some location work."

"Oh, I'd love to do that," Ramona said.

"You gotta learn to play to the camera," Deacon said as he leaned closer, sounding every bit like a Dutch uncle offering friendly advice. "How to use your face and your body." He ran his finger across Ramona's cheek. "You've got the right bone structure for the camera, and Hispanic women are a hot commodity right now."

"Can I see some of your location work?" Ramona asked, maintaining her eager smile.

"Sure, why not," Deacon said, getting to his feet. "But don't get ahead of yourself. That's not gonna be happening until you're about to graduate from the program."

Deacon swaggered his way into the studio and came back with some photo files. Ramona fed his ego with compliments as she looked at the pictures. She paused at the photograph of Sally Greer posing on the patio of the Santa Fe-style house. The one Deacon said he'd shot at the Indian resort and casino outside Ruidoso. Ramona knew better: she'd been to the casino and it didn't look anything like an adobe hacienda.

"Do you always go to the same places with Cassie's students?" she asked.

"Pretty much."

She tapped Sally's photo. "I have this really sexy little black cocktail dress. Maybe we could do something high-class at a place like this. You said I needed to get more comfortable in front of the camera."

"I thought you were short on money," Deacon said.

"I'm starting a new job in a week at The Players Club."

Deacon licked his lips. He'd figured all along that Bedlow had an agenda for the bitch, but hooking her up with a job at The Players Club sealed it. Bedlow and Tully were gonna turn this sweet thing into a whore, just like they did with Sally Greer and some other prime tail.

He put his hand on her thigh. "Yeah, you could use the practice."

Ramona ignored Deacon's hand and held up Sally's picture. "Is this place nearby? It looks like it was taken in Santa Fe."

"No, that was shot at a ranch owned by Cassie's brother."

"I couldn't afford to pay for your time to go there. But it's beautiful. Where is it?"

"Down in Lincoln County," Deacon said.

"I'd love to see that part of the state," Ramona said. "I've never been there."

"Maybe I could free up some time and drive you there for a shoot," Deacon said, slipping his hand further up her thigh. He wondered how long it would take to get the bitch high and naked with him in front of a video camera.

Ramona almost shuddered at Deacon's touch. Instead, she removed his hand and stood up. "Now, behave yourself, Mr. Deacon," she said primly, teasingly. "I have to go."

Deacon smiled. "Don't you want to stay and play with me?"

"I'm not *that* easy. How much do I owe you for the enlargements?"

"Forget about it. It's on the house."

After she walked out twitching her tight little ass, Deacon rolled a joint, took a hit, and shrugged off the bitch's rejection. The day would come when she would be *easy*.

Three blocks away from Deacon's house, Jeff Vialpando flashed his lights, and Ramona pulled to the curb. He got in her unit and Ramona handed him the wire she'd been wearing.

"That sucked," she said.

"I think it went well," Vialpando said.

"I'm talking about how I feel. He had his hand halfway up my crotch. I need a shower."

231

Jeff stayed silent. He'd learned from hard experience working with the female vice cops in his department that nothing he could say would wash Ramona's feeling of disgust away.

"I wish the bastard had incriminated himself," Ramona said.

"You did good," Jeff replied.

"Big deal. He shoots Bedlow's students on location at Norvell's ranch."

"It's another link in the chain," Jeff said.

"I would have liked to get a hell of a lot more."

"Are these your pictures?" Vialpando asked, reaching for the envelope on the dashboard.

"Don't touch."

He pulled his hand away. "I'd like to have one to show the guys who I'm dating."

Ramona's fierceness softened. "Oh, are we dating?"

"We will be, if you let me take you to dinner."

"Don't you have a date with Sally Greer?"

"Yeah, in three hours. Until then, I'm all yours."

"Dinner, huh?"

"Yep," Jeff said, pulling at the lapel of his best suit. "At a fancy restaurant. I already made the reservation."

"Pretty sure of yourself, aren't you?" Ramona said, breaking into a smile.

"Hopeful, optimistic."

"One question," Ramona said. "Are there any current girlfriends I need to know about?"

"I'm between relationships," Jeff replied.

"What does that mean?"

"It means I haven't been on a date in six months."

"That's worse than not having a girlfriend."

Vialpando laughed. "You're right. May I buy you dinner, Detective?"

"As long as you don't put your hand on my thigh."

"Agreed," Jeff said. "Now, about those pictures."

Ramona snatched the envelope off the dashboard. "In your dreams. You've got a long way to go before you'll get to see them, if ever."

"But there's a chance?"

"Maybe," Ramona replied.

Vialpando put his hand on the door latch. "Follow me. After dinner you can hang out and eavesdrop on my date with Greer, if you want to."

"I'd like that. Besides, somebody needs to keep an eye on you."

Vialpando laughed and went back to his car. Ramona dialed Chief Kerney's home number. He answered in a gruff voice, and she filled him in as Jeff swung ahead of the unit.

"I don't know if it means anything substantial," Ramona said.

"It's helpful," Kerney said tersely. "Thanks for the call, Detective."

Feeling a bit deflated by Kerney's tone, Ramona disconnected and closed the distance to Jeff's car, wondering what was eating at the chief.

Luis Rojas talked to the El Paso vice cop on the phone and watched Tyler Norvell drum his fingers on the black marble top of the kitchen island.

He disconnected and swung his bar stool to face Norvell straight on. "That Indian cop is still nosing around, but he won't get anywhere." He gave Norvell the scoop on Detective Brewer's phone call.

"And you were just telling me everything is going to be all right," Norvell said. "This doesn't cut it, Luis."

"What's the problem?" Rojas responded. "A cop asks

Cassie a couple of questions about Anna Marie and goes away. An Indian cop comes around nosing into my whereabouts the night of the murder in Ruidoso, gets his answers, and goes away."

"But this Indian cop hasn't gone away," Norvell said. "He's still investigating. He's got the names of two of our girls."

"He was told nothing that can come back at us. I'll have Shea take the girls to Juárez tonight. They can work there until things quiet down."

"And that solves everything?" Norvell snapped.

"If I asked the cop pretty please to stop, would that make you feel better?" Rojas moved off the stool, poured two mugs of freshly ground coffee, and brought them to the kitchen island.

"Cut the sarcasm," Norvell said, spooning sugar into his mug.

"In time, this will become just another unsolved cold case that's forgotten."

"Anna Marie's death hasn't been forgotten," Norvell said.

"Because they found her remains," Rojas said, settling back on his stool. "They had to reopen the case."

"Was it necessary to have Ulibarri killed?" Norvell asked.

"Of course it was, and Fidel did a good job of it. For five years, we used Harry Staggs's place to break in some of our new girls and never had a problem," Rojas said. "Ulibarri beat Greer up bad, for chrissake."

Rojas drank some coffee before continuing. "You know the rules: hurt our girls and you pay, threaten the partnership and you pay. Above all, we protect our investments. It's worked for over twenty years. Ulibarri

234

wasn't the first and he won't be the last. Remember Belinda Nieto?"

Norvell looked skeptical. "This is all happening too close to home."

"I told you to let me handle Montoya."

"There wasn't time for that," Norvell said. "She was going to bring everything down."

"Burying her body in a fruit stand in Lincoln County wasn't very smart," Rojas said. "I never should have listened to you when you said it was taken care of."

"She was fine just where she was, until a drunk got killed and the place was torched. I don't want to argue with you, Luis."

"So, stop. Do we have problems anywhere else in the organization? No. Everything is cool at Cassie's, at Tully's, and at your place. Things are running fine in Denver, Houston, San Antonio, Phoenix, and here. Nobody's questioning Silva or Barrett, Staggs is taken care of, Sally Greer is playing ball, and the Indian cop has nothing but the names of two whores who will be across the border as soon as I talk to Deborah."

"We should move Sally Greer," Norvell said.

"Fine. Have Cassie send her to Houston. The oil men will love her, especially the Arabs."

Norvell nodded agreement. "And neutralize the cop."

"I'll send Fidel up there tomorrow to kill him," Rojas said. "He'd like that."

Norvell's eyes widened. "You're joking, right?"

"Yes, I'm joking." Rojas stood, patted Norvell on the shoulder, and put his half-empty mug in the sink. "Killing cops isn't smart. Let's say we make him look dirty. Plant some money in his house that he can't explain away and make an anonymous tip to the state police."

"That would just make him more suspicious," Norvell said, sliding his empty mug across the kitchen island.

Rojas refilled it and pushed the mug back to Norvell. "Or get him fired. We don't do it right away. Give it a month, maybe two."

"Meanwhile, what?" Norvell asked as he reached for the sugar.

"We stay alert."

"That isn't good enough. We need to be proactive."

"Save the speech making for your constituents, Tyler," Rojas said. "If you're that worried, cancel the bookings at the ranch."

"I've already done it, and the clients aren't happy. Some of them made reservations up to a year ago."

"They'll come back," Rojas said. "We offer the best damn sex venue in the Southwest. We've got judges, lawyers, politicians, doctors, corporate executives, and celebrities from all over the country who come back year after year to be with their mistresses or favorite whores."

With a worried looked still firmly in place, Norvell sipped his coffee and said nothing.

"What else do you want to do, Ty?" Rojas asked.

"Keep tabs on the Indian cop," Norvell said. "That way we stay on top of the situation."

"That's not a half-bad idea."

"It has to be low-key, below the radar."

"I'll have Fidel do it," Rojas said. "But just for a couple of days. I'll send him up there tonight."

"I have to go," Norvell said.

"Stay in touch," Rojas said as he walked with Norvell to the front door.

Norvell drove away and Rojas went to find Deborah Shea. He found her in Fidel's bed, riding him hard with

236

obvious pleasure. She was a true nympho, who took her fill of Fidel every chance she got.

Rojas watched for a moment before interrupting. "When you two are finished," he said, "come to the kitchen."

Deborah nodded her head up and down vigorously without losing her rhythm.

By sunset Clayton had settled into a shallow gully that gave him adequate concealment and a clear line of sight into Rojas's driveway. The house sat at the boundary of the Franklin Mountains State Park, the largest range in Texas, all of it contained within the city limits.

The highest peak, pale pink in the last flicker of light, rose three thousand feet above the city. Rocky and treeless, from a distance the desert mountains looked barren, but through his binoculars Clayton had seen hawks circling in the sky and a wide range of different types of cactus plants on the hillsides.

Landscaping pretty much blocked Clayton's view of the house, although he could see a light from a room above the garage and another in the main residence.

The clear sky darkened, sapping away the heat of the day. Clayton pulled on his gloves and his ski mask, zipped up his sleeping bag, and adjusted his night-vision scope to draw in the maximum ambient light from the rising quarter moon. Above, he heard the distinctive sound of a bat winging by.

A car exited the driveway. Clayton locked in on the plate as it turned onto the road, and he almost let out a whistle. The vehicle carried the distinctive New Mexico license plate of the state senator from Lincoln County.

Clayton checked the make of the vehicle as it sped away. It was Senator Norvell's vehicle, for sure.

Clayton had seen it often on the highways traveling in and out of Ruidoso. What was Norvell doing with Rojas? Could it possibly have anything to do with the investigation? Maybe yes, maybe no, but certainly worth looking into.

He broke out a canteen and some trail mix from the backpack and waited to see what happened next. Within an hour two cars drove away from the house. He got license plate numbers, makes, and models, but couldn't see inside to spot the drivers.

Clayton waited, hoping for more action at the house. Except for an occasional vehicle passing by, everything stayed quiet. Finally, he decided to call it quits, drive home, catch some sleep, and check in with Sheriff Hewitt in the morning. He packed up his gear, belly crawled until the slope of the hill gave him enough cover to rise, and made a beeline for his unit.

Jeff Vialpando held the money out to Sally Greer—three hundred bucks—which was a fair price for an hour of her time, given her good looks and knockout body. When she slipped the bills in her clutch purse, he showed his shield and told her she was busted.

With a poor-me, dismayed look on her face, Greer sat on the hotel-room bed and tried hard not to cry, holding it back in small, tight gasps. Her reaction surprised him. Most hookers either played it nonchalant or put on the tough cookie role with cops.

Vialpando looked down the front of her skimpy dress. She wasn't wearing a bra, and there were faint bite marks on her breasts. The bruises on her arms had turned yellow, and makeup covered the mouse on her face.

"I have to call a lawyer," Greer said.

Vialpando sat next to her, thinking about her interesting choice of words. Why not *need to* or *want to*? That's what most of the working girls said when faced with arrest. Greer was a rookie.

Vialpando looked at her face. There wasn't anything hard about it, just a vacant sadness. He smiled sympathetically. "That might not be the wisest thing to do. It makes your situation more complicated."

"I can have a lawyer, can't I?" Greer asked pleadingly.

"Have you ever been arrested before?" Vialpando asked.

Greer shook her head.

"Here's the way it goes," Vialpando said. "I haven't read you your rights yet. If I do that, then you really are busted and I have to book you into jail. First off, you'll be strip-searched. They never show that part on TV. All your body cavities will be probed. Then you'll be dressed out in jail coveralls, fingerprinted, photographed, and locked in a tiny holding cell while I do the paperwork. It's got a concrete bunk, a toilet, a light that never goes off, and a small window in the door so you can be watched at all times. When I'm finished, you get to make one phone call. It's late by then, so the chances are good it will take the lawyer a couple of hours to arrange for your bail. Do you want that?"

Again, Greer shook her head.

"Let's say you get out on bail," Vialpando continued. "You'll still have a court date. If you show up, I'll make sure the newspapers cover it, especially your hometown paper. If you skip out, you become a fugitive from justice, which always carries jail time. While I'm waiting to see which way you decide to go, I'll put twenty-four-hour surveillance on you. Each time you meet a client, you'll get busted. See how complicated it can get when you ask for a lawyer?"

"What do you want me to do?" Greer asked.

"Talk to me, off the record."

"I can't do that."

"Do you want to be a whore?" Vialpando asked.

Greer dropped her head. "No, but I don't want to die, either."

"You won't, I promise."

Greer looked up. "I'm strung out."

"That won't kill you," Vialpando said.

"You don't understand."

"Make me understand."

Tears ran down Greer's face. She wiped them away. "I owe money to people."

"To Cassie Bedlow, I bet."

"You know?" Surprise filled her voice.

Vialpando nodded, got the desk chair, positioned it near the bed, sat, and leaned forward, not so close as to break into Greer's personal space, but close enough to keep her focused on him. It was time to get to the nitty-gritty.

"We know all about it," he said. "How she set you up with the tuition loan and reeled you in when you couldn't pay it back. Maybe even got you started on drugs. You're not the only one she's done it to."

"I know."

"But I don't think Bedlow would kill you."

"Not her," Greer said.

"Who?"

"This man, this boy."

"What happened?"

Greer took a deep breath to compose herself. "We were down in Ruidoso on location. The whole class. It

240

was kinda like a big deal because we were finishing school and the photos would complete our portfolios. Cassie told me I had to pay her back right away for the tuition, plus interest. I told her I couldn't, and she said I had to work it off, that she had a job for me."

"Then what?"

"This boy drove me to El Paso, where a man and a woman were waiting." Greer started sobbing, her face twisting into a look of disgust.

Vialpando gave her a minute before saying, "Go on."

"They did me, all three of them. The boy put a gun to my head while he was on top of me. He said if I ever failed to do what I was told, I'd be killed."

"Then he beat you," Vialpando said.

"No, that happened the next night in Ruidoso when I turned my first trick. They killed him for hurting me, I'm sure of it. It was in the papers. I went to Cassie and asked her about it. She said I would end up the same way if I ever said a word."

"I need names and places, Sally."

Greer gave him what specifics she had. The man was Luis Rojas. The woman was called Debbie, and the kid Fidel, but she didn't know their last names. The trick who'd beaten her was Felix, an Hispanic male. She'd picked him up at the Indian casino while Rojas and Fidel watched.

The house in El Paso was like an estate, and by the way Rojas acted, was probably owned by him. The cabin in Ruidoso was a rental, Casey's Cozy Cabins. Rojas had driven her there with the trick. Fidel, who was assigned to keep an eye on Greer, followed in another car.

"We're going to have to go over this again," Vialpando said, "in greater detail."

"Will I be safe?" Greer asked. The makeup covering the bruise on her cheek had been washed away by tears, and her eyes were red.

"I'll make sure you are," Jeff said gently, reaching out to pat her hand. "Who's the lawyer you were supposed to call?"

"Leo Silva," Greer replied.

The fifth partner, Vialpando thought as he opened the door and motioned for a detective to enter. "This officer will stay with you," he said. "I'll be back in a few minutes."

Sally Greer wasn't listening. She dropped to her knees at the side of the bed and curled up in a ball, crying in long, jerky sobs.

Vialpando stepped into the adjacent room just as Ramona took off the earphones and swiveled in his direction.

"Wow," she said, flashing him a smile. "You got more than I bargained for."

"What next?" Jeff asked. "It's your call."

"We need to get as much out of her as we can and then find a safe place to stash her under protective custody."

"I can arrange that."

"I'm worried that she may still be being watched. Can we use one of your female detectives to pose as Greer? We put her in Greer's car, wearing a wig and Greer's dress, and send her to the apartment. She picks up some clothes and personal items to make it look like Greer decided to bolt, and we give her backup in case she's followed."

"It will take about an hour to arrange it," Vialpando said. "I'll have to call in an off-duty detective. She's almost a perfect physical match to Greer. Did you catch

242

who her lawyer is?"

"I did."

"I'm going back in there for round two," Jeff said.

"You did real good," Ramona said.

"You're just saying that because we're dating."

The vice cop who'd been videotaping the conversation looked up and grinned at both of them.

Vialpando grinned at the cop and said, "Get Westgard for me. Tell her I need her here ASAP."

"Ten-four," the cop said, reaching for the phone.

"Go back to work," Ramona said. "I need to call my chief."

Sal Molina called before heading out to Kerney's house. The chief, who'd recently moved, gave him his new address, and Molina drove the quiet narrow road that wound up the canyon, past million-dollar properties. He knew the chief was rich, but because Kerney never made a big deal about it, Sal hadn't paid it much mind. That all changed as he swung into the driveway of a beautifully restored enormous adobe hacienda and parked in front of an equally charming guest house. From the size of it and the location, he guessed Kerney had to be putting out at least four grand a month in rent, which was quite a bit more than Molina's monthly take-home pay—a whole lot more.

Although it was past midnight, Kerney greeted him wide-eyed and awake, looking somewhat strained. He took Molina into a dimly lit, nicely furnished living room, where an almost full whiskey bottle and an empty glass sat on an end table next to an easy chair.

The whiskey bottle surprised Sal. He knew for a fact that Kerney wasn't much of a drinker, that the bullet wound to his gut had chewed up some of his intestines, destroyed part of his stomach, and made him cautious when it came to booze, so he wondered what was up.

"What have you got, Lieutenant?" Kerney asked.

"Information on Silva, Barrett, and Rojas," Molina said. "Plus some recent photographs of them."

Kerney nodded. "Run it down for me."

Molina spent ten minutes briefing Kerney, who looked at the photographs and listened silently, chin resting in his hand.

"You got questions, Chief?" Molina asked, as he closed his notebook.

"Not right now," Kerney replied. "A lot has happened and things are moving fast. I want a midday meeting tomorrow with you, Piño, that APD sergeant, Vialpando, plus two of your best detectives. Officers who can write flawless arrest and search-warrant affidavits. We'll put all the pieces we have together then and hammer out a plan of action. Set it up for me, will you?"

Molina nodded. "Want to tell me what's been happening?"

"Let's save it for the meeting."

Sal eyed the chief. Although his instructions were clear, there was something different about Kerney's tone. What was it? A blandness? A remoteness? Had the whiskey blunted Kerney's usual upbeat disposition?

Molina decided to risk asking. "Are you all right, Chief?"

"Yeah, I'm good, Sal," Kerney replied, pushing himself out of the chair. "Leave those photos behind, will you? I can use them in the morning."

Molina dropped the photos on the coffee table, said good night, and left, convinced that something was troubling the boss.

CHAPTER 12

FITFUL DREAMS AND A DULL HEADACHE WOKE KERNEY earlier than usual. In the predawn darkness, he reviewed the material the Lincoln County Sheriff's Department had sent up to Santa Fe: the autopsy report, forensic lab findings, and Clayton's field notes on the excavation of Anna Marie's body. Nothing had been uncovered that could tie Tyler Norvell, or any other unknown suspect, to the killing.

Kerney wasn't surprised; the victim had been murdered elsewhere and moved, and too much time had passed between the murder and the discovery of the body, which made the chances of finding any trace evidence almost nil.

Without physical evidence tying Norvell to the crime, Kerney would have to build a convincing circumstantial case. Anna Marie's letters and the fact that Norvell was in Santa Fe at the time of her murder put Kerney part of the way there. But he would need more persuasive information to convince the DA to approve an arrest affidavit for Norvell. He would have to develop the case in bits and pieces.

Kerney closed the files. Clayton had done a thorough job excavating Montoya's remains. He wondered if praising his son's good work would be worth the effort. Would Clayton simply respond with his usual cool disdain?

Kerney arrived for his follow-up interview with Helen Pearson curious to see how she'd held up overnight. Her hair was uncombed, her eyes were drained of emotion, and she moved in a distracted, almost awkward way.

"How long will this take?" she asked, her voice thin and troubled.

"Not long, I hope," Kerney answered, still feeling the headache that had dogged him since waking. He hadn't taken anything for it. The nagging throb kept his thoughts off Sara, so it served a good purpose.

The living room curtains, open yesterday, were closed, darkening the room. Helen Pearson sat in a chair where shadows hid her face. Kerney turned on a table lamp next to her and she blinked like a startled child caught doing mischief.

"Belinda Louise Nieto," Kerney said. "Tell me about her."

Pearson's mouth tightened, twisted. "I didn't know her."

"What do you know *about* her?" Kerney asked.

"She was just before my time," Pearson replied.

"And?"

"She's dead."

"You can do better than that."

She thought about her answer, rubbing her lips together as if it would make the words come out. "She was an object lesson to keep the girls in line."

"Why was that?"

"She booked dates on the side, held back money, met with clients who hadn't been screened, broke appointments, rejected bookings with men who didn't appeal to her, demanded additional payment for anything kinky, and sometimes refused to travel."

"She was murdered for not following the rules," Kerney said.

Pearson nodded. "The girls were told not to make the same mistakes Belinda did."

"Who killed her?"

Pearson shifted away from the lamp as if the glare was somehow hazardous. "Everyone figured it had to be Luis Rojas, or someone he sent to do it."

"Why?"

"Because he was the enforcer."

"Just for the girls?" Kerney asked.

"And clients who misbehaved."

"Were you warned about any other object lessons?"

"A girl in Houston, a client in Phoenix. There may be more, I don't know. It's been a long time since I've been in the life."

"So, Denver isn't the only base of operations."

"No. There's Phoenix, Houston, and El Paso, and probably a few more cities by now. Sex is a thriving business," she added sarcastically.

"Albuquerque?"

"I don't know."

"Did you know a woman named Anna Marie Montoya?" Kerney asked.

"The murdered woman who went missing from here years ago?"

"Yes."

"I never met her."

"Did Norvell ever mention her to you?"

"Not that I recall."

"Tell me about your clientele."

The request made Pearson angry. "Will knowing who I fucked for a living get you off?"

"I left here yesterday amazed at how you'd turned your life around," Kerney answered. "I'm still impressed."

"Sorry," Pearson said with a flicker of an apologetic smile. "It's hard to think about all of this. The men I saw were wealthy, well-known celebrities, or prominent people in their home communities. One was a network television journalist, another was a professional basketball player. The list goes on and on. I even saw a city police chief from Texas for a time. Does that surprise you?"

"Not really. Anyone from New Mexico?"

"Just one man Tyler set me up with. That's how I first came to Santa Fe. I spent three or four weekends with him over a period of about a year. His name was Raymond, but I think that was fictitious."

"Why do you say that?"

"Anything more than an evening in a hotel room usually happened away from the client's home turf. That means dinners out and being seen together without worry, a little shopping to buy the girl a present or two, taking in the sights. Raymond didn't want to do any of that. We just stayed at Tyler's house the whole time. Plus it was all a freebee. I was never paid a dime. Several other girls had the same experience with him."

"I'd like you to look at some pictures," Kerney said, handing over the photographs Sal Molina had left behind last night.

Pearson held the photos in the light. She shook her head at the one of Gene Barrett, identified Luis Rojas, and held up the last photo. "That's Raymond."

The image of archconservative state senator and attorney Leo Silva stared back at Kerney. According to Sal Molina, Silva was licensed to practice law in New Mexico, Colorado, Arizona, and Texas, and was affiliated with law firms in El Paso, Phoenix, Denver, and Houston.

He now knew that Piño and Vialpando were right, Silva was the fifth partner.

"I need you to write out a statement covering what we discussed yesterday and today," Kerney said.

"All of it?"

"Yes."

"Then what?"

"When the time comes, I'll present it to the district attorney and ask that you be treated as a confidential informant. He might agree to avoid bringing you before a grand jury."

"You can guarantee that?" Pearson asked.

"Not yet," Kerney replied. "But if I gather a few more facts it might be possible."

It took some time for Pearson to write her statement. Kerney sat with her at the kitchen table, refreshing her memory as needed. She kept her head down as she wrote, stopping to look up when Kerney spoke, absorbing what he said like a schoolgirl taking class notes. It made her look innocent and vulnerable.

Kerney decided there was a deep reservoir of goodness in Helen Pearson, and that she deserved to have her new life protected.

Kerney left Pearson and his headache behind with a promise to keep her informed. Outside, a stiff spring wind blew dust through the evergreens and rolled a few brittle leaves across the gravel driveway. Downtown, the thick stand of poplar and Russian olive trees surrounding the state capitol building swayed in the wind, bare branches clacking together in erratic patterns.

Bill Perkins, the legislative staffer who had pulled Norvell's per diem reimbursement voucher at Kerney's request, was in his office. A financial analyst, Perkins evaluated funding and appropriation requests for a number of state agencies, including the state police.

Kerney had worked with Perkins during his tenure as deputy chief of the department.

A cheery fellow, Perkins had a shock of curly brown hair and an exceedingly high forehead. He gladly made a copy of the paperwork and handed it over. According to the document Norvell had signed, the senator left Santa Fe just about the time Montoya disappeared.

"Do you archive office records for individual legislators?" Kerney asked, slipping the copy into a pocket.

"Only official documents, not their personal stuff."

"Who was Norvell's secretary back then?" Kerney asked.

"I don't know. Remember, office staffers for legislators are temporary personnel. They only work during regular or special legislative sessions. That information is in another office, and I'll have to look it up."

"I'll wait," Kerney said.

Perkins grinned. "Is that all you're going to tell me?"

"Can you do it on the q.t.?"

Perkins made a gimme motion with his hand. "Come on, Chief, fill me in."

"I wouldn't want to damage Senator Norvell's reputation by starting rumors that have no basis in fact," Kerney said.

"It's gotta be something."

"Yes, it does."

"Cops," Perkins said, shaking his head and getting to his feet. "They never tell you anything. Hang on, I'll pull the file."

Perkins came back with a name and address. "Alice Owen," he said. "She was a jewel. One of the best of the office staffers."

"Was?" Kerney asked.

"Retired," Perkins replied. "Hasn't worked the sessions for five, maybe six years. I see her around town every now and then. She's doing the grandmother thing and some charity work."

Kerney rang the bell at Alice Owen's house. The door opened partially, and a petite woman, probably in her seventies, with warm, intelligent brown eyes and gray hair cut short peered out at him.

"Yes?"

"Alice Owen?" Kerney asked, showing his shield. "May I ask you a few questions?"

"About?" Owen opened the door wider.

"Tyler Norvell."

"I really don't know the Senator very well," Owen replied. "I only worked for him during the session right after his first election."

"That's the time frame I'm interested in."

"Do you suspect that he's done something wrong?" Owen asked.

"Would it surprise you if he had?"

Owen hesitated. "We didn't hit it off particularly well. He was a young man who seemed quite full of himself. I've never found such people to be entirely trustworthy. What are your questions?"

"I'm trying to determine if he had any contact with a woman named Anna Marie Montoya."

Owen shook her head. "Oh my, I couldn't begin to know. So many people visit during the sessions, it's really quite chaotic. Constituents and lobbyists just stop by and mill about hoping for a few minutes of a legislator's time, or they drop off a letter or ask to use the telephone or make an appointment."

251

"You kept no records of visitors?" Kerney asked.

"Of course I did," Owen answered. "I maintained the appointment calendar and logged in all phone calls. But that didn't include people who left no messages or were simply dropping something off."

"Where would those records be?" Kerney asked.

"I have them," Owen replied, "for all the sessions I worked over the years."

She left Kerney waiting in the living room to search through some boxes. He spent his time looking at the photos of smiling children and grandchildren that were carefully grouped on tables and shelves around the room.

It made him think of the mess in his own family life, particularly Sara's scolding and Clayton's coldness. He tried to will back his headache to block off an overpowering desire to brood. Alice Owen saved him from the effort. She handed over a leather-bound appointment book and a loose-leaf binder. In the book he found an appointment for Anna Marie Montoya with a line drawn through it and a notation that the meeting had been canceled by *TN*. In the margin were the letters *WMPC*. Two copies of phone messages from Anna Marie were in the loose-leaf binder, both requesting that Norvell call her. All three were dated within weeks of her disappearance, but the canceled appointment was most recent.

With his finger on the appointment entry, Kerney showed it to Owen. "What do these letters mean?"

"Oh, that's my personal shorthand," Owen said. "They stand for 'will make personal contact.' "

"Who will make personal contact? You?"

"Oh, no. It meant that I didn't have to bother calling back to reschedule, the senator was going to do it himself."

With the evidence in hand and resisting an impulse to hug Alice Owen, Kerney called Bill Perkins on his way to his unit and asked where he might find old telephone records from Tyler Norvell's senate office.

"Tell me what you want specifically," Perkins said, "and I'll pull it from the financial accounting archives."

"It's for one month only," Kerney replied, giving Perkins the date. "Fax it to my office."

"When do you need it?"

"About eleven years ago," Kerney said.

"What?"

"ASAP, Bill, and thanks."

Jeff Vialpando's second interview with Sally Greer resulted in the full name and address of the other woman Ramona had seen in the hotel bar the night she'd tailed Greer from her apartment. The woman was Stacy Fowler, and she lived in a town-house complex in the North Valley close to the Rio Grande bosque a few miles from Old Town, site of the original Hispanic settlement founded during the Spanish reign in the Southwest.

After arranging protective custody at a safe location for Greer, Jeff and Ramona paid a visit to Fowler's residence, only to find her gone. They decided to stake out the town house and wait for Fowler to show.

Jeff took the first watch while Ramona catnapped, her head resting on her bundled-up jacket, which she'd wedged between the window and the car seat. He watched her sleep, studied her pretty face, and wondered what it would be like to wake up next to her in the morning. It was a pleasant thought that kept him occupied until he fell asleep.

253

The sun was in Jeff's face when Ramona shook him awake.

"She's here," Ramona said.

"How long have I been dozing?"

"An hour," Ramona replied. "You look cute when you're asleep. That goes on the plus side of the ledger."

"You're keeping score on me?" Jeff said, rubbing his face.

"You bet. Let's go."

An unhappy Stacy Fowler let them in and stood in the living room with her arms crossed, her chin stuck out in a pose of sassy defiance. Her round eyes protruded slightly, giving her face a baby-doll appearance.

"I don't know any Sally Greer," she said.

"That's funny," Ramona said. "There's a picture of you with Sally on the Internet."

"You got a warrant?" Fowler asked.

"We don't need one," Ramona replied. "You let us in, remember?"

"So now get out," Fowler said, casting her gaze at the door.

"We would all have to leave together," Ramona said.

"Why?"

"Jail," Vialpando said.

Fowler was silent for a minute, then she flipped her dark hair with a toss of her head. "Okay, let's go."

"This isn't a prostitution bust, Stacy," Ramona said.

"I don't know what you're talking about."

"We're talking about murder," Jeff said.

Fowler's plucked eyebrows arched. "That's crazy."

"It's not even a stretch," Ramona said. "You were with Greer in Ruidoso. We know she told you about the john that beat her up and got iced for it."

"What does that have to do with me?"

254

"That makes you a material witness."

Fowler gave Ramona a suspicious look. "What kind of bullshit is that?"

Ramona bluffed. "The kind that would make a judge agree to put you in jail without bail if you refuse to cooperate. You'd stay there until you talked."

"We can avoid all of that," Vialpando said.

"Talking to you wouldn't be good for my health."

"Not talking could make things worse for you," Jeff said.

"How's that?"

"We'll spread the word that you're our snitch."

"Jesus," Fowler said.

"You're new in town," Jeff said. "Did Tully bring you here, or was it Norvell?"

"Or Rojas?" Ramona added.

The names cracked Fowler's composure a bit more. She uncrossed her arms and put her hands out as if to ward off an attack. "What are you after?"

"The people who run the organization," Vialpando answered.

"They'd crucify me if I talked to you," Fowler said, her eyes searching for an escape. "You don't know how powerful they are."

"We know how powerful they think they are," Ramona said. "But unless you help us bring them down, you really don't have much of an option."

Vialpando stepped to Fowler and touched her arm. "Help us, and we'll help you," he said gently. "Sit down and talk to us."

Fowler nodded, reconsidered her decision, put on a false smile behind a scared expression, and said, "I do couples. Maybe . . ."

"Don't even go there," Vialpando said quickly. He

255

led Fowler to a chair and sat her down. "You worked out of Phoenix before coming here. Tell us about the organization."

Fowler frowned and bit her lip. "No bust, and I get a free ride?"

"Exactly," Jeff replied, sitting across from Fowler. "Plus protection for as long as you need it."

Fowler's lips twitched nervously. She reached for a pack of cigarettes on the end table and lit one. "Okay. Rojas runs Phoenix and all the Texas services. Tully does the same in Denver and here. Each city has a manager who oversees the day-to-day stuff—bookings, screening and billing clients, paying the girls, arranging housing."

"Who's the Albuquerque manager?" Ramona asked.

"Cassie Bedlow. She's been providing girls for the other locations through her modeling agency for years."

"What about Norvell?" Jeff asked.

"He supplies a venue for special occasions."

"What's that all about?" Ramona asked.

"He has a place where rich men can meet privately with a girl like for a vacation. You can't book it for less than a week, and it's expensive. Fifty grand for the cottage, and then whatever the girl costs. That can run between five and ten thousand a day, sometimes more. Some clients bring their own women with them. For that, they have to pay a hefty surcharge. It's got five or six cottages, and they're always full. I've never been there, but I've heard it brings in movie stars, politicians, celebrity jocks—men like that—from all over the country."

"So it's a place where rich guys can play house," Vialpando said.

Fowler smirked and blew smoke through her nose. "Yeah, along with their favorite sex games. S and M,

256

domination, fetishes, bondage—whatever they want, including drugs."

"Where is this place?" Ramona asked.

"Outside Ruidoso," Fowler replied. "I'm not sure where. It's on a ranch."

"How do the finances work?" Ramona asked. "Who pays the bills? Where does the money go?"

"I don't know. We get paid in cash weekly, plus any expenses. Tips and gifts we get to keep."

"What about drugs?" Vialpando asked.

"Whatever you want, but just for the girls and clients. There's no street selling or dealing. Mostly it's coke, crack, and pot, along with some meth. If a girl uses, the cost is deducted from her pay."

"Are you a user, Stacy?" Ramona asked.

"Sometimes." She stubbed out her smoke. "It makes going to work a whole lot easier."

"Are you strung out now?"

"A little bit."

"We'll get you into detox," Ramona said.

They wound up the interview and turned Fowler over to detectives who'd been waiting for their call. Jeff drove Ramona back to her unit.

"Next time we spend a night together, let's not do it in a car," Jeff said with a smile as he wheeled in behind Ramona's vehicle.

"Don't get ahead of yourself, Sergeant," Ramona said.

"I'm just suggesting a change in venue, nothing more."

Ramona laughed. "I'll see you in Santa Fe at the meeting."

Clayton woke to an empty house and checked the

bedside clock. It was after nine. Either he'd slept hard or Grace had tiptoed around, keeping the kids quiet before taking them off to day care and going to work. He put in a call to Paul Hewitt only to learn that the sheriff was out of the office until noon.

He went to the local newspaper's office and searched through back issues for anything that mentioned Tyler Norvell. There were plenty of stories on normal political activity: speeches he'd made, legislation he supported or opposed, positions he took on social problems. The guy was a right-to-work, anti-abortion, three-strikes-and-you're-out conservative. Judging from the voter sentiment discussed in the articles, he drew a lot of support from middle-class Texans who'd moved to Ruidoso looking for a less expensive Southwestern version of the Aspen lifestyle.

Clayton dug deeper and found a news item in the business section. A year before running for the state senate, Norvell had bought the Bluewater Canyon Ranch, a twenty-thousand-acre spread outside the small settlement of Arabella on the east side of the Capitan Mountains.

In his short time with the department Clayton had been to Arabella twice on routine patrols. There wasn't much to the place: a few whitewashed, shuttered adobe buildings, several old barns, a vacation cottage or two, maybe a half dozen year-round residences, and some outlying ranches along the paved road that ended at the village.

It was a pretty spot, a good seventeen miles off the main highway to Roswell, in rolling country against the sharp backdrop of the mountains.

In his unit Clayton consulted a government reference map that highlighted all publicly and privately owned land in the state. It was a useful tool for determining the boundaries for law-enforcement jurisdictions. He found Bluewater Canyon on private land a bit south of Arabella. There wasn't time to drive up and look around before the sheriff returned to the office, so Clayton decided to see what he could learn through official records.

If Norvell had turned the Bluewater Canyon Ranch into a secret sex playground, as Clayton suspected, then he had probably spent a pile of money on the project.

In the county assessor's office at the county courthouse, he located the file for the Bluewater Canyon Ranch. Since the date of purchase, Norvell's property had increased in taxable value by over five million dollars. The old ranch headquarters had been torn down and replaced by a ten-thousand-square-foot hacienda, along with six new guest houses of three thousand square feet each, horse stables, barns, a swimming pool with a cabana and hot tubs, garages, a caretaker's cottage, a bunkhouse, and something called a meditation center, which included a small movie theater.

Clayton went looking for the deputy county assessor, Marvin Rickland, and bumped into him in the hallway.

"Have you got a minute to tell me about the Bluewater Canyon Ranch?" he asked.

Rickland nodded. "What a place. It's amazing what money can buy. The senator sure hasn't spared any expense. I bet the landscaping alone set him back a half million or more."

"What does he use it for?"

"Right now, just for friends, family, business associates, clients, and his political pals. He caters to a lot of rich people who are looking to buy property through his real estate company and who want anonymity while they're here. The last time I talked to him he said eventually it was going to be a resort-type dude ranch. Why he doesn't open it up right now beats me."

"You've done all the property assessments," Clayton said. "Describe it to me."

"It's really spread out," Rickland replied. "Each guest house is at least a mile from the main residence and very private. The style is Santa Fe adobe, with portals, patios, courtyards and all those Southwest touches like corner fireplaces and beamed ceilings. Around the headquarters you've got the meditation center, the swimming pool, staff housing, and a horse barn and stables about a quarter mile away. He's even got an airstrip on the property, along with all-weather gravel roads, and a grader to keep them in good repair."

"Do you have any trouble getting in?"

Rickland laughed. "I was just talking to Ray Kelsey about that the other day. He's the general construction inspector for the state, who works out of Ruidoso. He was telling me the senator has submitted plans to build a sweat lodge and a pond along a creek bed and put in a Japanese-style garden. We were laughing about how we always have to call ahead and make an appointment to get on the property. It's completely fenced—the whole twenty thousand acres—and he has it patrolled regularly. Everybody who works there has to sign a confidentiality agreement not to talk about the guests or the ranch. Those rich people really like their privacy."

Clayton asked a few more questions and learned that an electronic gate with a speaker box controlled access to the ranch road, and the headquarters were about five miles beyond the gate. There were no neighbors within a ten-mile radius, and Rickland dealt with Norvell's

260

live-in manager when he needed to make a tax assessment inspection. Rickland had never seen any of Norvell's friends or clients during his visits, but there were usually cars parked at the guest houses and a plane or two on the landing strip.

Clayton thanked Rickland and went looking for the sheriff, who was due back in the office. His secretary told him Hewitt was running late and wouldn't be in until around two. He went to his hallway desk and started writing out his chronological report so he could have it ready when the sheriff arrived.

Until the Indian cop arrived at the county courthouse, Fidel was bored and restless. He'd left his motel room early, thinking it would be maybe an hour before the cop showed at work, and he'd wound up waiting almost all morning. Fidel didn't know why Rojas wanted him watched, but it would be fun to follow the cop around for a while, sneaky like. Of course, it would be way more cool to kill him.

He wondered why Rojas was worried about Istee. Did it have something to do with the hit at Casey's Cozy Cabins? That had been a bitching cool kill, and taking out Staggs had also been kick-ass. He'd made Staggs beg before blowing him away. The old man pissed in his pants and cried like a baby.

The thirty grand Fidel had taken off Staggs's body made it his most profitable hit yet, better than the Ulibarri job. He bet a cop would go for even more. Fidel smiled at the possibility.

Time passed and Fidel started getting bored again. Too bad Debbie Shea wasn't with him. It would be a kick to have her go down on him, parked fifty feet outside of the sheriff's office.

261

He slipped his semiautomatic out of the shoulder holster and checked the magazine. He'd always wanted to put a couple of caps in a cop. Maybe Rojas would change his mind.

He put the handgun away. A vehicle pulled into the parking space reserved for the sheriff, and a big guy dressed like a cowboy got out and went inside.

Cowboys and Indians, Fidel thought. Carrizozo was total fucking hicksville.

From his time with the state police Kerney knew that the state government telephone system was unique in certain ways. A computer recorded all the calls made from each individual phone, and a monthly report was distributed to supervisory personnel so that they could track personal calls made by employees at work and request reimbursement for any toll charges.

In his office Kerney compared the faxed telephone record of calls made from Senator Norvell's private legislative office phone against the information in the Montoya case file. Norvell had made an eight-minute call to Anna Marie's work number on the day her appointment with the senator had been canceled.

The case against Norvell was building, but Kerney still needed more.

Sal Molina had left updated information on his desk, and Kerney read the hurried notes Detective Piño had prepared from the interview she and the APD sergeant had conducted with a woman named Stacy Fowler. Along with what Kerney had learned from Helen Pearson and Molina's late-night briefing, it suggested that something more than a small team of detectives would be required to conduct the investigation from this point on. It would take a task force to get the job done

262

right.

He told Helen Muiz to push the meeting back by two hours, and started making phone calls. Once he explained his agenda, it didn't take much cajoling to get everyone on his list he could reach to agree to attend the meeting.

Kerney failed in his attempt to reach Paul Hewitt and secure his participation on the task force. He considered calling Clayton and dismissed the idea. As sheriff, only Hewitt had the authority to commit his department to Kerney's plan. Most likely, Paul would agree to come onboard, so Kerney decided to proceed under that assumption and talk to him after the meeting.

A little after two, he walked into the packed conference room, where the original team had been bolstered by his second-in-command, Larry Otero, two of Molina's detectives, the district attorney, the resident FBI agent, the APD deputy chief of police, a lawyer from the U.S. Attorney's office, an agent for the Internal Revenue Service, a supervising DEA special agent, and the commander of the state police criminal investigation bureau.

With Helen Muiz at his side taking notes, he got the meeting rolling with quick introductions, and then asked Molina, Piño, and Vialpando to make brief presentations highlighting their investigative findings to date. He wound up the overview with his own report, got a buy-in from everyone present to participate on the task force, and opened it up for discussion.

The IRS agent would coordinate a team to look at the partners' personal and corporate tax records. DEA would handle the drug-trafficking end of it in all known cities where the partners operated. The FBI would do the same on the out-of-state prostitution rackets, and seek wiretap warrants on all partner communications including Internet E-mail. State police agents would dig into money laundering. Their first targets would be State Senator Gene Barrett's CPA firm and Representative Leo Silva's law practice.

Additionally, agents from the state police district headquarters in Alamogordo and Roswell would be pulled into Lincoln County to target Tyler Norvell. APD vice, with Detective Piño as lead investigator, would go after Bedlow, Tully, and Deacon. The FBI would use El Paso special agents to nail down Rojas.

The DA agreed to supply a prosecutor full-time to work with detectives on the arrest and search warrant affidavits. He'd coordinate the effort with the U.S. attorney and other state DAs to get necessary judicial sign-offs. SFPD would be the lead agency, with Deputy Chief Larry Otero in charge. Molina and his two detectives would run the task-force casebooks and assemble and coordinate all documentation.

"Stay focused, people," Kerney said. "We're going for racketeering, drug trafficking, tax evasion, prostitution, money laundering, and related federal charges right now."

"What about the Montoya homicide?" Sal Molina asked, "and that murder Greer talked about in Ruidoso?"

"At present, Montoya is our weakest case," the DA said. "I doubt you could convince a judge to approve an arrest warrant based on what you have, although it's close."

"Agreed," Kerney said. "We need something that will connect Norvell to the crime scene where Montoya's body was found."

"That would do it for probable cause," the DA said.

"I'll handle the Montoya homicide follow-up," Kerney said. "I'm going down to Lincoln County tonight. I'll ask the sheriff and his investigator to join the task force and find out where they are with the Ulibarri homicide investigation."

Kerney closed his file and gave it to Helen. "Mrs. Muiz and her staff will prepare comprehensive task-force packets on everything we've got so far and distribute them to you ASAP. We have to move fast but carefully, ladies and gentlemen. Let's set a target date of one month from now to make our initial arrests. After that, we'll continue to file charges as the facts roll in. IRS and the state police will probably need more time to nail down the tax-evasion and money-laundering parts of it."

Kerney pushed back his chair and stood. "Everybody stay tight-lipped, and maintain a low profile. We don't want to telegraph our intentions to our targets. Do whatever is necessary within the scope of your authority to keep them off guard. From now on, need-to-know communication is limited to task-force members only and their immediate superiors. If any word about the task force leaks out we'll be facing a media circus and an army of defense attorneys. Good hunting, everyone."

There were smiles and approving nods throughout the room. Everyone was pumped and ready to go, and not just because some dirty politicians were going to be brought down. If all went well, the task force would be a career-making opportunity for every law-enforcement official in the room.

Ramona Piño walked with a frowning Jeff Vialpando to his unit parked outside the SFPD headquarters.

"I didn't want to bring it up during the meeting," he

said, "but we've got a slight problem."

"Yeah, I know," Ramona said. "We can't keep Stacy Fowler under wraps for thirty days without raising suspicions."

"So, what do we do about it?"

"Improvise," Ramona replied as she watched the state police criminal investigation commander drive away. "Would a faked one-car traffic fatality work? Perhaps a rollover investigated by the state police?"

"Would your chief go for that?" Jeff asked.

Ramona laughed. "Didn't you hear what he said about keeping the targets off guard? I think he'd be pissed if we didn't do it."

"Let's set it up," Vialpando said.

"Then I'll buy you an early dinner."

"Are you taking me on a date?" Jeff asked.

"That will have to wait until we're no longer working together, Sergeant," Ramona said, flashing a brilliant smile. "After all, I am the designated lead investigator now, which makes you my subordinate."

Vialpando groaned. "Are you telling me I have to wait months before I can date you?"

Ramona patted Jeff's arm. "You'll just have to suffer through it."

Paul Hewitt rolled a pencil on his desktop and thought hard before speaking. The last two hours had been spent listening to Clayton's verbal report and reading through all his extensive documentation.

"I'm not saying your assumptions about Norvell are flawed, Deputy Istee. But proving them is a whole different matter. For now, Luis Rojas is the prime suspect. If that leads us to some clear-cut evidence of Senator Norvell's involvement in this prostitution ring, then we can take action."

Clayton looked miffed.

"Speak your mind," Hewitt said.

"Are you talking to me as the sheriff, or as a politician?" Clayton asked.

"You really need to learn to be a bit more diplomatic, Deputy," Hewitt said firmly. "Norvell and I sit on opposite sides of the political fence. Even if that weren't the case, I wouldn't give a shit. First and foremost, I'm a cop. If he's dirty, then he's dirty."

Clayton dropped his gaze. "Sorry about that. I don't do very well at being subtle."

"No, you don't. Now, we're going to have to contain this investigation and keep it focused on the Ulibarri homicide. Since Staggs hasn't surfaced, your best bet is that Deborah Shea woman. Since she's a whore, she shouldn't be all that hard to find. She lied to alibi Rojas, so you need to pull her in and break her down."

Clayton nodded. "What about the prostitution ring?"

"That's way outside the scope of what we can handle on our own," Hewitt replied. "Besides, what's happening in El Paso is outside of our jurisdiction. When the time comes, we'll turn your findings over to the appropriate Texas state authorities, not the El Paso police."

The phone rang. Hewitt picked up, listened, and told his secretary to put the call through.

"How are you, Chief?" he said as he smiled and sat back in his chair.

Chief who? Clayton wondered, watching Hewitt's smile gradually fade. Hewitt reached for a pencil and started busily scribbling notes, his eyes signaling surprise as he listened.

Although the call didn't last long, time dragged as

267

Clayton waited.

Finally, Hewitt dropped his pencil and said, "We'll see you first thing in the morning."

He hung up and looked at Clayton. "Seems we don't have to worry about limiting our scope. The Santa Fe police investigation into the Montoya homicide has led to the creation of a multi-agency task force, and we're in on it. The targets are Rojas, Norvell, his sister, two Albuquerque state legislators, and a member of the Tully family. They're looking at a whole range of possible state and federal felony charges. Chief Kerney wants everything we have on Rojas, Norvell, and the Ulibarri homicide faxed to his deputy chief right away. Plus he wants your assistance on the Montoya case. He'll brief us here tomorrow at seven a.m."

Clayton looked at the thick file in his lap. "I better get started."

Fidel was restless and irritable. Except for a couple of quick trips to buy some food and take a leak, he'd been sitting outside the sheriff's office all afternoon, still waiting for the Indian cop to come out of the building.

He called Rojas with the news that nothing was happening, hoping he'd get to go home. Instead, Rojas wanted him to stick with the cop for one more day, which was a total downer.

Around dusk the cop got into his unit and drove away. Fidel followed at a distance. It was easy to keep the four-by-four police car in view with its high profile and rack of roof lights without trailing too close behind.

The cop turned off at the reservation village just as darkness fell. Fidel decided it was too risky to follow. He parked and waited across the road near a Catholic church for a couple of hours, in case the cop reappeared.

He played some music and counted passing cars to keep his mind occupied.

When the cop didn't show, Fidel decided to bail and head to his motel room. He'd be back at first light. Small-town cop work sure must be boring, he thought as he sped down the highway.

CHAPTER 13

KERNEY DIDN'T DO WELL IN MOTELS; HE MISSED HIS own bed and pillow. He'd rolled into Ruidoso last night at a reasonable hour, hoping to catch up on some sleep. But Sara's harsh annoyance about his bullheadedness and the prospect of facing Clayton's negativity made for troubled dreams that woke him off and on throughout the night.

At six a.m. Kerney called his office to get an update. Helen Muiz had pulled her people in at five a.m. to finish preparing the task-force packets. All participating agencies would have complete packets by noon. Larry Otero, who was also at work early, had ordered them hand-delivered by uniformed officers running silent Code Three to the out-of-town cop shops.

Kerney arrived promptly on time at the Lincoln County courthouse to find Paul Hewitt and Clayton waiting for him in the sheriff's office. After greetings, handshakes, and some small talk with Hewitt, they got down to business. Kerney kicked it off by detailing the breadth of the task force's mission, maintaining an equal amount of eye contact with both men so as not to give Clayton any reason to feel slighted.

When Kerney finished, Hewitt pulled at his chin in a failed attempt to hide a smile. "This could blow the roof off the state capitol, and put the good citizens of Lincoln County into an uproar. I wonder if Norvell and his political pals traded a week with a whore for votes from their legislative buddies."

"There's no telling," Kerney said as he handed out material on Sally Greer, Stacy Fowler, and Helen Pearson, who was described only as a confidential informant. "But discovering who their clients are will prove interesting. What I've just given you includes statements from three different women with personal knowledge about the operation, which has direct bearing on the Montoya case and Deputy Istee's homicide investigation. This is fresh information, gentlemen, gathered in the last thirty-six hours. You'll get full task-force packets as soon as they're completed."

Kerney watched as Hewitt and Clayton worked their way through the reports. The further Hewitt read, the more appalled he looked. Clayton seemed thoughtful and sober. He finished first.

"So Sally Greer was the woman with Ulibarri at the cabin," Clayton said, "and Fidel Narvaiz was nearby to keep an eye on her because Ulibarri was her first trick."

"That's what Greer says," Kerney replied.

"Did she witness the homicide?"

"No. Ulibarri paid in advance for twenty-four hours with Greer. When he went to the racetrack, Narvaiz checked on Greer and found her badly beaten. He got her out of there, took her to a motel room, and called Cassie Bedlow, who came and picked Greer up."

"I don't see that in these reports," Clayton said, tapping the pages with a finger.

"Greer's interviews were videotaped by APD vice officers," Kerney said. "The transcription of the second session wasn't completed by the time I left to come here. Greer did say, however, that Narvaiz left her with Bedlow at about eleven o'clock in the morning."

"Ulibarri was killed several hours later," Clayton said, "so Narvaiz had opportunity."

"What do you know about him?" Kerney asked.

"He lives on the Rojas estate and supposedly serves as a personal assistant to Rojas. The Debbie that Greer mentioned is Deborah Shea. According to an El Paso hotel security guy, she's a hooker. He also identified seven other prostitutes who probably work for Rojas. Initially, Shea alibied Rojas when I talked to both of them. Said she'd flown up to Ruidoso with him on his plane. Turns out that was BS."

"Tell me about it," Kerney said.

Clayton filled Kerney in on his inspection of Rojas's vacation cabin, which had exposed Shea's false statements.

Impressed with Clayton's good work, Kerney held back any praise and moved on to another subject. "And this Fidel Narvaiz, have you questioned him?"

"I've never met him," Clayton said.

"That's good," Kerney said.

"What's good about that?" Clayton asked. "At this point, he's our prime murder suspect."

"We need to work these cases without tipping our hand," Kerney replied. "Narvaiz was most likely ordered to kill Ulibarri by Rojas, so putting a murder charge on Rojas is a distinct possibility, if we can prove it. Did you get any hard physical evidence at the crime scene?"

"Ulibarri was strangled," Clayton said, "and we got some partial latents off the body around his throat that are good enough to make a match once we have something to match them to. And a few blond pubic

271

hairs probably left behind by Sally Greer."

"Those hairs can confirm Greer's story," Kerney said. "Let's ask for a DNA comparison."

"If you get me her fingerprints," Clayton said, "we might be able to put her in the cabin that way, also. We lifted a number of unknown latents at the crime scene."

"You'll have them today," Kerney said.

"You're sure Greer isn't the killer?" Clayton asked.

"I believe her story," Kerney said. "So do the detectives who interviewed her."

Clayton nodded. "That's good enough for me."

"What's next?" Hewitt asked.

"The Montoya case," Kerney replied. "I've got strong circumstantial evidence that Norvell killed her to keep her from exposing the racket, but I need more."

"Two of your reports mention Adam Tully," Paul Hewitt said, leaning forward to put his elbows on the desk.

"He and Norvell go way back," Kerney said. "They were boyhood friends."

"I haven't heard Adam's name in years," Hewitt said. "His father, Hiram, owns the fruit stand where we found Montoya's body."

"What do you know about Adam?" Kerney asked, his interest rising.

"He was the baby of the family—unexpected and spoiled rotten by Hiram. His mother died giving birth. She was in her forties at the time. His two sisters are a good twenty years older. Something happened when Adam was a teenager. The family doesn't talk about it, but Hiram kicked him out of the house, sent him to the New Mexico Military Institute in Roswell, then up to Albuquerque to the university. I don't think he's ever been back here since."

"What did folks think happened between Tully and his father?" Kerney asked.

"Oh, there were rumors that Adam had gotten some girl in trouble, stolen money from his father, was using drugs—stuff like that. But they were just rumors and there was no evidence anyone could point to. The family stayed tight-lipped, of course."

"Was Tyler Norvell mentioned in those rumors?" Kerney asked.

"Not as I recall," Hewitt replied. "But Deputy Istee saw Senator Norvell's car leave Rojas's house two nights ago."

Kerney turned to Clayton.

"And I know where the ranch is," Clayton said.

"Excellent. Have you had any contact with the Tully family?"

"Yeah. I interviewed Hiram, one of his daughters, and her husband, and a granddaughter." He passed his field notes to Kerney.

Kerney scanned through the papers. "I'd like to talk to these people."

"I'll take you around to see them," Clayton said. With a resigned look he retrieved his notes from Kerney's hand and held out his casebook. "I guess this is your investigation, now."

Kerney shook his head. With few resources, and virtually no help, Clayton had done an amazingly good job. "You don't get to bow out, Deputy," Kerney said. "The state police officers assigned to investigate Senator Norvell have been advised that the Lincoln County Sheriff's Office is in charge of this piece of the task force. As far as I'm concerned, you're the lead investigator, unless your boss says otherwise."

Clayton's look of resignation lightened into a smile

273

that he couldn't completely contain.

"I'm fine with that," Hewitt said. "How many agents and what's their ETA?"

"Four. They'll be briefed at noon. They should be here soon after that."

"I'd better get cracking," Hewitt said, rising from his chair. "Leave the casebook with me, Deputy. I'll free up some space in the building we can use as a command center, take care of the details, and have everything we've got ready to go."

Kerney stood. "You'll have the task-force packet in hand before the agents arrive. Thanks, Paul."

Hewitt hitched up his blue jeans and smiled. "No thanks are necessary, Kerney. Hell, this is one party I wouldn't want to miss."

Fidel, who had followed the cop from the highway turnoff to his house back to the county courthouse, waited for something to happen. It seemed like the Indian deputy and the cowboy sheriff went to work early so they could spend *more* time doing nothing. Ten minutes after parking, Fidel watched *another* cowboy—this one with a limp—park and go inside. Soon after that a few civilians and uniformed deputies arrived.

Fidel had hoped that the day would prove more interesting, but it wasn't turning out that way. It was, he decided, way beyond boring to be a cop in Lincoln County.

From his hallway desk Clayton put in calls to the people Kerney wanted to talk to while Kerney used his cell phone to ask to have Greer fingerprinted and provide some hair samples to be sent down for comparison to the evidence collected at the Ulibarri crime scene.

Page Seton, Hiram Tully's granddaughter, and her parents, Morris and Lily, were traveling out of state to attend a wedding in west Texas. Hiram Tully had been moved from the hospital to a state-run rehabilitation center in Roswell.

While Clayton called the rehab center to confirm that Tully could see them, Kerney stood with his back against the hallway wall thinking that the working conditions at the sheriff's department were abysmal. Clayton had no privacy, and the staffers from other county offices passing by had to step sideways behind Clayton's chair in order to get around him.

He didn't fault Paul Hewitt; sheriffs in rural counties pretty much always got the short end of the stick when it came to divvying up tax dollars.

The trip to Roswell with Clayton started out in silence. They passed the city park on the outskirts of town, a rather bleak-looking place bordering the highway that consisted of a poorly landscaped nine-hole golf course, some ball fields, picnic tables, and a scattering of trees. Soon after, Clayton slowed and pointed at the burned-out fruit stand up ahead.

"Want to take a look at the crime scene?" he asked.

"I would," Kerney replied.

Clayton pulled off the highway and together they walked to the building.

"At least the mud has dried up," Clayton said as he turned on his flashlight to show Kerney where Montoya's body had been found.

"It must have been a bitch to excavate the remains," Kerney said, peering into the cold-storage space from the doorway.

"Yeah," Clayton replied. "Why would Norvell, if he is the killer, put her body here?"

"I've thought a lot about that," Kerney said, stepping back from the doorway. "Let's say Montoya meets him at the shopping mall in Santa Fe and agrees to go someplace private where they can talk. Norvell takes her to some secluded spot and when he realizes she won't be dissuaded from unmasking him, he decides to kill her, except he doesn't have a gun, a knife, or the balls to strangle her. So he punches her, knocks her out, and uses a tire iron to kill her, hitting her not once, but twice. I asked for a forensic analysis of Montoya's skull. It showed that she suffered a hairline crack to the jaw along with two blows to the head consistent with a tire iron or similar object."

"But that still doesn't answer my question," Clayton said.

"I'm getting to it," Kerney said as he walked to the back of the building with Clayton following along. "So now he's got a dead body in his car, a long road trip ahead of him, and a big problem: what to do with the body. On top of that, he's probably not thinking very straight and is paranoid as hell about getting stopped by the police. He can't just dump Montoya out at the side of the road, or bury her on his own property. That would be too risky. So he thinks of places he knows where it might be safe to hide the body before he gets home."

"Even if you can prove Norvell knew about the abandoned fruit stand, have you got probable cause?" Clayton asked.

"That's the missing piece I need, according to the district attorney," Kerney replied, stepping back to look at the shell of the fruit stand. A parked car behind the structure wouldn't be seen from the highway.

He swung around and looked at the mountains. There were no houses or trailers in sight. "Norvell probably passed this place often during the years it sat unused. Maybe he even knew that Tully had no plans to reopen it. Or maybe he thought he'd come back later and move the body, but decided not to when time passed and the case turned cold."

"Have you seen enough?" Clayton asked.

"Yeah, let's go."

Clayton locked his gaze on Kerney's face. "One question: why did you back me as lead investigator with the sheriff?"

"Because you're the most knowledgeable about the case and you've done one hell of a job," Kerney replied.

The stern look on Clayton's face smoothed out slightly. "That's it? Nothing personal?"

"Part of it's personal, I guess," Kerney said. "You might think it's silly of me to say this, but I'm proud of what you've done."

The comment caught Clayton off guard. He swallowed hard and looked away.

"Let's go," Kerney said, taking the pressure off Clayton to respond.

All the phone taps, including land lines and cell phones, were up and running just before Cassie Bedlow arrived at her talent and modeling agency. In his APD uniform and driving a patrol car, Jeff Vialpando waited a few minutes before pulling up outside the building. Entering, he called out a hello and Bedlow appeared in her office doorway.

"Yes, Officer," she said, looking somewhat startled.

"Sorry to bother you, ma'am," Jeff said, taking off his hat. "But I need your help."

"Regarding?"

"A woman named Stacy Fowler died in an

277

automobile accident last night, and the state police asked if we'd help locate next of kin. They found your business card in her wallet. Did you know her?"

"Yes, but only slightly. I interviewed her a month or so ago for a modeling job, but it didn't pan out. How did it happen?"

"I'm not completely sure, ma'am," Jeff replied. "But I do know it was a rollover accident outside the city limits, and Ms. Fowler was alone in the vehicle at the time."

"Oh my goodness," Cassie said, shaking her head sadly. "I heard something about it on the radio as I was coming to work."

"Do you know anything about her family?" Jeff asked.

"No, I think she'd just moved here from the Midwest."

"Her car was registered in Arizona," Jeff said. "Did she mention any family members there?"

"We only talked once and it was purely about business."

"Thank you for your time," Jeff said.

"I'm so sorry I can't be of more help," Bedlow said. "I hope it won't take you long to notify her family."

"It probably will," Vialpando said with a shrug. "We don't have much to go on."

Once he was back in the unit, Ramona's voice came over his police radio. "She's talking to Tully right now."

"Saying?" Vialpando asked as he drove away.

"That Fowler is dead and Greer didn't keep her date last night."

"And?"

"She tried calling Greer from home and got no

answer. She's going to her apartment to look for her, then to Fowler's town house to make sure there's nothing incriminating for the police to find."

"Beautiful," Vialpando said. "That's even better than we expected. What else?"

"Tully's telling her to be careful. Bedlow's saying not to worry, the police are just investigating an accident, nothing more, and they don't know anything about Fowler. Tully just told her to act fast and call him back as soon as she's finished."

"I'm going home to change," Vialpando said.

"I'd like to send one of your detectives down to Fowler's town house to videotape Bedlow's comings and goings."

"Good idea. Use Alvarado. He's great with a camera and good at surveillance. Is Ault in place?"

"Ten-four."

Frustrated at not finding Sally Greer at home, Cassie Bedlow went to the resident manager's apartment, where Detective Allen Ault, unshaved and dressed in a sweatshirt and jeans, opened the door.

"If you're looking for the leasing office," he said, "it's in Building One. Just take a left at the corner. You can't miss it."

"I'm looking for Sally Greer," Bedlow said.

"She moved out yesterday," Ault said. "Didn't even leave a forwarding address for her cleaning deposit."

"Did you see her?"

"Yeah, she dropped off her key." Ault waved his finger at Bedlow. "Wait a minute. Are you Carrie?"

"Cassie," Bedlow said.

"Yeah, that's it. She left a letter for you."

Ault rummaged around on the coffee table and gave

Bedlow an envelope.

"Thank you," Bedlow said.

In her car Bedlow read the letter.

I figure that what you did to me and let others do to me more than pays you back the money you "lent" me. You've made me sick to my stomach about myself. But I'll never be as sick and twisted as you are. Don't worry, I won't cause you any trouble. I couldn't stand to have anyone find out what I did.

Bedlow dropped the letter on the car seat and called Adam on her cell phone. He and Luis could decide what do about Sally Greer.

The rehabilitation center was located on a former air force base just south of Roswell. The original building, a blocky, monotonous structure, had served as the base hospital. According to old-timers and locals, it had been built on the site where secret autopsies had allegedly been performed by military doctors on the bodies of aliens from outer space who'd crash-landed in a UFO outside of the city after World War II.

A single-story, modern addition that had been appended to the hospital created a jarring, somewhat schizoid blend of architectural styles. A wide expanse of lawn with trees planted here and there failed to soften the impression.

In a physical therapy suite housed in the new addition, Kerney and Clayton watched through a glass partition as Hiram Tully finished up his treatment. The stroke had affected the left side of his body, and Tully was doing a leg weight exercise to strengthen his calf

280

muscles. The old man was working hard, and Kerney knew from his own experience that the task wasn't easy. Soon he'd get to go through the experience all over again for his new knee.

After he completed his regimen the therapist walked Tully slowly out of the rehab room. His gaunt face glistened with perspiration, and his partially paralyzed arm dangled a bit at his side. They met with him in an empty nearby office, where Kerney introduced himself.

"I don't know why you're back here," Tully said haltingly to Clayton, as he lowered himself slowly onto a chair. "Couldn't tell you anything before, can't tell you anything now."

"We'd like to ask you about a friend of your son," Clayton said.

Tully stiffened and turned his head away as though he'd seen something despicable. "My son is dead to me."

"We're only interested in his friend," Clayton said.

"I don't know any of his friends," Tully said, working his mouth slowly to pronounce the words.

"A friend from a long time ago," Clayton said.

Tully gave him a sidelong glance. "Who?"

"Tyler Norvell," Kerney said.

Tully wiped a bit of drool from his lips. "I have nothing to say about him."

"Our questions aren't personal," Kerney said. "Did Norvell ever work for you?"

Tully nodded. "When he was in high school. I hired him as an apple picker. He worked after school and weekends in the fall."

"Did he ever work at the fruit stand near Carrizozo?"

"No."

"He had nothing to do with the fruit stand?" Kerney

asked.

"Deliveries, that's all. He'd go with Julio, my foreman, to restock apples and cider, and dispose of any spoilage."

"From the cold-storage cellar?" Kerney asked.

"Yes."

"How long did he work for you?" Kerney asked.

"Three harvest seasons."

A thought about the abandoned fruit stand clicked in Clayton's head. "Has Norvell ever offered to buy the property from you?"

Tully nodded. "He had a realtor make an offer through his company. I turned it down. Don't ask me why."

"When was that?"

"Ten years ago, maybe longer."

They thanked Tully and turned him over to a waiting aide, who walked him down the hall toward the old hospital.

"So when are you going to arrest Norvell for murder?" Clayton asked.

"All in due course," Kerney replied as they left the lobby.

Clayton shook his head. "I wonder what the deal is between Tully and his son."

"I'm glad we didn't have to find out," Kerney said.

Clayton unlocked his unit. "Why?"

Kerney thought about Vernon Langsford, the retired judge from Roswell who had been murdered by a deeply disturbed daughter because of a secret incestuous relationship he'd had with her decades earlier. "Because that kind of family stuff is usually pretty ugly, sometimes disgusting, and I've heard enough of it to last a lifetime."

"But saying a son is dead to you is really harsh."

"No harsher than a son saying it to a father," Kerney said deliberately as he strapped on his seat belt.

Clayton sat behind the steering wheel without reacting, letting Kerney's words sink in. When they'd learned about each other's existence, Clayton had come close to telling Kerney to completely butt out of his life. Was there that much difference between Tully's denial of a son and his own rejection of a father? Tully had raised his son, but he had never known Kerney as his father until recently. Still . . .

Clayton ran his forefinger over the edge of the wheel and said, "I guess that's true, in a way, isn't it?"

Fidel waited on a side street down from the rehab center, parked in front of a row of single-family dwellings which he figured once housed military personnel. Some of them were occupied and some had for-sale signs plunked down in dead grass under dead trees. The whole area on three sides of the center was filled with identical ugly concrete block houses. Some of them looked pretty trashed out.

He called Rojas and told him the Indian cop had done nothing, except go to work early, walk around a burned building, and take some crippled cowboy with a limp to a rehabilitation center in Roswell.

"I guess the Indian cop runs a taxi service when he's not busy drinking coffee and eating donuts," he said.

"What did the cop do at the fruit stand?" Rojas asked.

"Tour the guy with the limp around. They weren't there long."

"Did you recognize the other man?" Rojas asked.

"Never saw him before."

"Then nothing's happening," Rojas said. "That's

283

good."

"Yeah, but it's not keeping me entertained."

"If everything stays quiet, finish out the day and come home. Don't do anything stupid."

"I'll be cool, promise," Fidel replied.

He saw the Indian and the cowboy walking to the police vehicle, fired up the engine, and got ready to take another boring drive in the country.

As they left Roswell Kerney and Clayton shied away from talk about their troubled relationship and focused instead on business. Kerney got the distinct feeling that Clayton was loosening up a bit. He seemed more talkative and animated. It gave him a hopeful feeling.

"Do me a favor," Kerney said, looking at the brown desert hills and the mountains beyond rising up on the western horizon.

"What's that?" Clayton asked.

Traffic had thinned. Kerney checked the side-view mirror. "When the time comes, pick up Norvell for me. It will save me a trip down here."

"You're giving me the arrest?" Clayton asked, surprised. Kerney was offering to turn over *his* major felony bust to another officer outside his own department, which was almost unheard of.

"Why not?"

"I don't need a career boost from you," Clayton replied.

"No, you don't. Are you being sarcastic?"

Clayton shook his head. "I'm just saying you don't have to do me any favors."

"You're doing me the favor, remember?" Kerney tapped his right leg. "I've been recalled by my doctor for a replacement knee. The warranty has run out on the

284

old one. I go in for surgery next week. I doubt I'll be chasing any bad guys for a while."

Clayton looked at Kerney's leg. "You never told how you got hurt."

"You really want to hear the story?" Kerney asked, glancing at the side-view mirror.

"Yeah, I do."

Kerney told him how another cop—his best friend in the department and a secret boozer—had let him down when they were on a stakeout waiting for an arrest warrant to bust a drug dealer; how the perp had caught Kerney off guard because his friend had left his post to sneak a drink; how Kerney had taken one round to the stomach and one to the knee before he could put the perp down for good.

"Some friend," Clayton said.

"Well, he was. A good one, until the booze caught up with him," Kerney replied. He glanced at the side-view mirror once again and stretched his leg to ease the ache in his knee. "He's on the straight and narrow, now. In some ways, I think he's in more pain about what happened than I am. Although today I wouldn't bet on it. Did you know we're being followed?"

Clayton looked in the rearview mirror. "Which car?"

"Third one back," Kerney said. "The blue Camaro with Texas plates."

"Where did you pick it up?" Clayton asked.

"In Roswell, just outside the old air force base."

"Were you able to read the plate?"

"Not with these tired old eyes," Kerney replied.

"What do you want to do?" Clayton asked.

"Find out who our friend is," Kerney said.

They talked it over. Kerney suggested a traffic stop, using a state police patrol officer, who could ID the driver. Clayton agreed, adding that he thought it best to wait until they were back in Lincoln County. Kerney brought up the idea that their "friend" might not be very friendly at all. Clayton conceded the point and imagined that it might be best to use two uniforms to make the stop, doing it casually but treating it as high risk. Kerney felt that would work if they had the state police come up behind the Camaro while a second unit, preferably from a different department, passed by in the opposite direction, and then stopped to render assistance.

They crossed the county line with the blue Camaro still hanging back behind them. Clayton got on the horn to a state police officer and a patrol deputy, explained the situation, told them what he wanted to do, and where he wanted it to go down. They gave him a twenty-minute ETA.

"What do I write the driver for?" New Mexico State Police Officer Sonia Raney asked.

"I'll speed up when you're in position," Clayton said. "That should get you a legal stop."

"You said high risk but casual, right?"

"Ten-four, whatever that is," Clayton replied.

Officer Raney laughed.

"I'll do a thirty-second count after you pull him over," Deputy Dillingham said to Raney by radio. "Then I'll come into view and swing around behind you."

"Don't run Code Three," Clayton cautioned.

"Wouldn't think of it," Dillingham replied. "I can't act casual with my emergency lights on."

"Let me know when you're in position," Clayton said.

There were very few cars on the two-lane highway that ran from the Hondo turnoff to Carrizozo. Fidel kept his distance, letting the cop's police vehicle become a speck on the pavement up ahead. On the curves he sped up to regain visual contact. Through the village of Lincoln, the cop slowed, but tourist traffic on the road allowed Fidel to remain inconspicuous. He looked at the old buildings fronting the highway, wondering why anybody would want to stop and look at them. The place had nothing to offer: no bar, no gas station, not even a roadside diner or a convenience store.

In the hills past Lincoln the road curved and rose. The cop picked up speed, traveling well above the posted limit. Fidel hit the accelerator, and topped out on a plateau to find the cop nowhere in sight. He heard a siren behind him and saw flashing emergency lights in his rearview mirror. Had he been made?

He dropped down to the speed limit and watched the vehicle come up fast, hoping it would pass him. It was a black-and-white state police car. It slowed and flashed its lights in a signal for him to pull over.

He thought about taking off, decided not to, eased to the shoulder, and watched the squad car roll to a stop behind him. The cop, a woman, was talking on her radio, probably running his plate. He rolled down his window, killed the engine, took his semiautomatic out of the shoulder holster, stuck it under the seat, and waited.

He froze when a sheriff's vehicle came around a bend toward him, thinking it was the Indian cop. But it wasn't running with emergency lights or traveling very fast, and the only occupant was an Anglo uniformed deputy. The vehicle slowed, made a U-turn and pulled in behind the patrol vehicle.

Fidel let out a sigh, got his driver's license from his wallet, searched the glove box for his registration and insurance card, and waited.

Officer Raney keyed her microphone. "The car is registered to Fidel Narvaiz," she said to Clayton, who was parked up the road by an abandoned building that had once housed a bar with a bad reputation.

"Use extreme caution," Clayton replied, "and let me know the ID of the driver as soon as you can."

Raney dismounted her unit while Dillingham took up his backup position at the right rear fender. He had a clear view into the Camaro. He placed his hand on his belt next to the butt of his sidearm.

Raney approached the Camaro, stopped at the center post, and looked down at the driver, a young Hispanic male. His hands were empty, as were the center console, dashboard, and the passenger and rear seats.

Raney asked for his driver's license, registration, and proof of insurance. Fidel handed them out the window. Raney walked backward to her unit, stood behind the open driver's door, and called Clayton. "The driver is Narvaiz."

"Can you get me something with his fingerprints on it?" Clayton asked.

"Ten-four. Do you want me to write him?"

"Be nice, give him a written warning."

Raney wrote out the ticket, returned to Narvaiz, and explained that he wouldn't be cited, only issued a written warning. She handed the ticket book to him and asked him to sign.

"Thanks," Fidel said, smiling. He signed the form and handed the book back to the cop.

Raney tore out a copy, gave it to Narvaiz, and sent

him on his way.

"I've got his prints," Raney said into her handheld microphone. "They're all over my ticket book." She held it between a thumb and forefinger.

"Bag it, tag it, give it to Dillingham, and ask him to deliver it to Artie Gundersen," Clayton said. "Dillingham knows what case I'm working, and can tell you what's up."

"Ten-four."

At the sheriff's office, while Clayton huddled with Paul Hewitt, Kerney wrote out the arrest affidavit on Norvell. Because his evidence was wholly circumstantial, he took his time, making sure all the relevant facts were convincingly included. Then he faxed it to the private office of the DA in Santa Fe, along with a note to have a copy of the warrant sent to Deputy Istee.

He walked in on Clayton and Hewitt to learn that the task-force packet had arrived, and Narvaiz's fingerprints matched the partials found on Ulibarri's body.

"You've got your killer," Kerney said. "Congratulations. When are you going to arrest him?"

"All in due course," Clayton said, smiling slyly.

Kerney laughed. "Keep me informed. You've got my phone number."

"You're leaving?" Hewitt asked, rising to offer his hand.

Kerney shook it. "It's your show, Paul. You don't need me filling up space. That's something you don't have a lot of around here."

"Tell me about it," Hewitt said with a chuckle.

"I'll walk you out," Clayton said.

Outside, Kerney and Clayton looked for the blue Camaro and didn't see it. The clear day accented the

289

dull slate-colored mountains behind a sea of tall-stemmed soapweed yuccas that spread out across the high desert plains, rippling in low waves against a slight breeze.

"Grace was hoping you'd stay over, and come to dinner tonight," Clayton said.

"Another time," Kerney replied, smiling.

"The kids will be disappointed."

"You've got a great family."

"Good luck with your surgery," Clayton said.

"Thanks."

Hesitantly, Clayton extended his hand. "Give my best to your wife."

"Sara," Kerney said, gripping Clayton's hand. "I'll send her your good wishes."

"Yeah."

"Take care, and be careful," Kerney said.

"Yeah. You, too."

Clayton started to say more, but the moment passed, and he turned away. Kerney watched him disappear into the building. Maybe it wasn't a big breakthrough, but he felt a definite warming trend in the air.

As he passed the restored train caboose in the postage-stamp roadside park on the main drag that served as the chamber of commerce visitors' center, Kerney thought about Sara. As soon as he got home, he'd write her a love letter, even if he had to struggle halfway through the night to find the right words to tell her what she meant to him.

CHAPTER 14

A LITTLE MORE THAN FOUR WEEKS AFTER HIS SURGERY, Kerney had a new knee and a new limp, although it was much less pronounced and less painful, and was disappearing fast due to the punishing rehab program he'd set for himself. There were certain situations where bullheadedness wasn't a bad thing, and given the progress he'd made, this was one of them. Even Sara, who'd been getting daily progress reports from Kerney by phone, had conceded the point.

Tomorrow Sara graduated from the Command and General Staff College, and today Kerney was flying in to attend the ceremony at Fort Leavenworth. It was also the day when the task force would carry out a coordinated strike against the partners and their associates.

Amazingly, there had been no glitches or miscues during the massive, four-state investigation. Over sixty cops and prosecutors from ten local, state, and federal agencies had worked thousands of hours unraveling the inner workings of the prostitution ring, and gathering evidence with no leaks, no botched surveillance, and no blown undercover assignments.

At five o'clock in the morning, as Kerney packed for his trip, Paul Hewitt, Clayton, sheriff's deputies, and state police agents were arresting Norvell and his "guests" at his ranch, which had reopened for business several weeks ago. Six prominent men, including a foreign diplomat and the head of a national charity, were about to become front-page news.

Last night, Hewitt had called Kerney to say he was

291

planning to give Clayton a sergeant's shield and commendation for the work he'd done as soon as the cases were wrapped.

In Albuquerque Detective Piño, Sergeant Vialpando, and APD vice officers were rounding up Bedlow, Tully, Deacon, and all the known working girls, while IRS agents served search warrants on State Senator Leo Silva and Representative Gene Barrett to seize their financial and corporate records.

At seven o'clock, Kerney drove to his early therapy session on a perfect May morning just about the time federal agents were shutting down all the out-of-state prostitution operations, except El Paso, which would be the last to fall.

In an hour, after getting confirmation, Sal Molina was scheduled to make a personal visit to Walter and Lorraine Montoya to tell them that their daughter's murderer had been arrested.

Back home at ten after a long session with his physical therapist, Kerney showered, changed, and left for the Albuquerque airport. On the way he called Larry Otero and found that the schedule was holding: bank examiners and state investigators were just then seizing the records of Norvell's various Ruidoso enterprises.

Kerney checked the time as he boarded his flight. By now DEA agents should be picking up the Denver drug dealer who'd been supplying dope to hookers and their clients throughout the four-state region.

Later in the day around evening time, Clayton and agents from the Texas Special Crimes Unit would take down Rojas and Narvaiz on murder charges, when surveillance reported Rojas back in town and at home. Recorded conversations between the two men clearly showed that Rojas had ordered the murder of Felix

Ulibarri.

From his first-class window seat, Kerney could see the snow-covered crests of the Rocky Mountains, an awesome, remote barrier that spawned rivers, cut canyons, studded high valleys with lakes, and threw domes and sharp-edged peaks into the pale blue sky.

The plane turned east toward the prairie, and the spine of the mountains that had filled his eyes gave way to a panorama of open range, bending rivers, ribbons of paved roads dotted by farm villages surrounded with checkerboards of irrigated green fields and pale yellow pastures.

The change in the landscape below strengthened Kerney's resolve to be more open and more attentive to Sara. It was time to remove the self-imposed barriers that, over so many years of living alone, had eroded his ability to express his feelings.

He closed his eyes and touched his jacket pocket. In a jeweler's gift box was a pair of diamond earrings. Tonight, when they were alone, he would give them to Sara and tell her again all the reasons why he loved her.

With a no-knock warrant in hand, Clayton made assignments: three agents to the rear of the house, three to the front door with a battering ram, and two officers with him up the outside stairs over the garage to Narvaiz's apartment.

The house looked unoccupied, but Clayton knew better. Surveillance reports put Rojas and Narvaiz inside the compound, but where exactly the men were was another matter.

The team went in low and fast, using palm trees along the driveway as cover. Clayton hit the staircase at a full run, two steps at a time. He heard the sound of the battering ram against the heavy front door as he reached the landing. Narvaiz appeared suddenly in a doorway, semiautomatic in hand, blazing away. The first loud round hit Clayton's vest, spun him sideways. The second round knocked him on his back. His chest felt like a freight train had hit it. He lifted his head, spread his legs, raised his weapon, and watched Narvaiz walking toward him, grinning and firing at the agents crouched on the stairwell behind him. The officers returned fire, bullets screaming above Clayton's head.

He emptied his magazine at Narvaiz. Rounds from three weapons tore into Fidel's flesh and gouged holes in the open door on the landing. Blood splatter from a neck wound arched over the wrought-iron railing and cascaded down to the driveway below.

Clayton fed in another clip, aimed his weapon, and watched Narvaiz fall. He heard rounds shattering glass and pulverizing plaster walls inside the house and sent the two agents to lend support.

The firing stopped before they got down the stairs. They went in calling out names on their handheld radios, asking for status and location.

Clayton got to his feet on unsteady legs and walked to Narvaiz's body. He counted twelve bullet holes, all leaking either dark fluid or viscous gray matter. Was it adrenaline or just plain fear that had him shaking?

He waited for a feeling of revulsion to overwhelm him, but nothing came except an emptiness that made him feel dark and bleak.

His handheld hissed his call sign. Feebly he keyed the microphone and answered. Rojas was down, probably dying, and one officer had a superficial leg wound.

He stepped back from the body and ordered ambulances and crime scene techs to roll. Would he

294

ever be able to tell Grace about this? *Really* tell her?

He doubted it. But maybe one day he could tell Kerney.

ABOUT THE AUTHOR

Michael McGarrity is the author of the Anthony Award-nominated *Tularosa*, as well as *Mexican Hat, Serpent Gate, Hermit's Peak, The Judas Judge,* and *Under the Color of Law.* He is a former deputy sheriff for Santa Fe County, where he established the first Sex Crimes Unit. He has also served as an instructor at the New Mexico Law Enforcement Academy and as an investigator for the New Mexico Public Defender's Office. He lives in Santa Fe.

Dear Reader:

I hope you enjoyed reading this Large Print book. If you are interested in reading other Beeler Large Print titles, ask your librarian or write to me at

Thomas T. Beeler, *Publisher*
Post Office Box 659
Hampton Falls, New Hampshire 03844

You can also call me at 1-800-818-7574 and I will send you my latest catalogue.

Audrey Lesko and I choose the titles I publish in Large Print. Our aim is to provide good books by outstanding authors—books we both enjoyed reading and liked well enough to want to share. We warmly welcome any suggestions for new titles and authors.

Sincerely,